[LEAVING ATLANTA]

[LEAVING ATLANTA]

Tayari Jones

WARNER BOOKS

An AOL Time Warner Company

Copyright © 2002 by Tayari Jones
All rights reserved.

Warner Books, Inc., 1271 Avenue of the Americas, New York, NY 10020

Visit our Web site at www.twbookmark.com.

 An AOL Time Warner Company

Printed in the United States of America

First Printing: August 2002

10 9 8 7 6 5 4 3 2 1

Library of Congress Cataloging-in-Publication Data

Jones, Tayari.
    Leaving Atlanta / Tayari Jones.
       p. cm.
    ISBN 0-446-52830-7
        1. African American families—Fiction.   2. African American children—Fiction.
3. Serial murders—Fiction.   4. Atlanta (Ga.)—Fiction.   I. Title.

PS3610.O63 L43 2002
    813'.6—dc21   2001046524

Twenty-nine
and more

Acknowledgments

This novel, like all novels, and especially like all first novels, is a collaborative effort. I won't be able to thank all those who helped this novel make the arduous journey from my imagination to these pages, but I will try.

All of the Joneses: Barbara, Mack, Lumumba, Maxine, Bo, and Marcia have supported me since my first scribblings. My parents financed my eclectic education and cheered me on without (copious) complaint. My brother Patrice Lumumba, my first friend, treated me like a writer before I was one. I love all of you like a bunch of grapes.

The Opester, known to some as Opal Moore, gave deathbed line edits and lived to tell about it. Jewell Parker Rhodes convinced me to head west and kept every promise she ever made. The one hundred dollars Pearl Cleage paid me when she published my first story ten years ago is still the best money I ever made. My teacher and friend Demetria Martinez taught me about writing, life, and the writing life. Ron Carlson charmed me with opaque metaphors and showed me the way to a better book. Judith Ortiz Cofer and Kevin Young each guided my work without ever telling me where to take it.

Alice Erika Livingston read early drafts, cursed everyone who rejected the manuscript, and kept me laughing while we waited for good news from New York. Thanks for reminding that friendship is the whole point.

Marita Golden and the Hurston/Wright Foundation have been exceedingly kind, not only to me, but to many other fine writers. You really are *developing the world community of African writers.*

The generous support of the Robert C. Martindale Educational Foundation helped me survive a very long, hot Arizona summer.

There are many others who read ugly early drafts, coordinated kamikaze Xeroxing missions, gave money to help with postage, and/or offered to commission violence in lieu of more traditional routes of soliciting publishers. The names here are representative of the human landscape from which this story emerged: June Aldrige, Jafari Allen, LaKisha Anderson, J.B., Demetria Baker, Bryn Chancellor, Crystal Drake, Mabel Green, Kiyana Sakena Horton, Dolan Hubbard, Andrea Ivory, Doug Jones, Adrienne Maynard Melchor, Michael Ray McCauley Jr., Deborah McKinney, Kweku Pletcher, Kathryn Randall, Sanderia Smith, Peter B. Thornton II, David Van Fossen, Michelle Villanueva, Tonja Harding Ward, Anne Warner, Alma Faye Washington, Elizabeth Wetmore, Wille R. Wilburn II, Deborah E. Williams, Andrea Wren, and the Women of Giles Hall.

My magnificent agent, Jane Dystel, and my glorious editor, Caryn Karmatz Rudy: You ladies made it easy. No first novelist ever had more fun.

Finally, I must mention TaRessa Stovall who told me that black books always have long acknowledgment pages. I'd like to thank her for never being smug about the fact that she is always right.

[LEAVING ATLANTA]

PART 1

Magic Words

Hard, ugly, summer-vacation-spoiling rain fell for three straight months in 1979. Atlanta downpours destroyed hopscotch markers carefully chalked onto asphalt and stole the bounce from yellow tennis balls forgotten in backyards. On the few days the rain didn't fall, children scurried to play 1-2-3 Redlight under low-hanging gray clouds. Red Georgia clay clung to inexpensive canvas sneakers and the kids tracked it into light-carpeted living rooms. Mothers slapped their narrow behinds with leather belts before dabbing at the marked floors with wet rags, worrying about the expense of carpet cleaners or loss of deposits. When the rain fell, it did so to an accompaniment of growling thunder and purple zigzag lightning. Bored kids were told to sit still. *Be quiet. God is talking.* The children listened to the water smack against the window panes and figured that God's message must not have been meant for them to understand.

But on the first day of school, the students at Oglethorpe Elementary did not sweat inside yellow plastic jackets or carry umbrellas. The eight-A.M. sun winked as they tromped on broken sidewalks with brightly colored book satchels and lunch boxes. The unfamiliar light turned the girls' plastic barrettes into prisms, casting rainbows on their cheeks. Everybody wished the sun had come out the day before, when they had been free to chase the ice-cream man. But this, they kept to themselves.

Perhaps someone said under her breath, but still out loud, *Why the sun had to come out today when we got to go to school?* And maybe God heard. For although fifth-graders couldn't understand God's language, no one doubted that He knew theirs.

By recess, the sky was as gray as it had been the day before, but the fifth-graders went outside anyway. Although they had looked forward to moving to the trailers recently added to the rear of the old school building, and standing apart from the lower grades, the windowless metal room was claustrophobic and cheerless, foiling the bright bulletin boards' attempts to welcome them back. At noon, the children stampeded out to the damp playground, but LaTasha Renee Baxter was the last to leave the trailer, carrying the heavy jump rope that had been coiled since school let out last June.

Jumping rope had been the proving ground for girls as long as she could remember, and for equally as long, Tasha had been embarrassingly incompetent. This was fifth grade, the last year of grade school; next year she would go to Southwest Middle School, which was closer to her house. Her parents had chosen Oglethorpe Elementary School because it was near her mother's work, which was good when Tasha was little. Mama could get to the school in less than five minutes if need be. But now that Tasha was getting to be a young lady, Mama and Daddy thought that it would be better for her to be on her own side of town, rather than across the street from the projects.

Because this year would be her last chance to make a place for herself among the girls in her class, Tasha had devoted most of the vacation to improving her rope-jumping technique. Because of the summer's inclement weather, she had practiced in her basement, tying one end of the rope to a wooden chair and forcing her eight-year-old sister, De-Shaun, to turn the other end. Tasha had worked on all the skipping rhymes. She was best at "Ice Cream" and could get very near the end of the alphabet before losing her footing. But she had decided already that she would deliberately falter at "P" since there was no boy in her class whose name began with that initial.

After untangling the rope, she held one end in her hand and waited for someone else to grab the other, but no one did.

"Y'all don't want to jump?" she asked.

A small kneesocked cluster of girls shrugged in unison and looked toward Monica Fisher, the best rope skipper ever seen in Georgia. She had been born in Chicago where the girls skipped two ropes at once and chanted rhymes that sometimes included cuss words.

"Nah," said Monica. "I don't have time for that baby stuff. Y'all going to make me sweat out my hair." She stroked her straightened page boy, pulled off her face with a wide headband. Tasha noticed horizontal imprints where rollers had been fastened.

Tasha dropped the rope as if it were hot. She had washed her hair for the first day of school, but Mama had not subjected her to the torture of a pressing comb. Now she was unprepared. "That's alright," Tasha said. "I didn't really want to jump. There's just not nothing else to do."

"Look at her just lying," said Forsythia Collier, Monica's best friend. Forsythia's hair was also pressed, and her oily ringlets coiled all the way to her shoulders. "She probably practiced all summer."

Monica laughed a little louder than was appropriate and continued her cackle until the other girls joined her.

Tasha decided to laugh too. Didn't Mama tell her that a person needed to be able to laugh at herself? And besides, she didn't want to start a feud with Monica and Forsythia.

Then the rain started and Tasha was relieved, although she groaned along with everyone else as they ran toward the tin box that was their classroom this year. She even cried out, "My hair!" although her tight cornrows were impervious to climate.

Inside the trailer, the noise of the rain on the roof rose into magnificent crescendoes with the wind. "Let's play jacks," Tasha shouted over the weather.

"Okay," Monica said.

Tasha turned her head to hide her smile as she reached into her book bag for the purple felt sack that held twenty jacks and a purple rubber ball. Jumping rope wasn't the only thing she had practiced over the summer.

The girls made a clearing by pushing all of the desk chairs over to one corner. Most of the boys argued over comic books under the supervision of their new teacher, Mr. Harrell. Tasha sat cross-legged on the floor across from Monica while her classmates breathed over them with gumball breath. "Anybody else want to play? Up to five can play jacks."

"No," Monica said. "Let's just let it be us."

"Okay," Tasha said, tossing the tiny pieces of metal.

Tasha won, as she had planned to, but she meant to quit before whipping Monica's siditty tail. But she couldn't make herself stop showboating, demonstrating all the techniques she had perfected over the long, wet summer vacation. She even knew maneuvers that none of them had seen before, things Tasha's mother learned as a kid in Oklahoma. Midwestern jacks had an entirely different flavor.

The girls clapped when Tasha perfectly executed an around-the-world with double-bounce and tap. Even a few boys came over and watched.

"Dang," Roderick Palmer, the cutest boy in class, said behind his hand. "She *killing* Monica."

Tasha couldn't resist saying, "Wanna play again?" although it was clear that Monica had had enough.

Monica heaved herself from the floor and crossed her arms over her chest, hiding the outline of her training bra. "That's alright." She dusted off her pants with sharp whacks. "I just let you win because my mother told me that everyone is supposed to be nice to you because your parents are getting separated and everything."

"Uh-uh," Tasha clarified. "They're not *separated*. They're *living apart* right now. It's different." She paused for a minute, trying to explain what was different about her household and Monica's, or that of any of the other kids who didn't have a father anymore. She still had her daddy. He called her on the telephone almost every night and picked her up from ballet lessons on Tuesdays. *Separated* was different, harsher. Almost as bad as divorce. And not once had her parents used that word.

Monica laughed and touched Forsythia with her pointed elbow, soliciting a complicit chuckle.

"It's just for a little while," Tasha insisted. A warmth spread from her chest up to her face as she gathered the jacks. "So," she shouted at Monica's back, "my mother says your parents live outside their means!" No one watching responded to Tasha's comeback. Monica, who had taken a sudden interest in the boys' comic book wars, didn't even turn around. Only Rodney Green, the weirdest kid in class, seemed to ponder her remark. With his face extended by two cheeks full of bubble gum, he studied her with scrunched brows behind his glasses, until Tasha felt uncomfortable and turned away.

She went to the girls' room, sat in a stall, and rested her humiliation in the palms of her hands. Closing her eyes hard to stifle tears the way pressing down on a cut stops bleeding, Tasha felt dumb as a rock.

Two weeks earlier, Daddy *had* moved out. Tasha wasn't so dumb that she didn't realize this was trouble. At first, when he and Mama came to tell her, Tasha thought they were going to tell her they were having another baby. That was what happened to Tayari Jones just last year. Tayari told everyone in class that her parents had come into her room smiling and holding hands and—just like that—told her that there would be a new baby in the house in August. So what was Tasha to think when Mama and Daddy knocked softly on her bedroom door and silently stepped over the clutter, *holding hands?* They never held hands or really touched each other, except a quick smack on the lips on each other's birthdays. *Thank you, baby.* Then the kiss.

And true enough, they hadn't been smiling like Tayari's parents. Mama held Daddy's hand tight so that her knuckles stood out and her face had worn a sorry, stretched look, like her chin was too heavy and was pulling her round face into a sad oval.

But Tasha figured this was an appropriate precursor to news about an impending baby. Where in the world were they going to put it? In the guest room? It didn't seem fair that a baby should have a room to itself while she had to share with DeShaun. And if the guest room was to be full of baby, then where would Nana stay when she came to visit from Birmingham? She knew Mama and Daddy weren't going to suggest putting it in here with her and DeShaun. There was not enough room for their two canopy beds and a crib.

"What?" Tasha said, looking at Mama's abdomen.

Daddy pulled his hand from Mama's and touched Tasha's face. "Wait till DeShaun gets here."

Tasha climbed onto her bed and hugged her knees. This was serious. Twins? Oh, Jesus. (She could take the Lord's name in vain all she wanted to as long as she didn't do it out loud.) One little sister was more than enough, really. She could imagine twins in identical prams. People would be saying how precious they were and how cute. It would be like being the only regular girl in a class full of pretty people. She got enough of that feeling at school already; having it at home would be unbearable.

Tasha wished she had X-ray vision so she could look right in Mama's stomach and see what was going on under the brown blouse tucked into the waistband of her tan slacks. Her stomach poked out a little bit, but not any more than anyone else's mother's did. Or did it? Mama ran her hand across her front, flattening the pleats.

There was the sound of a toilet flushing and DeShaun came in.

"What?" the little girl said, looking from her parents to her older sister and back.

"We been waiting for you so we can find out," Tasha said.

"I was using the bathroom," DeShaun whined.

"Tasha," Mama said, "don't snap at her like that."

"All I said was——"

Daddy cleared his throat. "Delores." He took Mama's hand again, but she didn't wrap her fingers around his. He let go to touch the sisters on the crown of their heads. His fingernails were neat rectangles against their dark hair.

"Girls," he said, "I love you very much."

Especially DeShaun, Tasha thought. She could remember the time before DeShaun was born. Mama said she couldn't possibly since they were only twenty-three months apart, but Tasha did remember and she knew that people used to love her more back then. What would life be like after the twins? She turned her face toward the wall and Daddy gently twisted her head so she had to look at his sober and unhappy brown face.

"And I love your mother too." He turned toward Mama, who seemed to be studying her knees. "But your mother and I think that it is best if we live apart right now."

Tasha looked up at him quickly. There was no baby?

"For a while," he said, looking at Tasha before turning to look at Mama.

"For a while," Mama echoed. "Just to see how things work."

"Okay," Tasha said fast. Relieved.

Her little sister DeShaun pulled a piece of loose skin from her wobbly bottom lip.

Now, Tasha felt stupid. Monica was right. Tasha was *immature*. And Daddy was in the wrong too. He should have said, *Tasha, DeShaun, your mother and I have been playing with matches and your whole life is on fire.*

After school that first day, Tasha did not wipe her feet before coming into the house. After leaving her wet umbrella on the carpet, she tramped into the kitchen leaving mad, muddy, size-six prints on the floors. She drank juice from three different glasses and didn't rinse a single one out. Frustrated, she flopped onto the couch and put her feet up on it.

"You're not supposed to put your feet up on that sofa," DeShaun reminded her.

Ignoring her little sister, Tasha placed her glass on the coffee table without a coaster. "Did you know Mama and Daddy were separated?" she asked.

DeShaun bit down on a carrot stick. "What's that?"

Tasha searched her mind. "It's the same thing as divorce."

"I don't know what that is either."

"Divorce is when the parents aren't together anymore. When the dad lives someplace else."

"I already know that Daddy is living someplace else." DeShaun looked confused. "You know that too, right?"

"Yeah, I know that much." Tasha was insulted. "I'm asking you if you knew they were *separated.*"

"And I said *what's that,*" DeShaun protested.

Separated was kids who only had a mother to come and

hear them say a poem on Black History Day. Or the ones who had stepfathers that they called by their first names. Ayana McWhorter, Tasha's best friend, had one named Rex who didn't like Ayana or any of her friends. He was young, according to Mama, clicking her tongue against the back of her teeth, but Tasha couldn't see it. Rex was tall and thin with a narrow scar on the side of his face, which he tried to hide with a thick beard. (Unkempt, according to Mama.) Tasha wouldn't have noticed the scar at all if Ayana hadn't pointed it out: *That's where someone tried to kill him.* After that, Ayana always came over to Tasha's house to play because Tasha didn't like going over to her house and Mama didn't think much of the idea either. Last June, when Ayana had spent the afternoon, Mama had pulled them out from in front of the TV and spread construction paper out on the kitchen table.

"You girls need to do something productive," Mama said, putting down newspaper to protect the floor. "Since Father's Day is right around the corner, you all can make cards."

Tasha thought that it was a good idea. She loved arts and crafts.

"I'm not making a card for Rex," Ayana said, loud as back talk.

Tasha looked at Mama, expecting her to be mad, but Mama only touched the girl softly on the back of her neck.

"You can make a card for anyone. Your granddaddy, or an uncle."

"I don't want to make a card for anyone," Ayana murmured.

"Okay, you can just draw a picture."

Ayana didn't draw a picture. Instead she ate paste and then threw up all over the table, ruining the paper Tasha had neatly folded and glittered.

Mama had put a cold towel on Ayana's forehead and made soft clicks with her tongue.

Separated was regurgitated glue and sour spangles.

Tasha went to her room to wait for Mama to come home.

"LaTasha Renee Baxter," Mama bellowed. "Come down here right now."

When Tasha got down to the kitchen, DeShaun was pleading innocent.

"I had some juice, but I rinsed out my cup and put it right here in the dishwasher. And those aren't my footprints neither. My feet are littler than that; see?" She put her foot beside one of the dirty marks.

Mama, satisfied with the evidence, waved DeShaun into the other room.

"You are really trying my patience today," she started. She had taken off her high-heeled shoes and was gesturing with them. "What is your problem, Miss Lady?" She aimed the pointed toe of her pump at the empty juice glasses and the dirty floor. "I just mopped this floor last night. There is a mat—" She realized that Tasha was not paying attention. "Look at me when I talk to you."

Tasha raised her eyes to her mother's face. She tried to talk with her teeth closed like grown ladies did when they were really mad. "You didn't tell me you were separated."

Mama was caught off guard. Tasha could tell. "What?"

"Monica said that her mother told her that you were separated. You didn't tell that to me."

Mama sat down heavily in one of the wooden kitchen chairs and patted the one beside her.

"I don't want to sit down." She could hear her heart beating in the sides of her head.

"Tasha, Daddy and I told you and Shaun both that we would be living apart."

"But you didn't say *separated!*" Tasha had never raised her voice at an adult before.

Mama's face changed and Tasha ran, frightened, to her room and shut the door.

Half an hour later, Mama's voice climbed the stairs. "Dinner's on the table!" Tasha didn't answer and no one came upstairs to see about her.

The sounds of silverware clicking against plates she could endure, but the whirring of the blender made her put her face into her pillow and scream; Mama and DeShaun were downstairs enjoying milkshakes. Last week, DeShaun had refused her cabbage and Mama had coaxed her into eating it. *Just one little bite.* It was such a big deal that DeShaun might not get all her vitamins but no one cared if Tasha went to bed without any dinner at all.

She dug around in her closet until she came up with a small package of peanuts that Nana had given her from the airplane and a stale marshmallow egg left over from last year's Easter basket. She swallowed with great difficulty, choking on salty sadness and thirst.

I will not eat with them again, she promised herself. They can have milkshakes from now until kingdom come and I will not even eat one bite.

For two days Tasha kept her word. She ate ravenously at lunchtime and spirited away granola bars under her bed to tide her through the evenings. She chewed each bite slowly, trying to make it last.

"Tasha will eat when she gets hungry," Mama said into the telephone. "She's not going to sit up in that room and starve to death." She was quiet. "That's easy for you to say . . . Um-hum. Hold on." She hollered up the stairs. "Tasha, pick up the phone."

She went into her parents' room. "Hello."

"Hey, Ladybug." Daddy's voice was dark and smooth like a melted crayon.

She wanted to cry. "Hey, Daddy," she whispered.

"Your mother says you don't have much of an appetite."

"I'm not hungry."

"She's really worried about you. Why don't you just eat a little something so she won't have to worry."

"She's not worried about me."

"Don't say that," he said. "Your mother loves you."

"She don't act like it."

"What?"

"Nothing."

"So are you going to eat?" The timbre of his voice masked an undercurrent of pleading, as if her refusal to eat dinner made an adult difference.

"Yeah," Tasha said. She couldn't bring herself to disappoint or disobey him.

But she couldn't bring herself to eat dinner at the table set for only three.

The next day, Mama stopped ignoring her.

"Tasha, come down here and eat." She accented each angry syllable with a tap on the banister with a spatula.

"I'm not hungry," Tasha yelled through her closed door.

"Well just come down and sit at the table."

"I don't feel well."

"You looked pretty healthy ten minutes ago."

Tasha didn't answer. At the sound of Mama's feet tiredly coming up the stairs, she kicked off her shoes without undoing the buckles and sprawled across the bed, hoping to appear at least a little queasy. Mama came in, disregarding the handmade signs ordering PLEASE KNOCK and ENTER AT YOUR OWN RISK.

"Tasha," Mama said, sitting on the edge of the bed. "I'm tired. Come down and eat. I know you miss your daddy, but a hunger strike is not going to solve anything." She searched Tasha's face for a smile. "Come on, Tash, get up. I fixed cheese-dreams just for you."

Tasha sat up on her elbows, looking at her mother with a quizzical half turn of her head. Mama was blinking her eyes about a million miles an hour, like DeShaun did when she was about to cry. Tasha lowered her brows and pursed her lips. What was going on here? Was all of this an elaborate ploy just to get her to eat?

"Don't you want cheese-dreams?" Mama put her elbows on her thighs and leaned her face against her hand. The softness of her cheek bulged brown and gentle through the cracks between her fingers. Shutting her eyes, she said, "Don't you want cheese-dreams?"

Tasha heard it, a subtle change in pitch, the precursor to tears. She wanted to put her shoulder against whatever door was threatening to open and press hard. She wished she could put her finger in the hole like the Little Dutch Boy and save what was left of her life from the flood.

"I didn't know you made cheese-dreams," Tasha said,

hoping to make it seem like her refusal to eat had been a standoff over menu. She started toward the door, more spry than she felt, refusing to look at her overtired mother still sitting on the bed in her work-crumpled blouse and skirt.

"Come here," Mama said softly.

Tasha stopped walking but she didn't turn around; she didn't want to see.

"Give me a hug," Mama said.

Tasha could hear her exhausted misery. Turning on the balls of her feet, she moved toward her mother's unsteady voice. Mama's hug held a desperate fierceness that Tasha had not felt since she had narrowly missed being hit by a car four years earlier. Mama had gripped Tasha then in a melting embrace until she had felt herself disappear. She had been aware of the heavy pressure of Mama's lips on the part between her braids, her forehead, each of her cheeks, and her quivering lips; then she knew nothing but the outdoor smell of pine and Mama's neck.

Mama squeezed Tasha today with the same famished affection. She felt, this time, the intensity of grown folks' emotion and gasped with the heat of it. The hug lasted several unendurable moments more before Mama released her.

"Let's eat," she said.

Tasha and DeShaun sat at the table, staring at each other with curiosity. Having cheese-dreams itself was odd enough. Mama had declared more than once that grilled cheese sandwiches made with French toast and smothered in raspberry syrup was *not* a balanced meal. On the rare occasion that she would consent to serving this treat, the girls were forced to eat a green salad first. But today, not only were they not required to choke down anything leafy, but they evidently were going to be allowed to ration their own syrup. Tasha poured a generous dollop on the center of the sandwich. It rolled down the sides of the bread. No response from Mama. She squeezed the bottle, releasing another raspberry globule. No response. She squeezed a little more. Then she realized that she had no idea how much raspberry syrup was enough. She didn't stop pouring until the design on the plate was concealed and DeShaun was begging, "Give me it!"

Tasha carefully cut a triangular section of the cheese-dream and popped it into her mouth. She was overwhelmed by sugar and a faint food-color bitterness. Mama looked at her daughters, struggling with too much of a good thing, and laughed.

Her laugh was clean but heavy. The power of it shook her bosom, bouncing the gold locket around her neck. Tasha laughed too, although her favorite meal was all but ruined, drowning in sweetness. DeShaun giggled too.

Mama rescued the sandwiches from their gooey beds and set them on clean saucers. Putting them down in front of the girls, she said, "I do believe that we are going to be alright."

———

"Ouch," Tasha protested, as her mother fastened an elastic around a small, neatly partitioned section of her hair. It didn't hurt, but she howled as a preventive measure. De-Shaun never complained and, as a result, often went to school with her hair pulled back so tightly that her eyes slanted.

"You know this is not hurting you," Mama said, but she used a lighter touch.

"Why can't I fix my own hair?"

"Because you can't part straight and I can't have you going out of this house looking like a little pickaninny."

Tasha sighed, resting her face on the inside of Mama's thigh and running her hand up and down her pecan-colored shin, enjoying the texture of the stocking.

"Tasha, let my hose alone. I don't have time to change them when you put a run in them."

Tasha moved her hand, feeling rejected.

"Okay," Mama said, patting her daughter's shoulder. "I'm done."

Tasha went into the bathroom to inspect the job in the mirror over the sink. Her hair was just like DeShaun's. Evidently, Mama thought that it was cute for the two of them to be small and large versions of the same thing, like those dolls that nest inside each other. But it was entirely inappropriate, not to mention humiliating, for a fifth-grader to have the same hairdo as a little bitty third-grader.

Assuming an air of maturity, Tasha wiggled the silver key hanging on a shoestring like a pendant, from under her blouse to the outside. This, at least, would separate her from her sister; no little kids had keys and Tasha had only gotten hers this school year. Instead of staying with their neighbor, Mrs. Mahmud, she and Shaun went straight home after school and stayed alone until Mama got off from work.

Those two hours were Tasha's favorite time of day. She was *in charge*. Each day, she gravely insisted that she be the only one to touch anything mechanical.

"It's too dangerous," she had told her sister, as she adjusted the thermostat to seventy-four degrees.

She looked in the mirror a little longer. If the weather had been better, Tasha would have demanded some modification of her coif. But it was raining outside and she would be forced to wear a stupid hat anyway.

Tasha was sitting at her desk when her nose started to run. There was a long piece of bathroom tissue in her pocket, but Forsythia Collier, across the aisle, was dabbing at her nostrils with tiny Kleenexes from a cute little pouch. Too embarrassed to tear off a piece of crumpled toilet paper, Tasha inhaled deeply through her nostrils, hoping to reverse the flow without making noise.

Mr. Harrell looked at her with disapproval from in front of the class. "Miss Baxter," he said, "if you need to blow your nose, please go to the lavatory."

Tasha skulked out of the trailer appearing to concentrate intently on the white tile floor, flecked with black.

Although the walkway connecting the fifth-grade trailers to the main school building was covered, it was not enclosed. Wet air blew into Tasha's face. Just as she shoved her hands into her pockets, she saw Jashante Hamilton leaning against a pole. He rested his weight on one leg and angled his chin.

"What you get sent out here for?" he wanted to know.

"I'm just going to blow my nose." For some reason, Tasha felt as though she were pleading.

He was good-looking. Not in the same way as Roderick Palmer, who had pretty eyelashes like a girl, cute bowlegs, and skin soft brown like the wood around a pencil lead.

Jashante was tall and brown-red like a pair of penny-loafers.
His hair, shaved low to his head, was pomaded and brushed
into rows of even waves. There was something grown about
him. Tasha knew he was much older than the average fifth-
grader. (Way older than her, since she had a late birthday.)
Roderick Palmer claimed to have somehow seen Jashante's
permanent record, which said he was fifteen.

"Don't you have one of them little bitty Kleenexes in
your pocketbook like all the other fancy girls?" he asked.
His voice was slippery and almost deep.

Tasha was flattered that he thought that she was of the
same caliber as Forsythia Collier; in reality, she didn't even
carry a purse. She stuffed whatever she needed into her
pockets or in the front flap of her book bag.

"Oh. I left them at home."

Jashante didn't say anything. He looked at her slowly.
Tasha was fragmented as she watched him seeing her. He
took in the babyfied hairstyle, seeming to count each plastic barrette. Eyes lingered on the faint outline of an under-
shirt over a chest almost ready for a training bra. Her bony
wrists, a generic brown with no warming hints of red,
sticking out from the too-short sleeves of a striped turtleneck, narrow hips fastened into pink jeans.

"I gotta go," she said. "It's cold out here." She wanted the
sanctity of the girls' room where she could reassemble herself. She walked past him.

"Say," he said.

She pretended not to hear.

"Say, Fancy Girl. What your name is?"

By then Tasha had reached the swinging door. She
pushed it and went inside. Inside the warm, safe building,

she made an effort to breathe slowly. She felt tingly, itchy, and warm all at the same time, like she was loosely bound in a wool blanket.

The television, a small black-and-white with long antennae tipped with foil, was perched on top of the refrigerator. Tasha noticed it immediately when she and Shaun came down for dinner.

"What is that TV doing up there?" she asked. It hadn't been there an hour earlier, when Tasha had come home still crackling from the electricity of her hallway encounter.

"Surprise," said Mama.

"I thought you said we didn't need a TV in the kitchen." Her good mood was losing voltage fast.

"Well," Mama said, "I knew how much you wanted one. And I saw this one on sale. . . ."

This was bad, Tasha knew. When she had first brought up the subject of a kitchen television, three years ago, it was after she found out that Monica Fisher watched cartoons in the morning while she ate her breakfast. She could imagine Monica giggling contentedly as she downed countless bowls of Lucky Charms. Tasha, on the other hand, had to amuse herself by endlessly rereading the back of the box of Shredded Wheat. When she brought this inequity to her mother's attention, her request was unequivocally denied.

"This family," Mama had sniffed, "*talks* to one another while we are at the table. We don't need TV to keep us company."

"But what about in the morning? We don't talk then. All you and Daddy do is drink coffee. Me and Shaun end up reading the cereal box."

"Shaun and I," Mama corrected, and the case was closed.

Reversal of opinion was not Mama's style. This TV thing had to do with the separation. That was obvious. Since Daddy was gone, dinner conversation had dwindled to "pass this" and "eat your broccoli." The TV meant he was not coming back to lively up the evening meal with knock-knock jokes or funny stories from work. Daddy was gone for good and in his place was a raggedy little TV that probably couldn't even get Channel Forty-six good.

And Mama didn't even let them choose what to look at. She insisted that they watch the news at dinnertime.

"But we wanna watch *The Flintstones,*" DeShaun whined.

"No, *The Dating Game,*" Tasha complained.

"We are watching the news," Mama said, in her that's-final voice.

"But—"

"But nothing. You need to know what's going on in the world, or else, white people could reinstate slavery and you wouldn't know it until they came to take you away."

That was something that Daddy liked to say. Mama had been doing that a lot lately. Like in the morning when she woke them up, she said, "Get ready to greet the world!" instead of "Rise and shine." It was depressing to hear Mama say Daddy's lines. It was a pitiful substitution, like the time when she lost her shower cap and had to bathe with a freezer bag on her head.

As it turned out, the news wasn't so bad. It wasn't as interesting as *The Dating Game,* but it was neck and neck with *The Flintstones,* since she had seen all of the episodes already.

At least the news never played a rerun. There was a black lady on Channel Two whom Mama liked to call by her first name and critique on her appearance like she was somebody they actually knew. "Monica should know better than to pull her hair off her face like that," Mama might say, pouring melted Velveeta over broccoli.

Tasha was going to say, "I like that top Monica Kaufman has on," as soon as she finished chewing. But before she could swallow, the pictures of the children appeared on the screen. Nine photos that looked like school pictures were arranged in three rows like a tic-tac-toe game waiting to be played. Tasha stared hard at the TV. She had a mouth full of soft sweet fruit that she tried to swallow, but her throat was constricted and she coughed. Instead of patting her back, Mama said quietly, sternly, "Hush."

"Mama," DeShaun said.

"Hush."

Somebody had murdered all those kids. Two little girls, all the rest boys. What had happened? Tasha had seen a couple of people get murdered on TV. There was the noise of a gun and then the person lying on the floor with a big spot of ketchupy blood on his clothes. She wasn't sure how the gun killed people. A bullet was involved, yes. But a bullet was a teensy thing that could fit on just one of your fingers.

"All them kids are killed?" DeShaun asked. She was looking at the girl in the upper left-hand corner, who was about her same age. The girl was smiling with her mouth open, as if the photographer had been playing with puppets to make her laugh right before snapping the picture.

"Some of them," Tasha said, leaning forward to hear better.

DeShaun hooked her fingers between her bottom lip and teeth. She was about to cry; Tasha noted her little sister's fluttering eyelashes. She pushed the can of peaches toward her sister in an effort to hold off the gusher until the news was over because DeShaun didn't cry like regular people; she wailed, and nobody would be able to hear the news over that racket. When DeShaun opened her mouth to let out a whopper, the phone rang, choking her sobs in mid-bawl.

"Hello," Mama said. "Yeah, we're watching right now." She made a clicking sound with her tongue. "Of course they're home." Noisy exhale. "I haven't had a *chance* to talk to them yet. We get the news at six o'clock, same as you." Mama shifted the phone to her other ear and turned her eyes toward the ceiling. "Fine," she said. "Here's Tasha."

Daddy's voice was deep, like a hole that went all the way to China. "Hey, baby," he said. "You watching the news?"

"Yes, sir."

"Listen"—his voice was serious—"I want you and De-Shaun to come right home after school. Hold your sister's hand and don't talk to anybody. You hear me?"

"Yes, sir," Tasha said. He sounded like he was mad. That wasn't fair. She knew he wasn't going to talk to DeShaun like that. Tasha decided that she had a question for *him*. "Daddy, where are you?"

Mama looked at her sharply across the table. She opened her mouth but then she shut it again, pressing her lips together tightly as a warning. Tasha knew from careful eavesdropping that Daddy was "with his woman" but wanted to know exactly where.

"Not far," he said gently. "Don't you worry about that."

Tasha was about to press him for a little more specificity but DeShaun was trying to wrestle the receiver away.

"Ouch!" Tasha said. "Shaun *scratched* me."

"Give her the phone," Mama said.

"But I'm not through talking to Daddy. I was fixing to ask him—"

Mama pointed her slim index finger at Tasha and shook it wordlessly. Tasha gave the phone to DeShaun, mumbling, "It's not fair."

DeShaun held the phone with both hands and yelled into the mouthpiece as if she thought that she had to talk loud enough for him to hear her, wherever he was. "Daddy, can you come back? Somebody is getting the childrens!"

Tasha shook her head. Whenever DeShaun got scared, mad, or even really happy, she started talking like a baby. Her voice got all high, and she messed up even simple words.

Tasha didn't know exactly what Daddy said to Shaun, but she figured that it was something like he would not be coming home right that instant, because DeShaun knocked the can from the table to the floor. Thick syrup and orange peaches landed on the yellow linoleum and were smashed under Mama's shoes as she sprang to take the phone from DeShaun, who was begging her daddy to come back and save them. "I'll call you back," Mama said into the phone and hung up.

They slept with Mama that night. She had invited them after they followed her around the house all evening, not wanting to be left in a room without her protective adult presence. Sometimes Tasha would feel better if DeShaun was in the room too. But today, when she thought about going to her room with her little sister and listening to the record player, she realized that being in a room with De-Shaun was just about the same as being alone. If something scary happened, what would DeShaun do? Probably run to Tasha expecting her to be the one to save the day, since she was the oldest and everything.

Mama stepped on DeShaun twice while trying to fix the curtain rod in the den.

"DeShaun, baby," Mama had said, "don't stand up under me like that. I don't want to hurt you."

And DeShaun had balled her face up and cried. Mama got on her knees so they would be about the same height and hugged her little daughter, who stopped crying enough to say, "Scared."

Tasha was frightened too, but she didn't want to cry about it. As a matter of fact, she wished DeShaun would shut up. They wouldn't be able to hear it if an intruder knocked in the front door with a sledgehammer. No, they would not be aware of a single thing until the man came to take them away.

"Do you want to sleep in my room tonight?" Mama asked.

DeShaun nodded.

"What about you, Miss Lady?"

"Okay," Tasha said, relieved. "If you want me to."

At bedtime, Tasha lay on her father's side of the bed, awake while DeShaun and her mother dreamed. Tonight was different from the other nights she and her sister had gotten themselves so frightened that they were allowed to sleep in their parents' big bed. Last June, there had been a ferocious thunderstorm. A power line had been hit and the Snoopy night-light had gone dark.

"Mama!" DeShaun had called.

"Come on in here," Daddy had said, sounding sleepy but like he was laughing. Tasha had thought she heard Mama giggle.

The girls had crawled into the bed between them and slept breathing in Mama's gardenia talc and Daddy's Old Spice underarm deodorant.

Tasha remembered the thunderstorm night. Her parents on each side of the bed provided a barrier between them and—what? Not the thunder; it boomed away, oblivious to their sleeping arrangements. And she hadn't been scared of thunder. It was only a sound. She had been startled, but not scared. So when had she ever truly been afraid? After watching a movie about a swamp-monster, she had trouble sleeping for weeks. But what exactly had she been afraid of? That a swamp-monster would come into her room? She *had* opened her eyes at the slightest sound, expecting to be face-to-face with the gooey green beast. But if the monster did in fact come into her bedroom, what would it do that was so scary? In the movie, the swamp-monster had the white girl in his arms and was heading back toward the muck and the white girl was crying *Help!* Then her boyfriend came and shot the monster with a bow and arrow and kissed the girl. The movie didn't really show what the monster was going to do with the girl if the boyfriend hadn't shown up, and Tasha couldn't imagine.

But this was way worse than a swamp-monster with vague motives. If a child murderer came in the doorway, he would have to kill Mama, then DeShaun, and then Tasha.

But if he came in the window, Tasha would be first. And it could happen. Didn't Monica Kaufman say that one girl was taken through her window? And Tasha knew what had happened to her. She got asphyxiated. *What's that?* Tasha had asked. Mama shut her eyes. *Smothered,* she breathed.

Tasha pressed her face into her pillow to see what it was like to be smothered, to be deprived of something as necessary as air. After a few seconds, her heart moved harder and she felt a desperation in her chest. She held her face there as long as she could and then she lifted her head. Her body acted without her, drawing a long, deep breath as if it were making up for lost time.

———

The power of DeShaun's tears had long been, for Tasha, a source of mystery and envy. As soon as Shaun's lower lip started trembling and her eyelashes went to blinking, their parents sprang into motion. Tasha's tears, it seemed, only brought admonitions to be a big girl. But it was DeShaun's enchanting weeping on the night they found out about the child murders that brought Daddy back home.

It took a few weeks for DeShaun's magic to kick in. Tasha was fumbling with the lock on the front door—trying to remember if pushing or pulling would keep the bolt from sticking—when the door opened from the inside. Tasha dropped her lunch box and used her free hand to grab her little sister's wrist. The plastic container opened when it hit the porch and an apple rolled out, badly bruised.

"Who's that fooling with my door?" Daddy said, smiling broadly, stretching his arms wide enough for a double embrace.

DeShaun ran into the hug, shouting, "Daddy! Daddy!" like TV kids, but Tasha stood back. He folded one arm over DeShaun's back but left the other free, inviting.

"Ladybug, you're not glad to see your father?" He stopped smiling.

"You came back for your fishing rod, screwdrivers, and stuff?"

"No," he said. "I came back for you two."

"You're taking us with you?" Tasha said, alarmed. DeShaun fell limp in her half hug.

"No," he said, laughing. "I mean I'm back home. For good."

Tasha consented to the hug then, but she didn't believe him until she had snuck into her parents' room and seen his underwear stacked in the top dresser drawer, their striped waistbands facing outward.

They sat at the table that night in their usual positions; the only evidence of the weeks that had passed without him was the little TV, which displayed the pictures of the lost children. Tasha was aware of the words *hot line* and *task force* as she shoveled bright yellow corn into her mouth. She looked up at the little screen and took in a photo of the little girl. Her hair was fastened into an unruly ponytail just above her right temple.

"Daddy," Tasha said, "at school somebody said that they took that one girl out of her house when she was asleep."

"For real?" DeShaun said.

"That's what Monica said."

"That girl that was taken out of her house was different," Daddy said. "I believe that was her stepdaddy."

"Like Rex," Tasha said, interested.

Mama interrupted. "Tasha, don't even say that. Next thing you know, you'll be going around telling folks that Rex is going to kill Ayana."

"I wasn't going to say that," Tasha said, wondering how her mother could look right into her head and see what she was thinking.

"But somebody took her out of her bed?" DeShaun asked again.

"Carried her out of the window," Tasha added. "And nobody ever saw her again. They still don't know where she is."

"Tasha, stop," Mama said.

Daddy sat DeShaun on his lap and put his hands on either side of her toast-colored face, smoothing back the hair that had escaped her barrettes. "Nobody is going to take you out of this house. Nobody is going to hurt my family as long as I'm around."

"And anyway," said Tasha, "we have burglar bars."

But burglar bars were not enough to convince Mama and Daddy that the house was safe. When the number of faces on the news increased to an even dozen, they told the girls that their routine had to change. After school they were to go to Mrs. Mahmud's house, next door, like they had when they were little kids, and stay there until Mama got off work at five. Under no circumstances were they to go into the house alone. Tasha was relieved. Although she had once been especially proud of the silver key, she had begun to dread turning it in the door and entering the empty house with DeShaun. After school Tasha, in charge, would turn up the thermostat, get their snack from the counter and put it in their room (although they knew better than to eat in there). Then, the girls would go to the bathroom, each one sitting on the side of the bathtub keeping watch while the other was vulnerable. This completed, they would go to their room, shut the door and put a chair in front of it as an obstacle for child murderers who might be lurking in the house waiting for sisters coming home alone.

When Mrs. Mahmud opened the door for Tasha and DeShaun, the girls looked at each other quizzically. The lime-colored living room had been transformed. Before, Mrs. Mahmud's house had been full of knickknacks that children were forbidden to touch. The girls had sat on the living-room couch, still as mummies, until their parents came to retrieve them. Now, however, the fragile glass rocking horses had been removed and the carpet covered with a plastic sheath. Children were all over the place engaged in rainy-day activities. A group of four or so seventh-graders were playing Monopoly. Roy from across the street was in the kitchen frosting brownies with an unsteady hand. His brother, David, read quietly in the corner.

"Everybody is over here!" DeShaun said, wriggling out of her coat. She was right. They had spent so many afternoons locked in their room they hadn't noticed that none of the neighborhood kids played outside anymore.

"Let me hang up your coat," Mrs. Mahmud said, picking DeShaun's green plaid jacket up from the floor. Tasha was reluctant to remove hers. It was a pretty pink one with genuine rabbit fur around the hood and sleeves. Daddy had brought it home one day hanging from a little hook above

the window of the passenger seat of his car. Tasha had
thought that it was dry cleaning but the package was
opaque. And something about the way he handled it made
it clear that this was more than just his gray suit. He'd held
the garment with its hanger hooked over his index finger,
gone into his bedroom and shut the door.

Tasha had stood in front of the shut door and listened.
Mama was in the kitchen banging pots and pans, making
all sorts of distracting noise. But Tasha knew how to concentrate on what she was listening for. There was the sound
of rustling plastic. He was unwrapping the thing. She
wished that the door had a big keyhole like doors in stories.
But real-life doors locked with a little round button in the
center of doorknobs, and kids' rooms had no locks at all.

"Tash," Daddy called from inside the room.

How did he know she was out there? She had pretty
much accepted that Mama had eyes in the back of her head
and even X-ray vision sometimes. But not Daddy.

"Tasha!" he said louder, and she realized that he was just
calling her in the regular way. She scampered back to her
room to answer.

"Sir?"

"Come here for a minute."

"Okay, let me put my spelling words up."

The door was still closed when she reached her parents'
room. Should she knock on it or barge right in like she usually did? She tapped lightly on the door frame and went inside.

"Ta-dah!" Daddy said, with a grand swoop of his arm,
motioning toward the bed.

Tasha eyed the rose-colored satin incredulously. She whispered, "Did Mama see this yet?"

Daddy winked and shook his head.

"What about DeShaun?"

"Nope."

She giggled deliciously, sliding into the coat as Daddy held it. She turned on her toes in a complete circle before the full-length mirror twice before Daddy said, "Don't get dizzy and fall."

Monica Fisher was going to pass out with jealousy. This coat was not only trimmed in genuine rabbit fur, as the label verified, but it came with a matching muff to keep her pretty little hands warm.

Tasha had to let that fabulous coat rot in her closet for a month and a half as she waited for the weather to cool off. She was afraid that she would have to wait until Christmas and who knew how many girls would have new coats by then? But October brought a little nip to the morning air. Tasha wore the heavy coat although DeShaun only had on a windbreaker.

Mrs. Mahmud said, "Let me hang up that gorgeous coat in the hall closet by itself so that nothing happens to it."

Tasha wiggled out of the coat and headed to the living room and sat outside of a group of three kids playing Monopoly. They had all gotten to Mrs. Mahmud's at least an hour before since their school was in walking distance. She thought about asking them to start the game over so that she could play, but she didn't really know them all that well. Besides, she wasn't a big fan of Monopoly. She didn't want to play a board game. She wanted things to be like they were before, when she was in charge of her own house for two wonderful afternoon hours. This felt like being demoted to kindergarten.

Tasha quickly got tired of watching the Monopoly game. She wished she had brought something to read. She wandered into the kitchen where Mrs. Mahmud was on the telephone, laughing. When she saw Tasha, she shooed her away with a wide hand decorated with nail polish. Mrs. Mahmud was the kind of grown person that Tasha didn't really like, the kind that thought that kids weren't supposed to talk unless someone talked to them first. Her Great-Aunt Reatha was like that. She even went so far as to say, out loud, that "children should be seen and not heard," like they weren't really people at all.

Mama and Daddy were even getting to be like that now. Tasha didn't like it, but she kept quiet at dinner now. It hurt her feelings not to be allowed to contribute to the conversations, but it did have benefits. It seemed that when she was not heard, she was not seen either.

That night at dinner, she sucked saltine crackers until they were mushy and quietly swallowed them. Mama and Daddy were talking and she didn't want to disrupt their illusion of privacy. They spoke more freely when she and De-Shaun were not part of the discussion, so she let them have their space.

"It's got to be somebody white," Daddy said, shoving his peas around his plate with a slice of light bread.

"Might be," Mama said.

"Might nothing. Think about it. You ain't never heard of nobody black going around killing people for no reason. That's white people's shit."

"Daddy," said DeShaun, "you're not supposed to say bad words."

Her little voice broke her parents' intensity. They both looked across the table at the girls as if they had forgotten that they even had children.

Tasha wanted to thump DeShaun right in the middle of her shiny little forehead. She never could just shut up and listen. Tasha would have gone ahead and crunched on her crackers and slurped her milk like a regular person if she had known DeShaun was going to butt into the conversation, demonstrating beyond a doubt that little pitchers have big ears.

"Girls," said Mama, noticing their empty plates, "go to your rooms and finish your homework."

"We already finished," Tasha said, although she knew the situation was hopeless.

"Go and look it over. I'll be up in a minute to see if you know all your spelling words."

Tasha gave her sister a look-what-you-did look and walked out of the room. As soon as they had crossed the threshold, Daddy started talking again. Tasha paused, just out of sight, and listened.

"Think about it, Delores," he said. "Charles Manson, Son of Sam, all of that stuff. White folks."

"I've known some black folks to do some ugly things," said Mama.

"I ain't saying that niggers are harmless. I know a black man will cut you in a minute on a Saturday night over his money or his woman, something like that."

"Yeah, a real good reason like that."

"Delores, I am not saying that it's all right to stab somebody for two dollars. I'm saying that *we* gotta have a *reason* for killing someone. White folks just kill for the hell of it."

"Hold on, Charles," Mama said, holding up her hand. "Tasha, I know you are not in that hallway."

Now how did she know that? Tasha had not made a single sound. She even breathed half as fast as she regularly did.

"We weren't doing anything," Tasha protested, heading to her room. She wanted to hear more about the white killers. What were their names again? Daddy said them easily, like he was saying the name of somebody famous like Michael Jackson or El Debarge. Tasha wished she could recall the names, but asking Daddy to repeat himself was entirely out of the question. She thumped DeShaun behind the ear as they headed down the dark hallway. She'd just have to make do with the information she had.

———

At recess, the fifth-graders had formed a kind of ad hoc discussion group. They clustered under shady trees sitting cross-legged on the pine needles. A breeze, cold but heavy with baking bread, blew over from the Sunbeam factory and made their stomachs growl and reminded them that lunchtime was only thirty minutes away.

Tasha was sitting between Monica and Forsythia. The two of them were best friends, but sometimes they were nice to Tasha. As a matter of fact, she had been with the two of them all day. She was dying to tell them what Daddy had said, but she waited. Some information was too juicy to be wasted on mere small talk. The words were inside her and trying to get out. She adjusted her weight from side to side as if she had to go to the bathroom.

"Stop wiggling," Monica said, too loud, and everyone laughed.

"I was just getting comfortable," Tasha mumbled. "And I was getting ready to say something."

"Well say it then." Monica had a way of making everything sound like a invitation to fight.

"I was just fixing to say that it has to be somebody white that's doing it."

Some of the kids nodded. "That's what my mama says too," said Roderick Palmer.

Tasha, encouraged, went on. "Because black people don't do stuff like that."

"Black folks do too kill people. My uncle . . ."

Tasha tried to sound like Daddy: patient, authoritative, but a little annoyed. "I'm not talking about people killing people over money or their woman."

Jashante broke in: "I'd cut somebody for my lady." He looked meaningfully at Tasha and turned a piece of candy over in his mouth.

Monica touched Tasha with that pointy elbow of hers. She must have done the same thing on the other side because Forsythia let out a low giggle.

"Well, who do we know that's white?" Roderick addressed the group.

"Miss Russell," volunteered someone behind Tasha.

Miss Russell was the art teacher who came to their class on Tuesdays. Her hair, the color of acorns, was so long she could sit on it.

"Miss Russell is a lady, fool," Jashante said. "Ladies don't be killing people."

"A lady can't kill a man; they not big enough, but she could get a little ol' third-grader."

"Even when I was just a third-grader, I wouldn't let no white lady come and kill me."

Tasha imagined that he wouldn't.

The conversation deteriorated into fifth-grade macho, with the boys illustrating in competing detail how they would handle a homicidal white woman.

Tasha was bored. The only white woman she could think of was skinny Miss Russell with her paint and clay, and any idiot could see that she wasn't about to try and kill anyone. As a matter of fact, Tasha thought that she was really nice and even liked her. She felt guilty listening to the boys discuss hypothetical acts of violence toward the art teacher, even if it was in hypothetical self-defense. The recess bell finally rang and the sound of tennis shoes rustling pine needles drowned out Roderick's insistence on the ferocity of his karate chop.

Tasha walked about a pace and a half behind her companions.

"What you waiting for?" Monica asked.

"I'm not waiting," Tasha said, hoping to sound casual.

"Her boyfriend," Forsythia said. "I saw you looking at Jashante the whole time."

Tasha stared at the pretty girl incredulously. It was unspoken but accepted that Monica would be the one to initiate all teasing or ridicule. This was unprecedented; Tasha was unprepared.

"I was not looking at that boy." She shoved her hands into her fur muff.

"And he was looking right back at her."

"No he wasn't," Monica said. "Jashante wasn't studying Tasha."

Now Tasha was unsure if Monica was coming to her defense (also unprecedented) or if she was implying that Tasha wasn't cute enough for a boy to look at, even one like Jashante. Because of this double possibility, Tasha was unsure how to respond.

Monica continued. "Tasha wouldn't talk to somebody like that anyway. He been kept back so many times that even *he* don't know what grade he supposed to be in. And"—she lowered her voice—"he lives in the projects."

"So," Forsythia said. "She was still looking at him. You saw it too; that's why you elbowed me."

"Looking isn't the same as talking."

"She was smiling too."

"I was just trying to be nice," Tasha said.

Forsythia said, "My mama says you just can't *be* nice to some people."

Now what did that mean? There were some people that kids weren't nice to, like Octavia Fuller, who they called the Watusi; but Tasha figured that everyone could be nice to her if they felt like it. Maybe there were some people that you just *couldn't* be kind to, but she was pretty sure that she hadn't met any of them.

DeShaun wasn't scared anymore. She could eat an entire plate of spaghetti while the newscaster talked about the Missing and Murdered Children. Tasha watched her sucking the noodles into her figure-eight mouth; the end of each pasta string slapped her gently under her nose.

"You're not supposed to eat like that," Tasha told her. "You can choke like that."

"For real?"

"And when you choke, your lips turn blue. You'll be trying to call somebody to help you but you won't even have enough air to talk with—"

"Tasha, cut that out," Daddy said.

As soon as Daddy started paying attention, DeShaun started acting like she was really worried about choking.

"Do kids really choke on their spaghetti and die, Daddy?"

Daddy gave Tasha a long look that said that he was mad. She would have given DeShaun a hard pinch under the table if she thought she could get away with it. But there was nothing that she could do with Mama and Daddy both sitting right there.

At night, in their canopy beds, Tasha said to her sister, "I wonder what's happening to all those boys." There was no noise from DeShaun's side of the room. "Someone, or some *thing*, is hunting them."

"Some *thing?*" DeShaun said. "What do you mean by that?"

Tasha smiled in the gentle orange glow of the nightlight. "I mean that whatever is killing those kids might not be a person. It could be a creature or something."

"What kind of creature?"

"Oh, any kind of creature. There are a lot of different kinds. Especially around here. The only thing keeping the creature from getting us is Daddy."

"For real?"

"Think about it," Tasha said knowingly. "When somebody gets killed, they show just the mama crying on the TV. Those kids that got snatched, not one single one of them has a daddy."

"For real?"

"Um-hum. That's why Daddy came back. Remember he said 'Nobody will hurt you as long as I'm around'? That's what he was talking about. I'm just telling you what I know."

The girls lay uneasily in the darkness and almost quiet. The story she had told DeShaun was only half real, like chocolate Easter candy with just air in the middle. Little snuffly sounds made their way across the room.

"What's the matter?" Tasha said like she didn't know.

"Scared."

"Scared of what?"

"The creature."

Tasha felt cruel like that time she had poured salt on a snail and it had dissolved into a shell full of blood.

"That creature is not going to mess with you. Remember I said that it only bothers kids without dads."

"But Daddy left us that time. When they were separated."

DeShaun was getting smarter.

"Well," Tasha said, "if the creature tries to get you, all you have to do is say a magic word."

"What is it?"

Tasha started to make something up, run some syllables together, but she changed her mind. "I don't know yet."

"You could tell me. I won't tell anybody." DeShaun's voice collapsed like a house made out of Popsicle sticks falling in on itself.

"You can come over here if you want to," Tasha said, scooting against the wall to make space in her narrow bed.

———

October was dry and cool; the pine needles, brittle and sharp, blew across the playground, tumbling end over end, erasing footprints. Tasha leaned carefully against a dull silver pole and watched the boys run races. They crouched like the runners in the Olympics two years past. One knee on the ground, between their hands, the other leg stretched behind. Each boy looked straight ahead at the line scuffed in the red dirt with the toe of a sneaker. The winner would be the one who crossed this line first.

Monica said, "On your marks, get set, GO!" and the boys pushed themselves forward and ran. They beat the air with their tight fists and turned their faces upward as they struggled to get to the line, where Forsythia would declare the winner. Jashante was in front. He moved more freely than the other boys because no one forced him to wear a cumbersome jacket. His arms pumped powerfully in a thin pullover sweater as they kept time with his legs.

Tasha watched him propelling himself forward, sweating though coatless; she wondered with envy what it felt like to be fast and to be a boy.

"Let's do relay races," Monica suggested.

"Mixed teams," Forsythia added. "Girls and boys."

The two of them had on blue jeans and tennis shoes too. They had planned this. Tasha was wearing a navy blue jumper and her good coat. Why did Ayana have to go to private school? She and Tasha had been friends ever since kindergarten. Tasha looked down. She couldn't run in the shoes she had on, nice leather ones with side buckles. And mixed teams? What boy would want to run with her? Roderick had already made his way over to Forsythia. Tasha saw him pull on one of her long straightened braids.

She turned her back to the kids who were milling about trying to find partners. She saw Rodney Green, the weirdest kid in her class, maybe in the whole school even. He was the only person not watching the races. Some kids pretended not to watch, but Tasha knew they monitored the proceedings covertly. But Rodney was locked inside his own head. He sat alone on the cool red dirt with his back against the school building, pouring Alexander the Grapes into his mouth. Rodney had even fewer friends than Tasha, but he was so weird that he didn't even care. Maybe that was better.

She turned in response to a tap on her shoulder and saw Jashante standing there. "You want to be my partner, Fancy Girl?" he asked, reminding her of their walkway encounter.

He smiled, showing a chipped front tooth. He reached for her hand as if she had already agreed. "Come on."

"Oooh," Monica sang out omnisciently from somewhere. "Tasha and Jashante sitting in a tree—"

Tasha pulled her hand away. Jashante's sweat-and-grass smell was suddenly suffocating and she wanted to be away from him. "Somebody already asked me."

"Who?" The cute smile was gone.

Tasha couldn't answer.

"Ain't nobody ask you," he said, "ugly as you is." He put both of his hands on her shoulders, amplifying his green odor.

"You better get back from me," she said, hitting at him.

Jashante held her fists tightly and pulled her close to his chest. The buttons on his sweater pressed her face. "Why you don't want to be my partner? You think you too good to be my partner; that's what it is."

Tasha was pulling away from him with all of her strength and suddenly, he released her, causing her to fall backward in the red dirt. There was a rip as the pink thread underneath her arms gave way. She was aware of people laughing at her. She looked behind her and saw Roderick laughing so hard that fat tears sat on his pretty-as-a-girl lashes. Jashante was cracking up too. "You not too good now," he said.

Tasha got up and pushed her chest into Jashante's. The pressure of his body mashed the zipper on her shirt painfully into the space between her small breasts. While their faces were close she said, "I hope you die. I hope the man snatches you and . . ." She searched her mind for the word she had heard on the news. "I hope you get asphyxiated and when they find you you are going to be . . ." What was the other word? "Decomposed."

Jashante stepped back. His smile was gone and he looked at her with something that might have been hurt feelings. Then the sad expression vanished and he pushed her down easily with a swift thrust of his arms. "Forget you, then."

"What'd she say?" Tasha heard the students ask. "What

happened?" The laughter was over. Tasha heard a few un-easy titters like the last drops of water trickling from the faucet as they put together the ugly words she had said with what they had seen on the news.

"She put a curse on him!" Roderick spat out.

The entire fifth grade was shocked into silence until Monica spoke. "I never did like her anyway," she said.

"Me either," agreed Forsythia. "We were just trying to be nice to her, but my mama says that you just can't *be* nice to some people."

Tasha wished that she had gone ahead and run the relay race with Jashante like she wanted to in the first place. Being teased about going with a project boy wouldn't be as bad as being the one that nobody liked. Even Rodney Green had turned his attention away from his candy to stare at her in openmouthed horror, his tongue and teeth stained blue with candy. Tasha caught sight of the red stain of Georgia clay on the sleeve of her pretty coat. She twisted her arm around for a better look. Hot tears came. She should have just told him that she didn't want to run a relay race in her good coat. She sat crying and sweating on the concrete when the bell rang calling everyone back into the building.

Tasha was the last one into the cafeteria. She stood at the end of the line behind two girls that she didn't know very well. Their names were Tracie and Demetria, but she had never jumped rope with them or played jacks.

Tracie said, "That's the one."

"Her?" Demetria said. "I can't believe Shante was trying to talk to her in the first place."

Project girls were the only ones who shortened Jashante's name like that.

"He wasn't trying to talk to her. He was just asking her to run with him in the race."

"And then she said *that* to him?"

Tracie nodded, one hand on her hip.

"See, that's why I don't fool with siditty girls."

"If I was Shante I would've slapped her right there."

Tasha endured the abuse silently. She didn't know what to say to these girls who moved their necks when they spoke and chewed gum brazenly, even popping it, although it was against the rules to bring gum to school.

"Who she think she is, anyway?"

"I didn't mean it," Tasha managed to say.

Demetria spun around. "Excuse you."

Tracie followed suit, swiveling her neck with each syllable. "It is *rude* to get into other people's conversations."

Tasha took her tray and looked for a place to sit. She would have liked to have sat alone, but all of the tables were occupied. There was no choice but to share. She surveyed the scene. Monica was sitting by Jashante and was even eating French fries from his plate. He was sitting where she normally sat. Where to sit? Tracie and Demetria had an empty seat at the table where they were but that was out of the question. Rodney Green had a table all to himself. His blue book satchel occupied one of the empty chairs like a companion. She thought about sitting with him, but even he hated her now.

"Miss Baxter, please find a seat," Mr. Harrell ordered.

Little bubbles of laughter popped all over the room.

"You can sit with me."

She moved in the direction of the kind voice. She

looked at the faces of the kids she passed, trying to figure out who had invited her.

"Right here."

The offer had come from Octavia, the one the kids called the Watusi.

Tasha hesitated; if she was the person that nobody liked right now, then Octavia was the person that nobody ever liked. If she sat with Octavia today, she could never eat with Monica and Forsythia again. Unpopularity was terribly contagious.

"You don't have to sit here," said Octavia. "I was just trying to be nice."

Tasha set her tray down and slid onto the red stool. "No. I want to sit with you."

She shrugged as Tasha opened her milk carton.

"Thank you," Tasha said, eager to demonstrate that she was a person somebody could be nice to.

Tasha watched Octavia pick translucent pieces of onion off of her slice of pizza. She should turn her attention to her own plate before Octavia looked up and said *What you looking at?* and sent her away. But Tasha was suddenly consumed with an intense curiosity about her new lunch partner. Octavia was black—*black as night,* Roderick had said, laughing. That's why kids called her the Watusi, because she looked like a black African. Tasha had never really looked at Octavia closely enough to see more than that darkness. But now, two trays apart, Tasha saw that Octavia wasn't ugly. Her hair was a mess, though. It was all trying to go back into one ponytail but the hair around the edges wasn't long enough or straight enough to make it to the red rubber band; that hair stuck out around her face like the rays of the sun in a

kid's drawing. Last year, Mrs. Willingham got so tired of seeing Octavia come to school with her hair all over her head
that she took her into the teacher's lounge and plaited it herself. Or that's what Monica had said. But she had also said
that Octavia smelled worse than a black African because she
didn't have soap at home to wash with. But Octavia smelled
like lemonade.

Tasha carefully lifted the droopy rectangular slice of
pizza to her mouth but put it down, embarrassed, observ-
ing Octavia cutting hers into neat triangles.

"So why you not sitting with all your friends?" Octavia
asked.

Tasha shrugged and looked down at her green sectioned
plate. "I don't know."

Octavia gave Tasha a look that was so much like Mama's
that Tasha felt herself starting to confess in spite of herself.
"Jashante wanted to be my relay partner and I said no. So
then he pushed me down. I got up and said something bad
to him and now everybody is mad with me."

Tasha waited for Octavia to finish chewing.

"How come you didn't want to be his partner?" she
asked.

Tasha didn't say anything right away. Her big mouth had
gotten her into enough trouble for this one day. And besides, the truth was humiliating now. She opened her mouth
to say, "I didn't want to run in the race with my good coat
on," when she noticed Octavia's wrists protruding from the
sleeves of her turtleneck sweater. When Tasha's clothes
started fitting like that, Mama would pack them up and
send them to cousins in the country or to the Goodwill.
How could she even mention fur-trimmed pink satin, now

marked with red clay, to someone so obviously poor? Tasha couldn't say anything in her own defense. She felt hopelessly lost and unsure. She wanted her father.

"How come you didn't want to be partners with Shante?" Octavia asked again. Her voice was challenging.

"I just wasn't feeling well. That's all," Tasha said.

She had never been sadder. The tears came suddenly and deeply as the enormity of everything pressed her chest and stole her air. She cried for her father's empty dresser drawers and the TV pictures that had brought him back. Her tears were for deserted playgrounds, clothes that didn't look like they did in catalogs, and words that wouldn't be taken back. There was no air. Her mouth was open but there was no noise. No air. Asphyxiation. Octavia was out of her seat, shaking her shoulder, shouting, "Mr. Harrell! Mr. Harrell!" Tasha inhaled. Lemonade.

Mama came to pick Tasha up with the rapid worried clatter of heels against tile and the nervous jingle of keys.

"Tasha—" She said her name almost like a question as she entered the sick bay and sat on the edge of the narrow bed.

"Mama, it was such a bad day."

Mama pulled her onto her lap. Tasha was getting taller; her feet touched the ground as her mother rocked her gently. She smelled like coffee and peppermint. Tasha shut her eyes.

Mama whispered to the nurse, "Where are her things?"

"In her classroom," the nurse replied, looking up from her paperback.

"I don't want to go in there," Tasha said.

"It's okay," Mama said, rubbing her back in tiny circles.

"Will you stay home with me?" Mama was in charge of the payroll department at Pitman and Sons. She often complained that the whole place would fall apart if she took even a day off.

"Of course I'll stay with you." Mama kissed the top of Tasha's head.

"Mr. Pitman said it was okay?"

"You let me worry about Mr. Pitman. Family comes first."

Tasha closed her eyes until there was a tiny polite tap on the door.

"Come in," Mama said.

Monica came in carrying Tasha's book satchel. She put it on the cot.

"Hello, Monica," Mama said in a friendly voice.

Tasha squeezed her eyes tight. There was nothing she could do to keep Monica from witnessing her curled up in her mother's lap like a baby, but she didn't have to see Monica seeing her.

Mama felt Tasha stiffen and held her a little closer. Tasha never wanted to go to school again.

Monica put the red-and-white satchel on the floor near the bed. "I hope you feel better, Tasha."

She didn't open her eyes or reply, although she could feel Monica standing there, all innocent looking, waiting for some sort of response.

There was another knock. Tasha wiggled from the warm lap. She wasn't going to be humiliated twice.

Octavia opened the door. She looked a little startled to see so many people in the cramped sick bay.

"Her coat," she said. "Monica left it."

Mama said, "Thank you, young lady."

Octavia returned the smile and then looked at the floor. "I got to go. I got to get this hall pass back before I get into trouble."

Monica, standing by the door, mashed her lips together as if it were taking all of her strength to keep from lying on the floor laughing and banging her fists like kids in cartoons. Tasha wished that Monica were as concerned about returning *her* hall pass.

Mama said in the voice she used to talk to Tasha's friends, "Thank you very much for bringing the coat." Then to Tasha, "Is this nice young lady a friend of yours?"

Monica looked like the force of laughter held in would make her eyeballs shoot from their sockets. Tasha hated Monica. After all, she was the cause of all of this. If it hadn't been for Monica saying *separated* that day, none of this would be happening. And now, Monica standing by the door biting her lips was keeping Tasha from saying *Mama, this is my new friend, Octavia.*

Monica made a sound like the first noise of laughter breaking free from her glued-together lips.

"Is there a problem?" Mama asked Monica.

"No'm," Monica said.

Mama said again, "Is this your friend?"

"Kind of," Tasha mumbled.

Octavia hung the pink coat on the back of a chair. "I got to give the hall pass back," she said.

"Get well soon, Tasha," Monica sang.

Mama took the coat off the chair and helped Tasha into it.

"Good gracious," she said. "What happened to this coat?"

"I fell," Tasha said.

"This isn't going to come out," Mama said, as if she were talking to herself. "I told him not to spend all that money." She hit at the stain with her palm.

"It's ruined?" Tasha asked.

Mama changed her tone. "Maybe not ruined. We might be able to get it where you can still wear it, but I doubt that we can get all that clay out."

She zipped Tasha into the coat and they stepped out into autumn.

———

Monica came to class on Wednesday wearing a brand-new pair of Gloria Vanderbilt jeans, a yellow blouse with a white collar, and even matching yellow-and-white tennis shoes. Balanced delicately in the palm of her hand were nine pink envelopes, the color of stomach medicine, fastened with magenta foil hearts: She was having a slumber party. For the past two weeks, Tasha had eavesdropped as Monica and Forsythia had revised the guest list at lunchtime, scratching off names and adding others. Tasha tried not to appear anxious as Monica shuffled the envelopes, moving this one or that one to the middle from the top of the stack, as if she were alphabetizing them.

It was possible that one of the fancy envelopes had her name on it. After all, there were *ten* to be given out and Tasha had been very good friends with Monica up until last month. Hadn't Monica and Forsythia both come to her birthday party last year? It was rude to get an invitation and not send one back. Mama had said that was a *social obligation*.

Monica stood up and put one pink invitation on the corner of Forsythia's desk. Tasha put a check beside Forsythia's name on the list she had written, hoping to predict Monica's choices. There were seven girls sure to be invited, but six more would have to compete for the remaining three slots. Tasha put a little star by those names to mean *alternate* like they did when they listed the girls who would be on the cheerleading team.

Carmen Montgomery said sweetly, "Thank you, Monica," as she peeled back the magenta heart on her envelope.

Darn. Carmen was one of the alternates. As Monica came near, Tasha put her spelling book over her version of the list and tried to seem like she was too busy studying her words to be concerned over the possibility of receiving an invitation.

Mr. Harrell's sudden entrance sent Monica scurrying back to her chair. Her new sneakers squeaked as she scooted. Had she been heading Tasha's way? It was possible. Even though Tasha had not been asked to sit at their table since that day she had gotten into it with Jashante, things had gotten better. Hadn't they? Tasha didn't have to eat lunch with Octavia anymore. Now she sat with Tayari, who was fun to sit with because she was really good at imitating people's voices. Tayari was on the list of alternates.

After lunch, Monica had only one invitation left. She didn't even walk over to the lucky girl to deliver it. Instead, she handed it to the person next to her and whispered, "Pass it on." The person looked at the name, written in big loops and circles, and gave it to the next kid. Each project girl who handled the pink rectangle made an annoyed sound as she fairly threw it along. The boys seemed uneasy and quickly sent the frilly thing on. Tasha kept her eye on the prize as it came her way; it had to pass two alternates before it got to her. Angelite Armstrong passed it to Tayari and it stopped.

Maybe Tayari was just playing; after all, she was a cutup. Maybe she was going to hold it awhile, thank Monica in a funny voice, and then pass it on. Surely Monica and Forsythia weren't still mad about what Tasha had said to Jashante. They couldn't be. *Monica* had been the one who was talking about him living in the projects in the first place. And anyway, they didn't even like Jashante. He didn't eat lunch with them again after that first day. Part of it probably was that he hadn't been to school that much this month. But when he was here last week, he sat with some other boys and didn't even look over at Forsythia or Monica. Maybe he had forgotten all about that day. Tasha had said hi to him when she was on her way to the water fountain a couple of weeks ago. He didn't say hi back, but he lifted his head up and jutted his chin a little bit to show that he had heard her.

But what had Forsythia said that day? *I never did like her.* Monica had agreed. But that wasn't true. It couldn't be. The two of them had been to her house. Twice. They might not like her *now*, but they *used* to. And they might still. Tayari needed to stop playing around—she was really immature sometimes—and just pass Tasha that pretty invitation.

Tayari ripped open the envelope, not even bothering to save the sticky magenta heart. Tayari looked as surprised as Tasha. She spun her head on her neck, grinning so hard her molars showed. Tasha ran her finger down a column of spelling words, as if this week's quiz were the reason she was on the brink of tears.

"What's the matter?" Daddy asked.

"Nothing."

"Monica's having a party and Tasha didn't get an invitation," DeShaun said while stuffing the end of a hot dog into her mouth.

"I thought Monica was your friend," Daddy said.

Where had he been for the last month? On Mars?

"She used to be," Tasha said.

"Well," Mama said brightly, "let's all go bowling."

Bowling? Mama couldn't possibly think a *family outing* would be an acceptable substitute for a party, could she?

Daddy took a swallow of beer and said, "Tasha, if Monica doesn't want you at her party, then she was never your friend in the first place. Don't worry about it."

Tasha could tell from his tone that he was trying to be comforting, but she burst into tears anyway.

Mama gave Daddy a see-what-you-did look and he gave back his confused what-did-I-do? glance. DeShaun slurped up the last of the soda. "Ahh!" she said, like people on commercials.

Then, the phone rang. Mama answered.

"Hello? Why hello, Ayana," Mama stressed the name. She raised her eyebrows to say *Do you feel like talking?* Tasha nodded.

"Tasha's right here," Mama said, looking to see if Tasha was composed. "So how are you liking middle school?" she asked.

Tasha was hurriedly drying her eyes as if Ayana could see through the telephone wires.

"Hey!" Ayana said, when Tasha finally got to the phone. "I thought your mama was going to talk me to death!"

"She's just real friendly," Tasha said, feeling guilty that her mother had appeared inappropriately loquacious just to hide Tasha's tears.

"Anyway," Ayana said. "I was just calling to see if you want to go with me to Skate Towne."

"Hold on," Tasha said, covering the phone with her hand. "Can I go to Skate Towne with Ayana?"

Mama said, "Who's taking you?"

"Ayana, Mama wants to know who's taking us."

"Cookie."

"Cookie's gonna drive us."

Cookie was Ayana's seventeen-year-old cousin who wore lots of brass bangles that sounded like wind chimes when she walked.

"What *adult*," Mama said.

"But you let Cookie take us that other time!" Tasha reminded her, hoping to establish precedent.

"That was last year."

Tasha said into the phone, "My mama won't let me go."

"Aw. Cookie says I can't go unless I have someone to be with. She's going to meet her boyfriend up there so she doesn't want me hanging around her."

Tasha covered the phone again, "Pleeeeease."

Mama said, "Tasha, I'm just thinking about your safety."

"I'll take them," Daddy said, finishing his beer.

Tasha wasn't sure if this was a good idea or not. She needed to bounce it off Ayana.

"What if my daddy takes us?"

Ayana thought about it for a minute. "Will he be actually trying to skate or is he just going to be there making sure we don't get snatched or anything?"

"Daddy, you're not going to try to *skate,* are you?"

He laughed. "You are not ashamed of your father, are you? No. I'm just going to play pinball or something."

Tasha said, "He doesn't want to skate."

"Okay, he can come."

Daylight was almost gone by the time Tasha got dressed and ready to go. It was already dark when they got to Skate Towne. Daddy was complaining about the lighting.

"With all these kids that are around here, they need to install some lights." Daddy took Tasha's hand like she was a little girl; this was a potentially embarrassing situation. "This don't make no sense."

When they got to the window to pay the entry fee, the girl behind the counter said, "One dollar to get in. Two for skates." She was about Cookie's age, and very pretty, Tasha thought. That's what she wanted to look like when she got to be a teenager.

"Why is it so dark outside?" Daddy demanded.

The pretty girl said something like, "Because it's night-time."

Daddy didn't laugh. He lowered his eyebrows and said, "Excuse me, young lady?"

She said, "I don't know why it's so dark out."

"I need to talk to a manager."

The girl disappeared from the window and came back

with a man who was mostly bald. What hair he had left made a soft halo around the sides of his head.

"Is there a problem sir?"

Tasha could tell Daddy was mad. That girl was going to wish she had never gotten smart with him like that. *Pretty face, ugly attitude,* Mama would have said. But Daddy didn't even mention her. "I want to know why there isn't any lighting out in this parking lot. This place is crawling with kids. Common sense—"

"Sir," said the halo man, "I have a daughter myself." He smiled briefly at Tasha. "I opened this place back before all this started happening so that kids could have a safe place to go. So it's not that I don't care. I just can't afford to rewire that lot."

"But—" Daddy started.

"Let me finish," the halo man said. "I allow the parents free entry to try to get them to come on out with their kids. All of the lights in the world won't help if people won't supervise their children."

Tasha wished Daddy would just give the man his three dollars so she could go inside and look for Ayana.

"Man, I'm sorry if I came off wrong," Daddy said, finally going in his pocket for a roll of bills and peeling off three. "It's just that—"

"It's alright," the halo man said. "I understand. We got to look out for our own."

Ayana was easy to spot, sitting on a bench tying her skates. She had pulled her white button-down shirt out of her jeans and tied it up around her middle, exposing her neat navel. (If Daddy weren't here, Tasha might have tried the same thing.) When her skates were tight, Ayana reached a hand up and unraveled her braids, creating loose, even waves around her ears. Tasha's two braids were tacked to the top of her head like the Swiss Miss on the cocoa can. She wiggled a bobby pin that dug into her scalp. Lucky Ayana shook her head, making her pretty hair bounce.

Tasha had laced her own skates and was ready to step out onto the rink when Ayana said, "Let's go to the rest room and fix our faces."

Tasha said, "Makeup? I don't know." She pushed open the fuchsia door that said FOXES in loopy letters. She wondered how Ayana would get her hair back into neat plaits before her own mother saw her. Somehow, Ayana always got away with everything.

Ayana pulled out a small jar. "No. Just Vaseline."

Tasha was intrigued.

Ayana smoothed the thick white grease onto Tasha's eyelids. "See?" she said. "Now that will bring out your eyes."

Bring them out? What did that mean? Tasha looked in the mirror. The area below her eyebrows was shiny and it kind of looked like she had on eye shadow. Sort of. She dipped her finger in the Vaseline and smeared her lips. Cookie used something called Kissing Potion that made her lips glisten with the color and smell of strawberries. Vaseline was almost as good.

Tasha waited while Ayana finished primping. Although they were the same age, Ayana had been skipped a grade in school. At the middle school, Ayana was learning all kinds of tricks from the seventh- and eighth-graders while Tasha was still fooling around with elementary babies.

Ayana might have been more glamorous and experi-

enced, but she couldn't skate half as well as Tasha, who loved
roller-skating. The deejay turned the music up loud and
Tasha could feel the beat in her chest just like when a
marching band passed by in a parade. She moved her legs
easily with the rhythm and used her arms to go faster. As
she pushed into the glowing darkness, the reflections from
the disco ball were indoor winter fireflies. Tasha lowered her
eyes while she flowed, enjoying her breeze.

After a half hour or so, the girls were really hot—sweat
rolled down their scalps, plastering their baby hair to their
faces—but they sipped their icy Cokes slowly to keep from
getting headaches. Some boys came in the door, play-
fighting and laughing loud. The group of fathers sharing
pitchers of beer looked up from their plastic cups suspiciously.

The boys were old, Tasha thought. Old as Cookie, at
least. And where was Cookie, anyway? Tasha had noticed
her when they first got here, holding hands with her
boyfriend, but now she had disappeared.

"Where's Cookie?" Tasha asked Ayana.

Ayana shrugged.

"Do you think she's okay?" Tasha felt a little panicky, recalling the dark parking lot.

"Oh, she's alright," Ayana said, raising her eyebrows
twice. She had been using more and more nonverbal com-
munication since she started middle school. Tasha didn't
know what that eyebrow motion was meant to convey but
she raised hers back.

The six or so rowdy boys didn't skate. Instead, they
played pinball. Two of them tilted the machine backward if
the silver metal ball threatened to roll into the little hole at

the base, ending the game. This way, all of them were able to play with only a single quarter. The halo man kept a careful eye on them as he filled orders at the snack bar.

Tasha snuck peeks at them as she skated around the oval rink. She had to slow down in order to see more than boy-shaped blurs. There was a little guy with them. Clearly, his mother hadn't asked what adult when he had asked to go. He stood on his tiptoes in order to see the pinball game over the massive teenage shoulders. They moved as if he weren't even there; he had to jerk his head this way and that to avoid being carelessly elbowed in the nose. He should have brought a friend with him that was his own age. How old was he anyway? The flashing disco lights obscured details but Tasha figured that he was eleven, or maybe a little younger. On the next lap around, she was glad to see that he was given a turn at the machine.

Then, she fell. The lace of her left skate got caught up in the wheels and she fell flat on her behind. All of the big boys turned at once from the pinball machine, hooting and laughing. The little one turned to see what all the commotion was about. Evidently he lost the ball, because his friends started cursing him. Well, not exactly cursing; there was a large sign posted near the door declaring NO PROFANITY. They beat him about the head and shoulders with their baseball caps as Ayana helped Tasha to her feet and over to a bench.

It wasn't really that bad of a fall. Tasha was pretty sure that she wasn't bleeding but she checked for skinned knees anyway. People were less likely to tease a person if she seemed actually injured.

Ayana looked at the knee. "It's okay. But let's sit down for a while. This way we can see those cute guys over there."

Tasha was horrified. "They're teenagers!"

"All of them aren't. One looks thirteen or fourteen."

"Which one?"

She nodded toward the little one.

"Him? He's not more than twelve. I think maybe eleven."

"You must need glasses," Ayana said.

Tasha turned her head for a better look but Ayana pinched her arm. "Don't look. Here he comes."

Now what to do? Well, maybe nothing. He was probably coming to talk to Ayana. Or he could be just on his way to the bathroom or the concession stand.

When he said, "Hey," Tasha jumped because Ayana dug her pink frosted nails into the soft skin of her upper arm, and also because the voice was familiar.

"You alright, Fancy Girl?" Jashante glanced over his shoulder to the pinball teenagers.

"I'm okay," Tasha said, easing her arm from between Ayana's thumb and forefinger. She wished she and Ayana could communicate telepathically like twins. *This is the one I was telling you about* would echo in Ayana's head as clear as if she had spoken. But maybe Ayana already knew. And if she did, she didn't seem to be holding it against him.

He shoved his hands in his pockets and looked at his ragged tennis shoes. He glanced up at Ayana. "That's your sister?"

"No. This is Ayana, my play-cousin."

He didn't say anything. Ayana elbowed her.

"You wanna sit down?" Tasha scooted down on the bench. Would Ayana approve?

"No. That's alright," he said, looking back.

"What school do you go to?" He was talking to Ayana.

"Saint Anthony."

"Where that is?"

"Over by West End."

"That's the one where the girls wear blue skirts?"

"Yeah."

"I was wondering about that one time," he said.

He was paying a little too much attention to Ayana. Tasha regretted not tying her own shirt or loosening her hair.

"What grade?" he asked.

"Sixth," Ayana said. Tasha was sure she heard a note of pride.

"My friend, he in the eighth. He say you look good."

Tasha noticed a boy standing about ten feet away watching the proceedings closely. Jashante probably wasn't lying about his friend's grade, but Tasha thought somebody needed to ask how old he was. Tasha could detect the soft fuzzy beginning of a mustache.

"You wanna talk to him?" Jashante asked.

Ayana shrugged her shoulders in a way that Tasha thought was very sophisticated. It didn't say *I don't know*. It was more like *I don't care*. Impressive.

Jashante said to Tasha, "You want something from the concession stand?"

Tasha would have liked to duplicate Ayana's magnificently nonchalant shrug, but this was no time to experiment. She looked to her friend. Ayana did that indecipherable eyebrow thing again. As Tasha started to the snack bar with Jashante, the world's oldest eighth-grader slid onto the bench beside Ayana.

The short distance to the concession stand made for an awkward stroll since Tasha had her skates on. But Jashante didn't laugh at her as she walked on her toes, balancing on the skates' brakes.

"Want some candy?"

Tasha looked at the different candies in the glass display case. Was he saying that he was going to pay for her? He didn't seem to be making a move for his wallet and she didn't have any money at all. And if he did decide to pay, would that mean that this was a *date?* What if she chose something too expensive? He solved the problem by making a suggestion.

"M and Ms?"

Tasha nodded her head.

"Plain or peanut?"

"Plain?"

He asked the halo man for one of each and counted out six bright dimes from a huge handful of change he pulled from the front pocket of his jeans.

"How come you have so much change?" Tasha asked.

"Selling stuff."

"What kind of stuff?"

"Oh," he said seriously. "Stuff. Like this." He went into his back pocket and retrieved a car air freshener shaped like a Christmas tree. "Sold these for fifty cents each." He held it out to Tasha. "You can have this one."

She was pleased. "What do you do with all the money you make?"

"Most of it, I give to my mama, but I keep some for my lady." He smiled at Tasha, showing that cute chipped tooth.

Tasha grinned back as he handed her the dark brown package of M&Ms. She didn't want to eat them. This was her first gift from a boy and should be put in a scrapbook or a memory box. A boy had given Ayana an ink pen shaped like a candy cane and she had preserved it in a pretty case on her dresser. But what about edible mementos? Tasha was unsure of the rules here. Besides, Mama was strict about no food in the bedrooms. That's how people get bugs. Was he asking her to be his lady? But what would that involve? Sitting together at lunch? And anyway, she had the air freshener, which might technically be the first thing. But he didn't *buy* that. He just had it in his pocket.

"Thank you for the M and Ms," Tasha said.

Jashante had opened his candy and held a large misshapen yellow M&M between his thumb and forefinger. He was waiting on her to open hers. Tasha shook one flat chocolate pill onto her palm. She looked up at her date. He moved his hand toward his mouth and she did the same, carefully synchronizing their motions. They chomped into the sweet chocolate at precisely the same exact magical instant.

Tasha would have liked to have repeated their communion as many times as there were M&Ms in their little packages for as many packages as Jashante had dimes to buy. But he ate the rest of his candy without ceremony. The deejay announced Couples' Skate, as the opening notes of her favorite song, "I Call Your Name," filled the arena.

"You like this song?" he asked.

"Yeah. You?"

"Um-hum." Jashante smiled at her, then turned away. He looked at his foot for a minute and then he stared intently at her face. His gaze did not travel all over like that time outside of the classroom. Tasha recalled that encounter the way a person remembers her babyhood—as something indistinct but a memory not to be doubted.

Then Daddy was there. "Okay, Tasha, it's time to go." He held her pink coat for her to slip her arms in. Mama had sent it to the cleaners but the red clay mark was still visible, even in this light. Tasha hoped the coat wouldn't remind Jashante of their run-in.

"But, Daddy, I still have my skates on," Tasha complained.

"Well, go turn them in," he said, turning to break up Ayana's cozy conversation with her new friend.

Jashante mumbled, "Bye," and moved toward the gang at the pinball machine.

"See you Monday," Tasha called. If he heard her, she couldn't tell.

Daddy drove Ayana home in spite of her insistence that Cookie would be back any minute to pick her up. After Mrs. McWhorter shut the door behind Ayana, Daddy turned his attention to Tasha.

"Who was that boy you were talking to?"

"He's in my class at school."

"How old is he?"

"Eleven," Tasha said.

"Eleven times what?" Daddy asked over the clink of the turn signal.

"I don't know how old he is," Tasha admitted. She didn't

know how old he *was*, but she was pretty sure how old he *wasn't*. Was that enough to make it a lie?

"Look Ladybug," Daddy said, looking at her. They were at a red light. "Stay away from that boy. He ain't nothing but trouble. I know you think I'm an old man, but I used to be a boy myself, so I know what I'm talking about."

"Okay," Tasha said, hoping that her cooperation would end the discussion.

Daddy said under his breath, "That boy'll be lucky to see the other side of eighteen."

Tasha had heard him but pretended not to. She climbed into her yellow and blue bed with the air freshener in her hand.

"What's that?" DeShaun asked.

"I thought you were sleep." Tasha wished she had her own room.

"I was. But what's that you got?"

"None of your business."

Tasha put the little tree inside her pillowcase and, inhaling pine, dreamed of Christmas.

———

She got to school Monday morning with only seconds to spare. There was no time to run to the bathroom, unravel her braids, and smear Vaseline in all the right places. She paused a moment before entering the trailer. Would everyone take one look at her and know that she was somebody's lady? Would they be able to tell whose?

The jangle of the tardy bell ushered her into the room. She scanned the faces quickly. Jashante wasn't there. That was disappointing but then, the day wasn't over. He was known to come to school as late as ten o'clock.

Eight girls were huddled around Monica, speaking in hushed tones like people do at a funeral. Tasha heard their voices but she couldn't make out the words.

"What happened?" she asked Angelite, who had a way of knowing everything about everybody.

"Monica's slumber party got canceled," she reported with a giggle. "Her mama went out and got a cake and hot dogs and stuff but nobody came."

Tasha laughed a little bit too. "What happened?"

Angelite lowered her voice. "Tayari's mother called all of the other mothers and told them that the party wasn't supervised."

"For real?" Tasha couldn't believe it.

"See," Angelite explained, "Monica's mama works at night, so they would have been there alone."

"Oh," Tasha said. She was glad that she hadn't been invited; her mother probably would have done the very same thing and Tasha would have ended up like Tayari, looking at her math book, trying not to cry.

The group around Monica had swollen into twelve. Even people who had not been invited were offering condolences. Sherrie Evans, who had not even made Tasha's list of alternates, said, "I don't know why you invited her in the first place."

"I was trying to be nice," Monica whined.

"You just can't *be* nice to some people," Forsythia reminded her.

Tasha suddenly realized that she hated fifth grade. The feeling of revulsion came over her in exactly the same way that she had abruptly realized that a song playing on the radio was absolutely horrible. She had been riding along, thinking private thoughts when this truly unbearable song had forced its way into her consciousness. She had no idea how long it had been on, but she could not stand another note. She had stretched her arm to reach the controls of the radio and pressed a button, switching to another station.

"Hey!" Daddy had said. "I was listening to that!"

But there was no button to press to take her out of fifth grade. She would have to remain in this class, with these same people, until June, when they would all graduate and go on to middle school. Tasha wished that she was smart like Ayana so she could skip fifth grade altogether. But what about Jashante? He had done fifth grade once already. How could he stand it twice? No wonder he never came to school.

At lunchtime, Tayari ate with Octavia. Tasha sat alone.

———————

"This is ridiculous," Mama said. "You knew about this assignment for how long?"

Tasha bit her lip. It was almost eleven o'clock and she hadn't even looked at her math homework. She was still working on her book report. "Stop fussing at me," she growled.

Daddy walked into the kitchen, almost stepping on De-Shaun, who was snoozing in the corner, tucked into her sleeping bag. He turned on the TV. "What's going on?"

"Tasha waited until the last minute to do her homework," Mama reported. "DeShaun didn't want to sleep by herself, so she camped out in here."

"All while I was in the basement?" Daddy smiled and grabbed a handful of animal crackers from the box on the counter.

"A lot happens while you are down there," Tasha snapped.

"What's wrong with you, Ladybug?"

"Nothing."

"Growing pains," Mama told him.

Ever since Mama had presented her with a small pink bra, that had been her explanation for Tasha's every mood.

She was about to complain when Mama looked up at the black-and-white TV and said, "Sweet Jesus."

"That's our school," said DeShaun, from her nest on the floor.

A woman with a blue-and-white scarf sobbed into a microphone. *I kept telling him to come right on home after school. I told him the man was going to get him if he didn't come right on home.*

It was Jashante. The fuzzy snapshot had been taken before he chipped his front tooth. He looked like a little boy. The scarf woman was crying. *He didn't come home after school.*

"He didn't even come to school today," Tasha said.

A phone number on the bottom of the screen. *Call if you know anything. Call if you see anything. Someone out there knows something. Don't be afraid. Come forward.*

Tasha's chest squeezed smaller. She leaned forward and put her head on her knees. "It's alright, baby," Mama said. "Breathe slow. You're alright."

They showed the picture one more time. Missing, not

murdered. *There may still be time for this boy. Call us. Twenty-four hours.* Scarf woman crying again. Wiping her face with the back of her hand. *He always give me a lot of trouble but I didn't want nothing like this to happen to him.*

"I know that boy. He's in my class."

"Shh . . . Don't talk. Breathe. Get your air."

Daddy stood over her. Picked her up, carried her toward the back of the house. He was worried. His face near hers. "Breathe," he told her. "Daddy's here."

Tasha put her hand up to intercept his kiss. "You said he wasn't going to live to be eighteen. I heard you."

"I didn't mean— That's the same boy?" Daddy was looking at the TV. "But he looks like a little fella."

Mama put her arms around Tasha and she didn't fight her. "Mama, I'm so sorry. I didn't mean for this to happen."

"Shh, baby."

Monica Kaufman said, "The missing boy is thirteen years old."

When Tasha woke up the next morning there was a sweet moment of nothingness, but knowledge returned like a yo-yo snapping itself back hard into the palm of her hand. Jashante was missing. Somebody snatched him. Then the next thought, that Tasha herself had brought it upon him with her hateful words. *I hope the man snatches you. Asphyxiated. Decomposed.* And she had meant it when she said it. Mad about ruining her coat, stinging from the laughter of her classmates, she had meant it. And Daddy had cursed him too. *That boy'll be lucky to see the other side of eighteen.* Jashante wouldn't get to see the other side of fifth grade. And that was the saddest thought of all.

———

Recess was postponed indefinitely. No one announced it or made it official. The bell had just rung and nobody moved. Tasha was uneasy in the stillness. She searched her class-mates' faces. Did they remember that she was responsible? All of the kids wore weird expressions, like their eyes had been reversed and they were all staring inside their own heads.

Tasha's father joined a search party. They all wore white T-shirts trimmed in blue and headed out in the morning dark.

"Where are they going?" Tasha wanted to know.

"They are looking out in the woods," Mama said.

"Why would those kids be in the woods?" DeShaun asked.

Mama didn't say anything and Tasha already knew that they were not looking for anyone alive. She opened her mouth to say this when her mother gave her a look and said, "Button it."

The three of them lay in Mama's big bed waiting for Daddy to come back. DeShaun complained of a sore throat and fell asleep soon after swallowing a big spoonful of pur-ple medicine. When DeShaun started breathing in quiet snores, Mama spoke.

"How are you feeling, Tasha?"

"I'm okay. My throat's not sore."

Mama smoothed Tasha's hair with her soft palm. "I mean how are you feeling on the inside? That boy from your class, Jashante?"

Mama said his name with uncertainty, like she wasn't sure how to pronounce it.

"He was my friend," Tasha said.

"Baby, sometimes things happen and we don't know why—"

But Tasha knew why. Her need to confess was as fundamental as her need for air. "I know why."

"You can't know."

"Yes, I do," Tasha said. "It's not a *growing pain*."

"Tell me, then," Mama said.

"It's me," she said. "He pushed me down and I got mad and said that I hoped the man gets him, and now he's gone."

It felt good to tell someone, especially Mama, who had the power to punish and the authority to absolve. "I promise to be more careful with my words," Tasha said solemnly, looking up at her mother expecting to see anger or even revulsion.

"Oh, sweetie," Mama said. "You don't think that you— You don't think that it's your fault, do you?"

"It *is*," Tasha insisted. Her contrition was turning to anger.

"Tasha, I understand that you feel bad about what you said to your friend, but you didn't kill—" She paused. "You didn't make this happen. A very sick person is responsible for this. It has nothing to do with you. Do you understand me?"

Tasha pulled fuzz from the blanket, but didn't speak.

"Listen," Mama said. "How many times have you wished for something to happen and it didn't?"

Just last week, she had wished for a pretty pink envelope with a magenta heart.

Mama waited a few seconds before she spoke again. "See, baby, things just happen in spite of our wishes."

"Well, what about prayers?" Tasha asked.

"Prayers are different."

But Tasha didn't think so. After all, what were prayers but wishes addressed directly to God?

Mama suggested that they say a prayer for Jashante. Tasha bowed her head and said "Amen" when Mama stopped talking; but she knew it wasn't going to work.

Daddy returned that evening different. Dinner was cooling in bowls on the table as the girls and their mother sat waiting for him to come downstairs. They could hear the shower running long after the bowls stopped steaming. He came and sat at his place.

"Let us pray," he said.

Tasha looked at her mother. They prayed over Sunday and holiday dinners, but ordinary meals like this one usually went unblessed. Instead of the usual grace thanking God for the food we receive for the nourishment of our bodies, Daddy slowly recited The Lord's Prayer. Tasha listened carefully. *Forgive us our trespasses.* She moved her lips silently around the words. After they soberly said "Amen," he said, "Don't turn that TV on tonight."

"Where did you go?" Tasha asked quietly. This was as close as she could get to her real question: *Did you see my friend? Was he dead?*

Daddy spoke to his hands, which were situated in the center of his empty plate. "The group I was with went way north, all the way where white people stay. All of us were packed in a bus like little kids going on a field trip. When we got out there, some of them were ready to help us search. Their wives—churches, or whoever—had fixed sack lunches for us, but I didn't eat none of it." He looked at Mama. "I am not prejudiced. Delores, you know that."

Mama didn't speak.

"Don't look at me like that," he said.

Tasha carefully set her glass down on the table without a click. She wanted to hear his confession.

"Does a man have to be prejudiced to see what is right in front of his face?"

Mama was still quiet.

"I'm asking," Daddy said, staring at her.

"All I'm saying is that you don't know." She spoke the words slowly, pronouncing each letter.

Yes, you *can* know; Tasha felt her pulse accelerate. It knocked hard against her temples. Let Daddy talk.

"Well, let me tell you what I do know. I know that a black preschool blew up just six months ago."

"What happened at Bowen Homes was an accident. The boiler exploded."

"An accident like Birmingham," Daddy spat. "Nothing has changed. When they found that little light-skinned boy, the one that was just down here visiting from Ohio, all I could think about was Emmett Till."

"Who?" DeShaun asked.

Mama looked over at the girls. Before she could send them away, Daddy answered the question.

"Emmett Till was a little brother in Mississippi; white folks killed him for no reason. Hung him and—"

"Charles. Hush now."

"No," Daddy said. "Don't hush me like I'm a child. I

won't hush. That's the problem. We been hushed up too long. These children don't know nothing about lynching. They don't know about white folks burning niggers alive. That's why we had to go out today—This whole thing is because black kids don't have sense enough to be scared of a strange white man."

He was shouting. His voice, losing its richness, was ragged and mean. He punctuated his speech with a fist brought down hard on the glass table, upsetting a blue tumbler of water and ice.

DeShaun's eyes were filling up. She thought the rage and the hate were directed at her. Tasha touched her sister's leg under the table. Daddy should know better. Shaun was too little to understand that he was cursing something way older than the girls. Something he had seen. And Mama had seen it too.

"Enough," Mama said, with one eye on DeShaun. "Alright, Charles?" She spoke quietly. "Enough."

The air in the kitchen was stretched tight like a rubber band. Daddy set both of his elbows on the table and covered each eye with the heel of a hand. Suddenly, Tasha wanted him to hold her on his lap, kiss her forehead, and say that everything was all right. But he didn't even look at her. He stared into the cave his hands made like somebody stuck in the middle of a game of peekaboo. Mama sent the girls to their rooms and Daddy didn't move.

Tasha stood in the darkened hallway. Waiting. There was more. Daddy's face was weighted in a way that Tasha almost recognized.

"Tasha," DeShaun whispered.

She had almost forgotten that her little sister was with her. "Shush," she said gently.

DeShaun moved so close that Tasha could smell the Kool-Aid on her sister's breath as they watched their parents.

"Delores," Daddy said, in a small voice.

"Come here," Mama said, without moving.

Daddy got up slowly, taking careful steps like his feet hurt and stopped in front of Mama's chair. She smoothed her skirt across her lap and he slowly sank, putting each knee delicately on the yellow linoleum. Their faces were level.

"Sh . . ." Mama said. She put her hands on the sides of his face. Her nails were clean and white-tipped against his skin.

"Don't shush me," he pleaded. "I need to talk."

He rested his head in her lap like he was horribly tired. She rubbed the story out of his head in gentle circles.

"Out there where we went, is like where I grew up. It's a trip. Twenty-five miles outside of Atlanta and *bam*, back in Alabama." He made a sound that was something like a laugh. "White folks looking at you half mean, half scared. The ones who came out to help us look were decent; I'll admit that. But most of them didn't lift a finger. Just stayed in their houses.

"They paired us up. I got put with this white guy named John or Jim. I don't remember. We didn't say anything to each other, which was probably for the best. I can't think of anything that he could have said that wouldn't have made me want to hit him. I think that he could tell that's how I felt. Sometimes those decent white folks can understand that we can't forgive them. Especially not at a time like this."

In the hall, Tasha wondered about herself, Daddy, and even Monica and Forsythia. Could they be forgiven? Maybe not at a time like this, but ever, at all?

"So me and Jim were in the woods, turning over bunches of leaves with our poles. It was cool and dry out but the leaves underneath were wet and gummed up. Decaying. Nasty. The whole time I was wishing I was home. I even wanted to hurt my feet on those damn jacks Tasha's always leaving on the floor for me to step on. But I had to keep looking. You know? I watch the TV and I see parents at their own kids' funerals. So I have to go on looking. I have to help. How can I say I can't stand to look under a pile of soggy leaves when I know whatever I find can only be so bad because my girls are at home sleep?"

Was it Jashante? Tasha could only picture him like he was in the photo on the news. She imagined him fuzzy, out of focus, and asphyxiated in a garbage bag.

"Shh . . ." said Mama. "I know. You don't have to talk about it." She rocked him like a grumpy baby.

"Mama, let him say it," Tasha whispered. Only words can undo words. Kids say that to take something back you have to say it backward. Like a filmstrip run the wrong way. *Die you hope I. Eighteen of side other. People some to nice be can't you.*

"That's what I'm talking about. How can I say that I can't stand to talk about it? And how can you say that you can't stand to *hear* it when other people are *living* it?"

Tasha couldn't see her father's face. She heard the strange muffled voice, and for a moment she didn't believe that it was him. She needed to see his mouth make the words.

"I was turning over the leaves." Daddy went on. "Shamed,

you know, and at the same time thanking God when there was nothing but worms and dirt out there. Then we came across something foul in a hefty bag."

Mama rubbed his neck until the words came out.

"The bag was about the right size and there was something dead in there, that much I knew. Only one thing smells like that. I wanted to let it alone or call one of the group leaders to come and handle it. But that white boy was looking at me; I could feel it. I took my pole and poked the bag open.

"It was nothing but a dead dog."

"Was that all you found?" Mama's voice was steady like when she said *Hold still* before pulling off a Band-Aid stuck to a wound.

What was out there to see? Pretty envelopes. Red dirt, pink satin. Shiny dimes and M&Ms. Magenta heart, torn open.

"Me?" Daddy said. "Yeah. That's all I saw. But the other group, they came across that little girl."

"Lord," said Mama. "Where?"

"That's the thing," Daddy said. "It was right around here. I didn't realize it at first. Word got around that they found a body, a skeleton really, around a lake."

"Around here?" Mama said. Her hand stopped its soothing circles.

"I saw a policeman. A brother. He said they found her at Niskey Lake. I said 'Where the hell is that?' and he told me. I said, 'Man, that's not far from where I stay. I never heard of no lake off of Cascade Road.' He said, 'Somebody did.'"

They were silent then. The heater hummed on as her father knelt with his head in her mother's lap. Tasha pulled

DeShaun's hand and they moved quietly into the black dark of their bedroom.

———

Tasha pressed her face against her window and saw the dark night through burglar bars. She looked across the lawn; it was too dark to see the trees, naked without their leaves, but she knew they were there. Jashante was out there too, but the night was huge. She saw one star. Tasha closed her eyes but didn't wish.

"Tasha," DeShaun said sleepily, "what's the magic word?"

"Huh?" Tasha said, distracted.

"Remember you said that there was a magic word to keep you safe."

"Oh, *that* magic word," Tasha said, as if there were only one. Words could be magic, but not in the abracadabra way that DeShaun believed. The magic that came from lips could be as cruel as children and as erratic as a rubber ball ricocheting off concrete.

"Shaun," Tasha said, "there's no such thing as a magic word."

"Not at all?"

"Not like you mean."

"Oh," DeShaun said, with almost tangible disappointment.

"Well," Tasha told her, "there is power. But—" She stopped, wanting to comfort her sister with more than flawed, uncontrollable words.

"But what?" DeShaun pressed.

"It's not a word; it's a charm."

Tasha retrieved Jashante's air freshener from her pillow-case. She pressed it to her lips and was overcome by its green scent as she handed it to her little sister. "Put this under your pillow and you'll be alright."

In autumn, oak trees drop acorns on Atlanta lawns and cover them with a quilt of decaying leaves. LaTasha Renee Baxter held her little sister's hand after school as they walked across their lawn, forcing the acorns under their feet into the red earth. The air stank of leaves burning in barrels, but Tasha recalled the clean outdoor smell of pine.

PART 2

The Direction Opposite of Home

Morning begins the moment Father swings his cracked feet over the side of the bed and stands. With the grace of the blind, he dresses in the dark of his and Mother's bedroom. You hear a crisp sound like pages turning as he pulls his starched coveralls around himself and fastens the zipper.

You are tense between your Snoopy sheets as he heads to the kitchen. When he pauses before your room, his body blocks the yellow light that arches underneath your door. Is he standing there recalling some criticism he forgot to deliver yesterday? You imagine him making a mental note to berate you tonight, over dinner. He continues down the hallway as you study the ceiling over your bed, wondering who arranged the tiny stalagmites in such an intricate pattern, and wondering why your father hates you.

Father's small A.M. radio belches out WAOK. The shrieking teakettle cannot muffle Ron Sailor's funereal report from the newsroom. One of your classmates, Jashante Hamilton, has been missing for two weeks. You do not miss Jashante; he had terrorized you for most of your elementary-school career. But you do not want to know that he has been found murdered, for whoever could kill Jashante, could destroy you effortlessly.

As you chant nursery rhymes to distract yourself from the news report, Father stacks his breakfast dishes in the sink and shuts off the radio. Father rattles the back burglar door, assuring himself that it is as locked now as it was last night when he turned the key and checked it twice. Exiting through the front door, he turns the double dead bolt behind him with a responsible clunk. You close your eyes and stop humming. He's gone to work. You can dream again.

At daybreak, Mother whisks into your room in a long satin robe, waking you with a contrived coloratura, "Good morning, Rodney." Ignoring her salutation, you do not stir. "Wake up," she sings, shaking you with hands that smell faintly of glue. You emit a grunting surrender to discourage her from tickling you or covering your face with cold-creamed kisses. Satisfied that you are awake, she leaves you alone. Her blue robe swishes with inappropriate elegance as she moves to Sister's room.

As you pull on your favorite pair of Toughskins, you notice the morning air is not heavy with too-crispy bacon and scorched eggs. A long assessing breath detects rubber cement. You take another guilty inhalation, savoring the smell in the same way that you enjoy damp ditto sheets held briefly to your face at school. But intoxicating or not, this is no breakfast smell. You make your way to the kitchen, picking up the odor of paint as well.

Mother frets over a sequined shoe box in the center of the sturdy oak kitchen table. It is a diorama, Sister's fall project. Mr. Harrell ordered you fifth-graders to create festive posters illustrating the theme, "Reaching as we climb." The purple mimeographed sheet with the instructions is crumpled in the sticky bottom of your book bag.

Sister's pretty little brow is creased as she carefully prints her name on the pencil line beside the word *by*. "Right here, honey," Mother says. Sister is six years old and very obedient.

"Your poster is in the living room," Mother tells you as she carefully encloses the diorama in bubble wrap.

You are surprised, but you shouldn't be. This is hardly the first time that your mother's industry has thwarted your strides toward underachievement. But what else has she found rifling through your bag? Has she seen the candy wrappers? Maybe, but that doesn't prove anything. Furthermore, Mother is not predisposed to think ill of either of her children by virtue of love liberally mingled with instability. You walk to the living room and retrieve the poster without comment.

"I'm hungry," says Sister, not unpleasantly.

The kitchen is covered with putty, spangles, twine, and toxic solvents. Mother glances at the daisy-shaped clock over the stove. "I have a hair appointment at eight. You'll have to get breakfast at school."

"What?" you sputter although you hadn't intended to say anything. Since your words are almost invariably misinterpreted, you avoid speech in general and abstain entirely from rhetorical questions.

"We're going to eat at school!" Sister is happy, partly because she is a naturally effervescent little girl, but also because the cafeteria ladies love her and give her extra cartons of chocolate milk. You have not made such a good impression on the heavy women whose round faces are framed by hair nets. They actually *dislike* you, demonstrating this antipathy by a subtle twist of the wrist, ensuring that your serving of casserole never has cheese on top.

And besides, school breakfast is eaten nearly exclusively

by kids whose families are so poor that they don't have anything to eat at home. They carry meal cards, given out at the first of the week, marked FREE so they receive their trays without paying. You'd rather not be associated with this group, but you don't mention this to your mother. She would accuse you of pretension. Never mind that the shoe box she chose to make your sister's diorama conspicuously bears the label of her only Italian pumps.

Arriving at school, you head toward the cafeteria, but pause in the hallway in front of a huge cardboard tree. Dangling from the branches are construction-paper apples bearing the names of the Students of the Month. No apple reads RODNEY GREEN. Mother once demanded a conference with the principal to discuss this oversight. She arrived for the meeting smartly dressed, clutching a copy of your standardized test scores in a gloved hand.

"We tend to reward achievement rather than aptitude," the principal explained, ushering her out.

You are starving. Why not push the cafeteria doors, walk in casually, and get yourself a tray? Every student is allowed to eat. Hadn't Mother said that you should be the *most* welcome because your family pays the taxes that make the breakfast possible? But sponsoring the meal does not erase the stigma of actually eating it, so you stay hungrily in the hall.

When the project kids file out of the cafeteria, you offer them the courtesy of not looking into their faces. For some reason, they hesitate a moment when they see you. Are they looking at your clothes? Can they tell that your socks, though similar, are not an exact match? Or is it your howling stomach that attracts such attention? Finally, you realize that in the hallway's fluorescent light, your poster—Mother's masterpiece—is magnificently luminous like the pulsing lights of a parking lot carnival.

You ignore the spectacle in your hands, and look at the toes of your shoes. They still look new although you have walked countless laps around your living room to rid them of that Stride Rite shine. As you meditate on the condition of your penny loafers, one of the breakfast eaters says, "Hi, Rodney." You are so startled that you swallow whole a double wad of bubble gum, still cinnamon sweet.

It is Octavia, who has always occupied the desk in front of yours. (Teachers are certain that alphabetic seating accelerates the learning process.) You are not surprised to discover that she is a breakfast eater. Having sat behind her for five going on six years of education, you know that her lunch card is stamped REDUCED so that she pays for her meal with a dime while you pay forty cents. She sometimes comes to school very early, even before breakfast; Mrs. Willingham or one of the other teachers gives her soap to wash with. Since you are one of the nicer boys in class, you never speak to her.

"Hey, Octavia," you mumble, noticing that she is also carrying a decorated posterboard.

It is not as ornate as yours because she made it herself. Her smile fades a little bit as she sees that your design is carefully shaded to create an illusion of depth.

"You'll probably win a prize," she says.

You feel that you should say something nice about her creation. Reciprocity is the cornerstone of good manners. But fifth-grade social institutions discourage mingling freely. Poor Octavia is drowning in a sea of untouchability and you don't want to be submerged as she thrashes.

Leon Simmons is about twenty feet from you; his new shoes look much less new than yours. He cracks his knuckles expressively as you speak to Octavia. His face is turned up on one side. A snicker? Smirk? You doubt he is just admiring your mother's handiwork. You want to turn all the way around so that your view of Leon is not obstructed by the handle of your glasses. But to look closely is the very same thing as admission, so you continue to examine your shoe.

You report to your classroom, pausing a moment at the door. Mr. Harrell is writing on the chalkboard. You hate him. In an unusual moment of candor you told this to your mother and were scolded.

"Hate is a strong word," she said, as if you didn't know this already.

Your distaste for this narrow man began the moment you laid eyes on him. You had been expecting pretty Miss Maddox, whom you met last year when you were sent out into the hallway for some inconsequential social transgression. She walked by with a dainty clattering of high heels and said, "I know that a handsome boy like you hasn't been causing trouble." And from that moment, you looked forward to starting fifth grade. But when you walked into your classroom on the first day, bearing several sharpened number-two pencils to impress her, you found out that lovely Miss Maddox had gotten married and moved to Arizona.

In her place is Mr. Harrell, who insists on addressing the students by Mr. and Miss. You missed your turn the first time he called roll because you are accustomed to being called by your first name.

"Did you say Rodney Green?" you asked, realizing that you had been passed. "I'm here."

"Tardy," Mr. Harrell pronounced, with a malevolent stroke of his red pen.

"But I've been here since before the first bell."

"In body maybe. But apparently, your mind has just arrived."

You slumped in your chair mumbling truncated obscenities. Mr. Harrell tapped the corner of your desk with his ruler. "Do you have something to say to me, Mr. Green?"

"No sir," you said, over Forsythia Collier's wind-chime laughter.

Mr. Harrell turns from the blackboard as you enter. Your eyes travel downward in what looks like humility but is not. His shoes, buffed to a high gloss, are identical to your own.

"For me?" he says, reaching for the poster as if it were a gift. "Very nice, Mr. Green. I am glad to see that you have decided to take your schoolwork more seriously."

It is hard to tell if he is being sarcastic or just stupid, so you say nothing.

He reaches behind you to Octavia, who is holding her project, with the decorated side toward the floor. Mr. Harrell examines it without enthusiasm. "Not bad, Miss Fuller."

You have made it to your seat and are covertly studying Octavia's hair when Mr. Harrell bangs his ruler on his desk. The gesture is dramatic, but not unusual, so you do not move your eyes from Octavia's mesmerizing braids, which travel an intricate winding path along her scalp. He brings the ruler down hard again. You reluctantly leave your scopophilic trance.

"Our guest today is Officer Brown from the Atlanta Police Department." Mr. Harrell sounds like Bob Barker. "He is going to talk to us about personal safety."

Cautious excitement spreads through the class. No child in this room has felt safe since Jashante disappeared.

Officer Brown is softer and rounder than you imagine a police officer should be. His wide toothy smile is naggingly familiar. Was he the man inside the clown suit at your sister's party last year?

"Hi, kids," he says. "Let's talk about safety. I have a feeling that this might be a topic on your mind lately. Am I right?"

The class stares at him. He looks at Mr. Harrell, who then glares at all of you.

"Not everyone at once," the officer says, with a stiff laugh much like a snort. "Okay." He claps his hands together. "How about you tell me what you already know."

No one speaks. What all of you already know is too terrible to trust to unreliable words. Officer Brown tries again. "I am sure that you guys watch the news with your parents. What have you seen that has to do with kids and safety?" He points at Angelite Armstrong; her long braids always attract attention. "I don't know," she whispers.

"Well, who knows?" He aims his finger at Cinque Freeman. "You look like a sharp young man."

Cinque is not flattered, but he condescends to reply. "Everybody knows somebody is killing black kids."

Officer Brown looks suddenly taken aback as if he only now notices that he is white. You wonder how long it will be before he realizes that he is fat. He looks quickly at Mr. Harrell but gets no reaction. Officer Brown presses his smile, displaying bluish teeth set in pink gums. He looks away from Cinque. "Yes, little lady, you have something to say?"

LaTasha Baxter says, "It's too late to talk to us. Somebody from this class is already—" She bites on her lip and looks at the ceiling as if the word for the unknowable is spelled out in the fluorescent lights. She shakes her head at the officer.

"Jashante," Cinque says. "My cousin."

"He got killed," someone shouted.

This is the first time since Jashante was added to the list of Missing and Murdered Children that he is mentioned at school. Now the syllables of his name are everywhere. Octavia's lips are moving privately, as if in prayer. You hear thirty-two-part harmony.

Officer Brown extends his hands in front of him as if he were saying, playfully, *Don't shoot.* Mr. Harrell bangs his gavel and the class comes to order.

"I am familiar with the Hamilton case," says Officer Brown. "But to my knowledge, Jashante is only missing. Lots of missing children are found each day and returned to their parents."

Not around here. Not this year. You now know, as undeniably as if you had read it in the World Book Encyclopedia, that Officer Brown has nothing useful to share. As a matter of fact, you are more fearful than ever to know that this man is all that stands between your generation and an early death.

"My daddy say it's the police that's doing it," Cinque shouts from the back of the room.

The class is instantly silenced. Of course, you have long since concluded that the police are ineffective at best. After all, twelve children have been abducted. But could the police actually be responsible?

"How else a white man going to get a kid to get in a car with him?"

A good point. The class turns its head toward Officer Brown like spectators at a tennis match. The pudgy man does not respond.

Mr. Harrell intervenes. "Mr. Freeman, out in the hall."

"Man," Cinque complains, slamming his desk shut. "He *my* cousin. I'm just trying to tell y'all what I know."

Officer Brown composes himself. "Wait, young man. Sit back down."

The eyes swing to the teacher. Is he going to allow this rotund white man to reverse his command? And what about Cinque? Will he be broken by the iron will of the law?

"No," says Cinque. "Man done put me out and I'm gone."

Heads turn again to Mr. Harrell. "Take your seat, Mr. Freeman."

Cinque obeys, but not without complaint. "Folks need to make up they mind."

Officer Brown clears his throat and speaks. "Listen, kids. Don't rule anyone out. If we don't know who *is* responsible, then we don't know who's *not*." Now his tone becomes deliberately authoritative, not unlike the voice that omnisciently declares that four out of five dentists surveyed recommend sugarless gum for their patients who chew gum. "But we *do* know that each Atlanta police officer has taken a sacred oath to protect the public, not harm it." He pauses dramatically and looks toward the American flag flaccid in its perch on top of the file cabinet.

"There may be some individuals *impersonating* officers of the law. But the impostor will not have this!" He dips into his pocket and triumphantly produces a glossy piece of metal. "This," he announces, displaying his shield between his thumb and forefinger, "is the official badge of the Atlanta P.D." He gives it to Angelite and indicates that she should pass it around. "Take a good look. Run your hands across it and feel the raised letters. I've seen a lot of fakes, and not one of them has had the letters raised up so high that you can read it with your fingers."

This man is clearly delusional, so you do not point out that a criminal who could steal an official police *uniform* certainly would not neglect to take an official police *badge*. Furthermore, it is nearly time for recess.

The bell rings and everyone files outside. Last year, your classmates would have sprinted to the playground. But that was before last summer's rains changed the girls. They reported to school on the first day of fifth grade taller than the boys and older, too. They were all fastened into pink training bras that you could see through the thin cotton of their button-up blouses. Their hair was straightened and turned into tight oily curls. When a group of them stands together, the combined scent of Jean Naté and singed hair makes you dizzy.

This year, all playground activities have become spectator sports. Kick-ballers worry about form as they round the bases. Jump-rope girls are careful not to pant with open mouths. You used to sit by the back fence daydreaming; but the idea of being watched as you think aggravates your sensitive stomach.

So you stand all alone during the thirty minutes of freedom before lunch. You never have liked to participate in the races since the consensus is that you are slow as dirt. And now, the competition to the finish line is intensified by the metamorphosed girls who whisper behind lotioned hands as the boys demonstrate their speed.

Octavia sits with her back against the building. She doesn't glance toward the lower field, where the boys kick up gritty disorderly clouds of red dust as they struggle to win. Her eyes focus on the pages of a worn paperback. From where you are standing, you see the small piece of brown cardboard covering a hole in the bottom of her shoe. You turn away, embarrassed to glimpse something as intimate as poverty. You turn your eyes to her again as she blows on her thin fingers, warming them.

She looks up from her hands, smiles at you and perhaps waves. Maybe she is just wiggling her fingers to stimulate circulation. No. Her second movement is clearly a wave. You wave back—discreetly, you hope—and look away.

She stands up, adjusting her shoe, and walks toward you. "Do you think Mr. Harrell is going to tell us who won?"

"Huh?"

"The posters. Do you think he's going to judge them today?"

You forgot about the fall competition.

"I thought that mine was good. I stayed up until ten

trying to get the border right. But yours is the best." She smiles, showing a tiny row of crooked teeth. "How long did it take you to make it? I wanted to work on mine longer, but my mama made me go to bed."

You shrug, feeling vaguely dishonest.

"But he might give something for second place," she muses.

Neither of you says anything for several moments as you look out across the playground. The races are over and the girls have disbanded their tight giggly cluster to chat with individual boys.

Leon Simmons is talking to Candida Winters, a tall, big-boned girl who chews Wild Cherry Bubblicious with her mouth open. She makes fantastic noises with the gooey wad, despite the fact that gum chewing is not only against the rules but also most unladylike. You had a crush on Candida for several days at the start of the school year, even going so far as to carefully pen a note expressing your admiration. You folded your confession carefully around two sticks of Fruit Stripe gum. Ultimately, you *ate* the note rather than have it fall into the wrong hands. Now, whenever you see pretty Candida, the back of your mouth sours with the remembered taste of blue-lined paper and black erasable ink.

You sigh as you watch her laugh as Leon whispers.

"They talking about us," Octavia says.

"Huh?" You are taken aback.

"I can't stand neither one of them. Always messing with me."

If this is the case, why hadn't Octavia said, "They talking about *me*." She had very deliberately said *us*. You know that unpopularity is dreadfully contagious, but you'd no idea that the incubation period is so brief. You feel unbearably conspicuous and must get away from Octavia as quickly as you can.

"That policeman today was stupid." She suddenly changes the subject.

Her characterization of the experience is so succinct and comprehensive that there is nothing worthwhile to add to the exchange, so you just shrug.

"Why you so shy?"

Did she actually want to know why, or did she merely want you to know that she noticed? But you are not shy. You simply have nothing to say. But now you are too shy to tell her this.

Leon Simmons sings, "Rodney and Watusi sitting in a tree, K-I-S-S-I-N-G."

Octavia stands suddenly. "You better shut your mouth, ol' ugly boy." She picks up a small rock from the ground and pitches it toward Leon's pointed head. She misses.

Leon laughs and performs a jerking parody of an African dance. He chants, "Watusi, Watusi. Wa-Wa-Watusi!"

Octavia hurls another rock. Leon ducks.

"I ain't no Watusi," she shouts, looking around for more ammunition.

There are two small stones near your shoe, which would be perfect to chasten Leon. But handing her a rock will fall short of chivalry. And besides, her aim is terrible. But if you are a gentleman and throw the rock yourself, Leon will no doubt respond with his fists, and you can't fight.

She finds the rocks on her own and connects with the side of his head, just above his jutting ear.

"That didn't hurt," he declares, though the spot is turning red fast. Then he addresses you. "You better be glad it's daytime because she so black that you can't even see her at night." Encouraged by Candida's affirmative gum-popping, he adds, "When she walk by, the streetlight come on."

Octavia is furious now. She picks up a handful of pebbles and flings them, showering both Leon and Candida with a barrage of stinging pellets.

"So," she hollers, "your hair so nappy that the BB shots in the back look like you screwed them in one at a time."

"Least I don't live in the projects."

"Least my mama ain't had to come up to the school to beat my behind because of stealing."

Octavia's face glows with perspiration in spite of the nip in the air. "I got him good, didn't I?"

You stare at her in wonderment. How could she react so quickly, compellingly, brazenly, and conspicuously? Not once did she look to see who was watching. She didn't measure her words but shouted with irresistible spontaneous rudeness. The vicarious thrill heats your face and fogs your glasses.

Octavia takes your openmouthed silence as disapproval. "He started it."

The bell rings and the breathless fifth-graders file into the building. You have stood behind Octavia in the lunch line as you have for as long as you can remember. But today you notice that the soft hair at the back of her neck grows into a gentle V. She is taller than you. Has this always been the case or is it only recently important?

"Chili-mac?" asks the woman behind the counter.

"Yes'm," Octavia says. She is given a large portion generously topped with gooey cheddar.

"Chili-mac?"

You nod. Your plate is served with an austere scoop of reddish casserole. Cheeseless. You look at the woman with a face full of hurt, but she ignores you.

Octavia pays her dime after whispering the word "reduced." You pretend not to notice as you fumble in your pockets for a quarter, dime, and nickel.

The cafeteria buzzes with complicated conversations. Today you don't want to sit at the last table on the right where you normally take your lunch alone. Octavia looks at you welcomingly; her face brims with a frightening expectation as she nods slightly toward the empty stool beside her own. The strap of her new training bra peeks pink below the sleeve of her shirt. To sit beside her requires a bravery you can't muster.

But there is an empty stool beside LaTasha Baxter. You move in her direction. She doesn't seem horrified. As a matter of fact, she looks away with disinterest and rifles through her little red-and-white purse. As you relax your arms to set your tray down, Leon appears from nowhere, bumping your elbows as he plunks down gracelessly beside Tasha, who pulls a round mirror from her bag and studies her own lips.

"Go and sit with your own girlfriend," he says, aiming the top of his pointy head at Octavia. Thirty pairs of appraising eyes wait for your response.

"That ain't none of my girlfriend," you squawk.

The cafeteria explodes with concentrated laughter. You wish that you had only said that you didn't *have* a girlfriend. But the words tumbled out just as you felt them.

Octavia rises from her stool, walks to the front of the cafeteria, and dumps her dime lunch into the large trash can without taking care to see that the tray is saved. The cardboard in her shoe is slick and she nearly loses her footing as she walks to the door. But Octavia doesn't fall. As she leaves, the door shuts almost silently in the mocking laughter.

Back in the classroom, you clandestinely place two rolls of Life Savers and a purple ring candy on her desk. Octavia sweeps the candy to the floor like the debris from an eraser; sitting as if she has somehow found herself in the room alone.

Mr. Harrell announces that there will be a spelling test ten minutes before the bell. Until this moment you stared at the clock, attempting to move the hands along by the sheer force of your guilty will. Now, you concentrate your energy in the opposite direction.

You have not memorized the word-rules that will ensure you a passing grade. You have tried, even allowing Mother to drill on the proper order of letters in words you never use. But the information will not adhere to your brain. It falls off like over-licked stamps.

But still you try to write the words as Mr. Harrell reads them in his hearty baritone. He pronounces the words slowly, emphasizing their sounds, encouraging you to write them out just as you hear them. You do, but he has chosen the list deliberately to defy phonetics. You will fail. Again.

The bell rings at three o'clock as scheduled.

You linger a moment at the coat rack, hoping to see Octavia. The antidote for words must be a spoken one. You stand between her and her coat and say her name.

She looks up and says, "Rodney Green, you better get out of my way before I have to hurt your feelings."

Although her face suggests that *her* feelings have been injured, you are shaken by this threat and don't disturb her as she retrieves her balding corduroy coat.

Across from the school building, in the middle of the block, is a corner store. Lewis's Market is a poorly lit box stuffed with overpriced miniatures of the products your mother buys at the large Kroger near Greenbriar mall. A tiny jar of mayonnaise good for no more than ten sandwiches sits beside an even tinier jar of mustard. One of the small cartons of laundry detergent has fallen from the shelf and burst, emptying a cup or two of white powder flecked with blue onto the black floor. The entire place smells like clean sheets. Mrs. Lewis, the shopkeeper, looks up from her *Jet* magazine when the brass bells attached to the door handle announce your arrival.

"Hello there, Rodney," she says.

"Hi, Miz Lewis," you reply, heading for the back of the store, ignoring the sign demanding that patrons leave all bags at the front counter. She doesn't object. After all, you are not the type of boy who steals. Boys who steal do not attend Greater Hayes AME Zion. They are not members of the Youth Branch of the NAACP. Boys who take things from stores without paying don't wear corrective lenses for astigmatism, say *ma'am*, or fear their fathers. In other words, they are not well brought up. Mrs. Lewis has known your father since the two of them were barefoot children in Plain Dealing, Louisiana, so she is convinced that your honesty is guaranteed by superior genetic material reinforced by corporal punishment.

The candy on the back row isn't shrunk to doll-house proportions like everything else in the store. Full and even king-size sweets are stacked carefully in bins and buckets. You steal a glance at Mrs. Lewis, who holds her magazine inches from her face as if she plans to lick the words right off the pages. You cross your eyes. She turns the page. You scratch the side of your face with your middle finger. You lift the finger cautiously from your temple and give Mrs. Lewis the bird. She looks up.

"You need something, Rodney?"

"No'm," you tell her, putting your hand on a mysterious palm-size candy that is pink and studded with peanuts.

Father once came into the store and chuckled at the sight of this odd-looking confection.

"Virginia," he exclaimed, "tell me this ain't what I think it is."

Mrs. Lewis laughed from behind the counter. "Claude L, don't tell me you got so old that you don't know a peanut patty when you see one."

Father laughed so deeply that he became unrecognizable. "I haven't seen one of these here since Hector was a pup!"

Mrs. Lewis said, "Go on and get one. Take one home to Beverly, too."

"Naw," Father said. "She from Chicago. She don't know nothing about this here."

"Well, let lil Rodney pick something out for himself."

Father nodded toward the candy display. "Pick something."

You looked up and down the aisle slowly. No decision is inconsequential. You pointed in the general direction of the bottom shelf, hoping your father would betray some suggestion as to the nature of this test. He set his jaw to offer you no clues. What is an appropriate desire? Not the dainty jewel candies. Laffy Taffy? Too soft. You put your hand on a small box that features a drawing of a grape dressed for combat.

"What's that?" Father wanted to know.

"Alexander the Grape."

"See, Virginia," he said with a disdainful sneer. "This boy is standing right here in front of this good peanut patty and he wants some mess called Alexander the Great."

"The *Grape*," you corrected him.

He made a nasty sound, indicating his opinion of this semantic distinction.

You attempted to put the tiny box back on the shelf.

"No," Father said. "That's what you say you wanted. Don't get shamed now."

"Claude L, let that boy alone," Mrs. Lewis said, enjoying your humiliation.

While Mrs. Lewis put Father's peanut patty in a tiny brown paper sack, you slipped a box of Boston Baked Beans into your jacket pocket. You felt a jolt as if the sugar had somehow passed directly to your bloodstream from the pocket of your red windbreaker, bypassing your mouth and stomach. Your heart churned. Your shallow panting breaths were sweet.

————

Now you stare at the peanut patty in your hand and ponder the previously unthinkable oxymoron of an unappetizing piece of candy. You put it back in its place, pick up three boxes of Lemonheads and drop them silently in your book satchel.

The doorbells clang as Leon Simmons enters the shop. You use the brassy jangle to drown out the cellophane crackle of the half-dozen Chick-O-Sticks packed into your pencil pouch.

"Leave that bag right here," Mrs. Lewis says.

Leon's eyes are on you as he extends his arms behind him and squeezes his shoulder blades together, causing his green army-surplus backpack to slither to the floor.

"I wasn't going to steal nothing," he lies, walking toward you. He plants his sneaker in the spilled laundry detergent; the smell of artificial spring rises to your nose.

"Say, miss," Leon calls to the front of the store. "You need to sweep this up before somebody fall and call they lawyer on you."

"Don't track that washing powder all over this floor, boy."

"I'm just trying to help you," says Leon, as if his feelings are hurt. "Some people around here believe in some *suits*."

Leon approaches you as he speaks. His body radiates heat and a saltwater smell detectable over the scent of the detergent. Will he expose you? Your fingers are wrapped around a fistful of jewel candies but you don't put them in your pocket. He nods slightly, freeing you from paralysis. You put the candies in your pocket.

He smiles and heads to the counter and begins to tell Mrs. Lewis all about his litigious relatives and neighbors.

"Some people just aren't willing to work for what they want," she tells him. "They think the world owes them something."

Her speech is crisply enunciated and grammatically flawless. There are no traces of the easy vernacular she used when talking to your father that day about those nasty peanut patties. She speaks to Leon with the deliberate correctness that some people reserve for speaking to bill collectors or other white folks. You leave the store as Leon demonstrates an affected limp.

The autumn wind shuts the door hard behind you. It is cold for November. You want to fasten your coat, but pulling the brown tweed together will crush the translucent lollipops carefully stashed in a hole in the lining.

You return to the school door just as Sister exits holding her teacher's hand. She likes to stay late to pound the erasers and clean the blackboard. With her missing front teeth, Sister looks like an advertisement for Sealtest ice cream. When you were her age, you resembled a jack-o'-lantern carved by an arthritic hand. Your baby sister smiles and you wonder how your father's eyes look so sweet in her little face.

"Brother!" She races toward you in saddle oxfords. When she sees your parents she will greet each of them with the same unchecked glee.

You give her a candy necklace and an Astro Pop. She cannot help being good.

Although you don't hold Sister's hand as you walk to the bus stop, you hover protectively near. A parental mandate recently issued requires that you actually wrap your fingers around hers to thwart child-nappers. You understand the sentiment behind the decree but you are too well aware of the flaws in its logic.

You'd have assumed that your parents would have noticed by now that nearly all of the bodies found in Atlanta's woods, creeks, and fields are male. Someone should be assigned to hold *your* hand. Nevertheless, you keep an eye on Sister. Last spring, she came close to being flattened by a dilapidated Impala as she darted into the street to retrieve a runaway dodge ball in a burst of near-fatal altruism.

You are in sight of the bus stop when you become aware of the regular thump of footsteps on cold red clay. The earth absorbs the sound but you feel the tremors through the thin soles of your loafers. Sister, looking for her reflection in a lollipop, doesn't notice. You take her hand. Lining the street are small wooden houses in need of paint. Should you run onto one of the porches? Maybe not. Officer Brown is right: If you don't know who it is, you don't know who it's not. The noise of running feet behind you is more urgent. Sister looks up at you with a question on her heart-shaped face.

"Don't look back," you tell her.

The only choice is to flee on foot, although you are the second-to-the-slowest boy in the entire fifth grade. Some even say that you run like a girl; poor Sister runs like a *little* girl, but you've no other recourse.

"Sister, we have to—"

The hand on your neck is not as heavy as you imagine the hand of death to be. Nor is it particularly clammy.

"Rodney! Wait up."

You turn around to see Leon smiling broadly. Although the air is cold enough to turn his panting breaths white against the gray day, Leon's jacket is open; little drops of sweat stand out on his face like beads of water on the waxed hood of Father's car. His skinny ankles poke beneath his too-short trouser legs before disappearing into huge sneakers.

"That was you behind us?" You are relieved enough to weep.

"Yeah. Who you thought it was?"

He looks at your faces and knows. Leon looks at his big shoes for a respectful and apologetic moment. Then he abruptly announces the reason for his intrusion.

"Say," he says. "Ain't you going to give me some of that what you got?" Leon leans closer and speaks almost without moving his lips.

"Huh," you say.

"You should give me some of that candy seeing as I'm the one who kept that lady busy while you was handling business."

He speaks cryptically for Sister's sake. You appreciate his discretion.

"But—" you begin, meaning to inform him that you take candy from Mrs. Lewis's store at least thrice weekly without any help.

"What?" Leon says. "You mad 'cause of what I said to Octavia today? I was just messing with her. She live down the street from me. Where you stay at?"

"Over by Mosely Park," you say, pointing west.

"All the way over there?" Leon is incredulous.

"It's just a little while on the bus," Sister tells him. "We get home right before *Family Feud*."

"That what I'm talking about," Leon says to you. "All the way over there, you don't know how we do it over here.

Octavia know I was just fooling with her. Both of us, we just stay around the corner from here."

"She—" You want to say something on her behalf.

"Anyway, I was just trying to look out for you. You don't want people going around saying that you going with the Watusi."

"She's not—"

"I *know* she not your girlfriend. That's what I'm saying. Anyway, she's mean. Maybe even crazy. Look at my ear where she chunked that rock at me. That hurted."

"She's nice." This is inadequate but it is all you can muster.

"That's what I'm *saying*." Leon gestures toward your bag. "We gonna be friends or what?"

This is quite a proposition. You have never had a friend before, at least not one formally declared. What would this alliance involve? You are not sure that you even *want* a running buddy. Will Leon approach you at recess while you are working on your drawings, putting his salty, sweaty arm around your shoulder declaring you to be his "ace boon coon"?

"Man," Leon says, turning with an angry flourish. "I can't believe you gonna do me like that." He kicks the brown leaves as he heads in the other direction.

"Wait," you say. "Get whatever you want." New friends are much easier to accommodate than new enemies.

"Dang!" Leon exclaims, opening your bag. "Did you take the whole store?" He is easily impressed. "Mike and Ike's, Bit-O-Honey, Gobstoppers. You got *everything*." He unwraps a blow-pop and puts it between his teeth and cheek. It juts from his face like a tumor. "That old lady so

busy watching me that she let you clean out the place."
Leon shakes his head. "Don't know why she thinks you don't
like candy as much as everybody else." Leon makes a basket
out of his shirttail. "She even makes *girls* leave their bags up
front."

This bit of information smarts, but you don't comment.
The implication hangs in the air like smoke.

Leon has taken more than his share, but he still digs
through your bag. "Where the candy corn?" He looks at
you, annoyed.

You didn't realize that you had been filling an invoice.
"There might be some in there."

"No it ain't. I looked. I can't believe you forgot the candy
corn." He ties the ends of his shirt together, securing his
haul. "Don't worry," he says brightly. "We'll get some tomorrow."

You have heard of an epidemic of disappearing black fathers, but you know you will never be as lucky. Yours
comes home *every* evening from a long day spent lying on
his back underneath malfunctioning automobiles. *I'm my
own boss,* he likes to boast. If he were someone else's boss,
perhaps he wouldn't get so dirty that dinner can never be
served until he has spent most of an hour in the bath re-
moving the evidence of his unsupervised labor. The meal
overcooks in aluminum pots as his voice from the bathroom sings, "Take my arms, I'll never use them."

By the time he gets to the table, he seems incapable of
song. He approaches your mother's cooking with a resigned

martyrdom. Mother switches on the television. Father looks at the screen and says simply, "Bastard."

"Claude L!" Mother is always shocked by bad language.

Your designated chair is not situated to provide a view of the black-and-white television. You can only wonder which bastard he is talking about. Perhaps it is the president. You twist your body counterclockwise and crane your neck to see what looks like Mayor Jackson sitting before a table heaped with money.

"Excuse my French," Father says, as he mercilessly rips a corn muffin in two. "I can't stand to see that yellow bastard up there acting like he care about black children. It makes me sick to my stomach."

You take a muffin and pull it apart carefully, searching for bits of eggshells. You see a white fleck and gingerly dislodge it.

"He didn't care nothing about Joe's kids when Joe and them said they didn't want to work for free. He didn't want to give them a decent wage to feed their family. But he's acting like he is so worried about the children."

Your Uncle Joe nearly lost his house last spring when the sanitation workers went on strike. Your mother baked improbable casseroles and took them to your cousins once a week. Father slapped a green-and-white sticker on your notebook that said THE MAYOR'S WORD IS GARBAGE.

Your mother takes in a sharp breath. Double negatives inflate her blood pressure.

"What's all that money for?" Sister asks.

"It's reward money," Mother explains. "If someone can catch the bad man who is taking the children, Mayor Jackson will give them the money."

"Don't say that SOB's name in this house. It wouldn't surprise me one bit to find out that money ain't worth the paper it's printed on," Father pronounces, sawing angrily at a fried-hard pork chop.

"Claude L! Your language!" For Mother, *ain't* is a worse word than *nigger*. Her freshly straightened hair trembles with outrage.

You cut your pork chop into salty bits and scatter them all over your plate.

"Officer Friendly came to our class today," Sister says.

"Did he?" Mother replies.

"He taught us a song. Want me to sing it?"

No one answers. Father still mumbles under his breath. You listen to the disembodied voice of the first black newscaster ever on Atlanta TV. She announces that another child's body has been found.

"Wanna hear me sing the Safety Song?" Sister asks again. Without waiting for permission, she begins.

"Kids don't go with strangers . . . They never go with strangers . . ."

"Did they say whose body it was?" you ask, loud enough to be heard over Sister's warbling.

There has been much conversation lately about finding bodies, as if a person's physical self could be misplaced as easily as a catcher's mitt. As if Jashante might say *You found my body? Where it was?* Would he pull it on like a sweater or step into it like a pair of pants? But you know better. Bodies are like the turnstile at Kmart: Once you pass through you can't change your mind and go back the other way.

Sister is still singing. "Kids don't go with strangers, that's a fact. Get back, Jack!

"You want me to sing it again?"

"That's alright, baby," Mother says with her hands covering her mouth as she watches the television. Father shakes his head and closes his eyes. "This don't make no kinda sense," he says.

Sister sings, "Kids don't go with strangers."

That night, you lie in bed trying to remember the time before you were born. Father said once, "Boy, we talking about things that happened before you were even *thought* about." This is the time that you want to recapture. You are curious about the state of not being, because this is certainly where people go when they leave their bodies in the woods for the police to find.

Mother claims that people are baby angels before God dispatches them to some family. But you aren't sure if you believe that such an impractical concept as the angel system could be the product of a divine mind. If Mother's theory is true, heaven would be crowded with all the people that are already dead and those waiting for their turn to be born. And why aren't baby angels the little ones who die in their cribs, like your two baby aunts Grandmother says she lost?

You lie there hoping for a peaceful prenatal memory to assure you that death is nothing to fear. That you shouldn't be afraid to go to the mailbox after dark because the worst thing that could happen would be that you would be returned to the place that you were. That you would be sent back to a condition where there is no father, no mother, no candy or school. But you still wonder about the process of leaving the body behind, dying. Monica Kaufman said that the missing children had been asphyxiated. Your children's dictionary (which you hate) does not include this important word, so you consulted the real one in the family room. Asphyxiate is to smother, which is almost the same as drowning.

You nearly drowned when you were about four. Mother's stomach was large with Sister. Her belly button protruded. Father held his large hands under you as you lay, trusting, near the surface of the cool, chlorinated water.

"Kick," he commanded, and you did.

He laughed. "Look, Beverly," he shouted over his hairy shoulder. "This boy might be ready for the Olympics in seventy-six!"

He took his hands away. "Keep on kicking."

You sank. The water in the motel pool closed over your head like a glass elevator door. You tried to remember the lessons you had just learned. *Kick your legs. Cup your hands. Blow bubbles. That's my boy.* But the fake blue water rushed in your nostrils, setting fires in your sinuses, and there was no air with which to cry.

Powerful hands with calluses softened by cool water lifted you through the blue glass. You twined your legs around Father's waist. Wiry chest hair scratched your trembling stomach.

"What happened?" he asked, prying you from his torso so that your faces were level. "You were swimming good until you saw that my hands were gone. Then you went under like a lead balloon."

He laughed a little bit, but you cried. "Oh, come on." Father gave you a rough shake. "Don't act like a little girl."

You looked to Mother, who struggled to rise from a green-striped pool chair. "Claude L, is he alright?"

"He's fine. We gonna try it again."

"He looks cold," Mother noticed. "Bring him over here so I can dry him off."

"Beverly, you gonna make this boy into a sissy," Father said, but he delivered you to Mother, who rubbed the tiny chill bumps on your arms with a yellow beach towel that was heated by the sun-warmed concrete. You wanted to climb on her lap, but her huge stomach rested on her thighs, leaving no space for your narrow bottom. Even hugging was awkward, so she held your hand and kissed your forehead.

———

When you awaken the next morning dark clouds filled with water shroud the sky, obscuring the fading stars. The drumming of water on earth and brick and glass is hypnotic. Your father knocks twice on your closed bedroom door before you answer.

"Sir?" You are suddenly tense between your Snoopy sheets.

He thrusts his squarish head into your room. You are glad that the lights are out so he cannot see the socks peeking out from half-closed dresser drawers. "Put on your shoes and get your raincoat. I need some help."

"Outside?" You reach for your glasses on the night table.

"Drain pipe came aloose again. I need you to hold it still while I strap it in place."

The door closes. You stare at it. It opens again.

"When you get home from school today, clean up this snake pit."

You stare at the door again, but thankfully, it stays shut.

Apprehension envelops you, permeating even your bones. Father never solicits your assistance in such decidedly male endeavors. What did rotund Officer Brown say? *If you don't know who it is, you don't know who it's not.* One dead girl was taken out of her window. The barbershop consensus indicts her stepfather. "Who else could get a child out the house without her screaming and carrying on?" the men wanted to know, as clippers buzzed against their necks. And who else besides a father, of some kind, could harbor such malevolence, you mused, sitting very still in the red-cushioned chair.

Now you are uncertain how to proceed. Your yellow slicker is zipped over your green-and-white pajamas and you lace on your sneakers without socks. Father is waiting. You call upon wisdom culled through close readings of the Hardy Boys series. On a sheet of lined notebook paper you write, *My father has taken me out of the house early on Tuesday morning.* You fold the sheet into quarters, then eighths. Then, you carefully print, *OCTAVIA.*

You can't see the ground upon which you plant your canvas sneakers. You press down hard with every step, hoping to leave a trail, but the rain rinses your footprints away like birds eating a path of bread crumbs. Father, walking several paces ahead of you, curses the weather but does not look back.

The offending drainage pipe rests against the side of the new den, added on last spring. It is painted a cheerful green to match the shutters.

"See that?" Father says. "We need to tape the plastic pipe on the end to send the water away from the house, before the basement gets flooded."

The plastic pipe is flexible with accordion pleats. Father positions it to guide the runoff into the neighbor's yard. You decide against sparking a debate on the ethical implications of this act. You don't care much for those neighbors anyway.

You feel the water coursing though the pipe like gallons of blood through a giant artery as you hold it in place. Father breathes heavily as he encircles the pipe with four layers of gray tape. You watch the adhesive give way only seconds after Father's satisfied, "That should do it."

"Shit," he says. "Hold it again."

You do. Father applies more tape. Your feet are going numb from the cold stagnant water in your shoes, but you enjoy the pain as you witness Father's sheer ineptitude. How long will it be before he realizes that "duct tape" is a misnomer?

"Damn," he mutters. He cut his finger with his pocket knife. You concentrate on your frozen ears to keep from laughing as he sticks his injured thumb in his mouth and sucks like a baby.

Since it is raining, Mother drives you and Sister the five miles to school. Because she takes an early bird yoga class at the YWCA, she drops you at school thirty minutes before the first bell. Sister dashes into the building to see if she can be of aid to her teacher, while you stand on the porch watching the orange rivers adjacent to curbs.

"Where you been?" Leon looks like a raisin. His head, arms, and legs jut from the crumpled garbage bag that serves as his raincoat.

"Me?"

"Yeah, you. Wasn't we supposed to do something this morning?"

You don't recall any appointments.

"The candy corn?" Leon prompts. "Come on." He heads toward Lewis's Market. "We only got fifteen minutes before the first bell."

"But it's raining," you protest.

"So." Leon looks back as you tie the drawstring around the hood of your sunshine-yellow raincoat.

"Don't be laughing at me because I'm wearing this Hefty bag. I got a yellow coat just like yours at home. It just wasn't raining when I left the house. When it starts coming down, I see this Hefty bag by the side of the road and put it to good use." He spins around now. "You can't mess with a boy as smart as me."

You nod, although the concept is hardly ingenious. Leon's head is soaked by the time you get to the store. His faded jeans are stained deep blue with rain.

Mrs. Lewis looks up as the two of you enter. "Good morning, boys."

"Morning."

"Leave those wet coats and bags up here. I don't want you dripping water all over my floor."

"Yes'm." You slowly remove your jacket. This is completely unprecedented. Does Leon expect you to follow through even though you are deprived of your tools? You put your book bag on the counter and gingerly walk to the back of the store.

Mrs. Lewis declares Leon too wet to go any farther than the front counter.

"But miss, I wanted to buy something," he complains.

"Just tell Rodney. He'll bring it up here for you."

The sound of your name startles you. The small bag of candy corn falls to the floor.

You bend to retrieve it. The little sack is made of your least favorite packaging. Stupid Leon has no understanding of the logistics of shoplifting. Why can't he ask for Pixie Sticks, which come wrapped in soft cardboard that slides noiselessly into one's pocket? Or even Life Savers in discreet wax-lined foil? Candy corn comes in cheap cellophane, which crackles like burning logs. You carefully put the pouch into the front pocket of your Toughskins. You are going to have to walk gap-legged until you get out of the store.

"Rodney!" Leon calls. "Bring me some candy corn. She won't let me come back there."

You do not enjoy this type of improvisation, but you pick up another packet of candy corn and head toward the counter. You shove it wordlessly toward Leon.

Mrs. Lewis says, "What did you get for yourself?" She looks at you with narrowed eyes, as if she were trying to read the words off your sweatshirt without her glasses. The lines at the side of her mouth look like sideways exclamation marks.

"Wasn't none back there," you mumble.

"Beg your pardon?"

"There aren't any back there." You hope her disapproval is rooted in your failure to meet her grammatical expectations.

"What are you looking for? I just stocked up yesterday."

You mentally whiz through the candy aisle like an accelerated film strip. She is right. Everything is back there.

"Pop Rocks," you say, because you remember they had been taken off the market because they had somehow caused children in Maine to die.

"We can't sell those anymore," she says.

Leon says, "We gonna be late."

"Ten cents." Mrs. Lewis opens the cash register.

"I don't have no money." Leon pats his sodden pockets. "You got a dime, Rodney?"

All you have is your lunch money but you reach into your pockets. There is no way you can get the money out without disturbing the stolen packet of candy corn. You shake your head no.

"What did y'all come in here for if you don't have money?" The question is clearly rhetorical. She looks at Leon. "Get on out of here, boy." He shoots out of the door, into the rain, without bothering to retrieve his black garbage-bag coat.

"And you, Mr. Rodney," she says. "I'm telling you this because you are like one of my own." She leans over the counter so your faces are nearly level. Breakfast is heavy on her breath. "Don't fall in with the wrong crowd. That boy you come in here with never had nothing and ain't never going to get nothing. Look at this." She holds up the wet Hefty bag and shakes it, sending lukewarm raindrops onto your cold face. "Is this all you want out of life?"

You are not quite certain what she is asking, but clearly the appropriate answer is no, so you say it. "No."

"Pardon me?"

"No ma'am."

"Now, put on your coat and run over to school before you get in trouble."

———————

Miss Russell, the art teacher, comes to your class one Tuesday a month. You enjoy the freedom of art class but you are ambivalent about Miss Russell. Her thin brown hair tends to hang in her face, obscuring her spooky hazel eyes.

Octavia uses the easel beside yours. She stares at her canvas for a long time before she dips her brush into the yellow paint and dabs carefully. Her bottom lip is caught gently between her teeth.

You don't want her to see you studying her artwork for fear she will make good on yesterday's threat to hurt your feelings. Turning your attention to your own canvas, you paint fluidly, moving your arm in broad arcs and strokes, dragging the brush behind, forgetting to rinse it before dipping into a fresh color. The hues on your canvas are bruised hybrids.

You take a couple of steps back from your easel to see what you've made. Your hand brushes Miss Russell's arm.

"Ooh," she says, looking at your canvas from under her visor of hair. "My." She pauses and then peeks again. "What do you want to be when you grow up?" she asks.

You understand that she likes your picture. Her question is one of two ways adults have of starting conversations with children. The other, of course, is *how old are you,* which you prefer since a one-word answer will suffice.

You try to formulate an answer. Picturing yourself as an adult requires more imagination than you can muster on such short notice. Your body would be stretched tall like a piece of bubble gum pulled out of shape. But that would make you big, rather than grown. Being grown meant that you wouldn't always be relegated to the drumsticks when your mother bought a bucket of chicken. You have to chew through the stringy veins and rubbery cartilage while Father happily tears through the breast.

Miss Russell nudges you. Her limp hair is the color of acorns. "Do you want to be a policeman? A fireman?" She laughs a little bit. "An artist?"

Why doesn't she just ask you how old you are and move on? Tayari Jones, two aisles over, is sniffing rubber cement and could use a little adult supervision. But Miss Russell squats beside you and leans forward as if your vocational leanings are of some consequence.

You know she doesn't want to know what you want to *eat* when you grow up, but you can't take your mind away from the dinner table. Just yesterday you were forced—at the threat of whipping—to eat several mushy mouthfuls of au gratin spinach that smelled of feet. Father hadn't even put any on his plate. Instead, Mother had served him three tiny red potatoes glistening with butter and dotted with flecks of parsley.

"Hmm?" Miss Russell says.

"A father," you say finally.

"A fireman," she says. "How nice. I'm sure you'll be a very good one."

Octavia looks up from her work and communicates nonverbally that she thinks your ambition is ridiculous. You dunk your brush, heavy and red, into the paper cup of black paint. The mix of colors is like a beetle squashed underfoot. Her eyes are on you still.

"That's pretty, what you made," you tell her.

"What is it then?" she challenges.

You study the configuration of splotches the colors of marigolds and daffodils. You are sincere in your compliment, but the painting bears little resemblance to anything you recognize.

"See, you don't even know what it is."

"A butterfly?"

"No, stupid." Her hand is on her hip. "It's a plate of scrambled eggs and cheese."

No one has ever called you stupid before. You are pleased. You laugh and she joins you, covering her mouth with her hand, smearing spring colors on her dark cheeks.

You don't win first prize for your fall project. Mr. Harrell pins a purple-blue ribbon on Tayari Jones's collar. Evidently, her mother is more talented than yours. Tayari's project includes moving cardboard parts.

Octavia sucks her teeth as a beaming Tayari pulls a little lever that causes a miniature hiker to climb up her posterboard. Her sweater is turned inside out.

"It's not fair," Octavia complains. "You know her mother made that for her."

You nod, eager to agree with her.

"Yours is good," she continues. "Better than mine. But you can still tell that a kid did it."

You smile at the unintentional insult to your mother. You resolve to sit with her at lunch today, if she asks you.

Octavia, in front of you in line, is as quiet as she has ever been. She stands rigidly and takes each advancing step as a regrettable but unavoidable necessity. Your eyes are trained on her neck as your feet move to some choreography that you can't understand. You want to speak and disrupt the lunch-line conveyor belt.

"What are they having today?" you open your mouth to say, but the words get tangled in your inner machinery and are deposited in your stomach.

Today is yesterday. The milk in the cooler is still warmer than ideal but you will drink it anyway. The cafeteria ladies' hair nets still bite into their foreheads. You will exchange forty cents for your lunch, Octavia, only a dime.

"Tetrazzini?" says the cafeteria lady.

"Yes'm," from Octavia.

"Tetrazzini?"

You nod.

She plunges her heavy spoon into the casserole and plops a sprawling portion onto your green sectioned plate. The noodles shine orange with oil and cheese. You open your mouth to express your astonished gratitude, but she's serving the next tray.

Octavia sits alone at a round table with red stools attached. She does not lift her eyes to see where you will sit. She uses her fork to spear a single kernel of corn.

"Is somebody sitting here?" The words make it out of your mouth after first passing through your gut.

"I don't see nobody." She impales another kernel.

You set your tray beside hers.

Leon Simmons calls, "Rodney, I got you a seat over here."

You obediently carry your tray toward the sound of his voice.

"I thought you and me was supposed to be friends. You

don't have to sit there with that Watusi." Leon nudges Candida, who chews hard on gum that is pink as a wound.

You reach in your pocket and pull out the packet of candy corn. It is warm with the heat of your thigh.

"Here go your stuff." You slide it across the table before lifting your tray again.

Octavia is no longer sitting alone. Trina Littlejohn sits unhappily across from her, poking at the turkey Tetrazzini. Should you join them? Sitting with one girl suggests you are going together. Sharing a table with two of them means you're weird.

"Mr. Green, please take a seat," Mr. Harrell orders.

You put your tray beside Octavia's again. "Are you saving this seat?"

She shakes her head no and Trina stops frowning long enough to giggle.

The girls had been talking before you arrived but now they stare silently at you. Trina shovels gigantic scoops of cheesy noodles into her mouth as Octavia eats her corn yellow kernel by yellow kernel. You finish lunch wondering if cafeteria casseroles taste better without cheese after all.

Sister is in an especially good mood after school today. She grabs your hand and swings it as you walk the quarter mile to the bus stop.

"Know why it's not raining no more?" she says.

You shake your head no, as you try to disentangle your fingers from hers.

"'Cause we got our report cards!" she sings, holding tight to your sticky hand.

You've received your report card too. It is sealed like a

state secret in an envelope squashed in the bottom of your book bag.

"What's the matter, Brother?" she asks you, over the hiss of the opening bus door.

"Nothing," you say, sitting aboard the bus, heading in the direction of home. Sister, you know, believes that a progress report is merely an occasion for gift-giving. Last term, she was given a doll that wept. You, on the other hand, understand that the Cs written in Mr. Harrell's careful hand will only remind Father why he hates you.

You could do better. Some of your classmates, whom standardized testing deem to be barely above average, take home exemplary grades. But you, despite your ability, do not memorize multiplication tables or spelling words, although the rote drills are all that stand between you and a student-of-the-month award. They could protect you from Father's belt.

"We're here." Sister tugs your hand. You follow her to the front of the bus. When she exits the city bus, drivers of cars in both directions are pleased to stop although the law does not require this. Sister walks quickly; the plastic barrettes on the ends of her ten or so neat braids click charmingly as she makes her way.

When you come in the house, Sister has already hung her red-and-white jumper dress in her closet and is sitting at the table in her slip polishing an apple with a napkin. In the center of the table is a white envelope. You see it, sigh, and take a similar one from your own backpack. It is gummed with residue of purple candy, but you put it on the table next to hers. The contrast is almost humiliating.

"I hope that's good news!" Mother is cheerful as she eyes the tattered envelope.

She knows full well that it is not, but you say nothing. *It's alright* is what you said last time, but lately you have become bored with the ritualistic lies.

"Your sister is going to do some reading before dinner. Don't you want to read for a few minutes before your father gets home?" Mother has read somewhere that children who read at least an hour a day are somehow better than those who don't. Sister absently chews a green apple as she looks at her kids' book with big letters. You read too, but you are not an exhibitionist.

Three hours later, Father arrives, reeking of hard work. "Did you clean your room like I told you?"

You shake your head. "Homework." Luckily you have an open book on your lap to appease Mother.

Father exhales. He is disappointed that he has nothing better for a son. A boy who is not only too short but *trifling, lazy, sloven, and spoiled.*

"Little overdue for a haircut, boy," he says, as if it is a moral defect. You say nothing because you are sure that eventually it will dawn upon him that you are too young to drive and that he is the person ultimately responsible for your upkeep in all matters male. "My daddy told me never to trust a man without a decent edge up," he says emphatically. You hunch your shoulders to hide the two nappy trails of hair running down your neck.

When dinner is served you are full of stolen candy. Mother, a terrible cook, is unaware of her culinary limitations and misprepares complex dishes without remorse. Sis-

ter asks for another serving of vichyssoise. Father wipes his
mouth with a blue paper napkin and reaches for the envelopes in the center of the table. He takes the clean one
first. Sister smiles down at her plate as he rips through the
adhesive with his square fingernail.

"Look at this, Beverly," he says. "Almost all Es. And look
here. A note on the bottom. It says her report was excellent."
Mother now looks down at *her* plate shyly. You know that it
is because she did most of the work on that particular project. All Sister did was hand her the glue or the construction paper.

Father opens the second envelope. He looks at it quickly
and hands it to your mother. He wants to know what your
problem is. You shrug but offer no response.

"He's not challenged," Mother says in your defense.

"Challenged?" Spittle flies from his lips. "This boy's
problem is he never had to pick cotton. When you pick cotton you don't sit out there and see if you can be *challenged* by
the cotton. You don't bring your bag in empty at the end of
the day and tell that white man that the cotton didn't *chal-
lenge* you. You just pick the goddamn cotton!"

"Daddy!" Sister says. "You said a bad word."

He apologizes, kissing the top of her lovely head. You
stare at your plate, plot murder, say nothing.

Father will beat you tonight. The tiny column of letters de-
facing your report card mandates that he pull his belt from
its loops and swing it hard. His pants will fall below his
waist revealing clean white undershorts as he swings at
your shins, forcing you to dance a humiliating jig. There is
a boy in the special ed class whose legs are immobilized by

braces of reinforced metal. Father's belt coils around your
left thigh, the buckle collides with your knee. You wish you
were a special boy whose legs could not move and could not
dance to the rhythm of the licks.

"You have to learn to get your lesson," he says.

You cry despite your resolve to be impassive.

"Never going to amount to nothing." Each word is ac-
centuated by a whack.

You recall Octavia hurling rocks at Leon's head. What
would she do if she were in your place? Then, you remember that people say that she has no father. The envy leaves a
taste in your mouth that is as bitter as blood.

Father is exhausted now. He takes his air in gulps as he
fastens his belt around his trousers. Both of your faces shine
with saltwater.

"Let's not let this happen again," he says, opening your
bedroom door.

Mother is in the hallway. "Did you hurt him?"

"No," Father assures her. "I hurt his feelings, that's all."

———◆———

On Wednesday morning, your full bladder forces you
out of bed. You open your bedroom door and dart across
the hall to the bathroom. In the clean and bright room, you
use the toilet, being careful not to splash the green tile.
Mother has complained to Father about your bad aim. "Get
a little closer next time," he told you, as you rubbed the
floor with a soapy sponge. "It's not as long as you think it
is."

You are on your way back to bed when your parents' door opens. Father is ready for breakfast.

"Well, looka here," he says. "What you doing up?"

You point at the bathroom door and stare longingly at your bedroom.

"Come on in the kitchen and talk to me while I get me some breakfast."

You stand in the hallway barefoot and vulnerable in your Snoopy pajamas. He smiles as if he hadn't hit you with his belt just hours earlier. Will he swing it again if you refuse his invitation?

"Okay," you say.

Father is cheerful as he turns on the radio and shuts it off again. "Don't need that since I got my boy to talk to this morning."

The teakettle shrieks and Father turns brown pebbles into coffee. "Kids don't like coffee, right?"

You don't.

"What it is y'all drink? Hot chocolate? Tea?"

"Hot chocolate is okay."

He rummages in the cabinet. "I don't see none. How about a Coke?"

You shrug. You have not brushed your teeth yet; whatever you drink will taste terrible.

You watch Father's broad back as he breaks three eggs into a little bowl and beats them with a fork. He slurps coffee while dotting slices of white bread with golden margarine. He doesn't turn around before he starts to speak.

"My daddy worked in the sawmill. He couldn't read. He would turn over in his grave if he could hear me because he worked so hard to keep people from knowing. Daddy could

write his name as good as a schoolteacher. But that was all."
Now Father turns to look at you. "I hate that he died before you could get to know him."

"Yes sir," you say.

"The reason I know that he couldn't read, is that he used
to bring me books when I was a boy. I don't even want to
think about where he must've gotten them from." Father
stirs the eggs in the little black skillet, shaking his head gently from side to side. He takes a big gulp from his mug. "But
the reason I know he couldn't read those books is that some
of them were straight pornography." He turns and grins at
you before lifting perfect slices of toast from the oven. Yellow splotches make the bread look like dice. He hands you
two slices on a white saucer trimmed in silver.

"Jelly?" he asks.

"No sir."

"I thought kids were supposed to like sweet stuff." Sitting at the table, he chases his eggs around the plate with
the perfect toast. There are crumbs in his mustache.

"Now Daddy was a religious man—we spent all *day*
Sunday in church. I know that if he had even a little piece
of an idea what was in them books, he never would have let
me have them." He laughs and looks at you, expecting a
smile. You show your teeth and he continues. "He wanted
me to have things a little better. He didn't want me to end
up at the sawmill, you see?"

You nod. But you are confused. Father has never given
you a book.

"He always made sure I got my lesson, you see."

Your throat tightens and you cannot swallow your toast.

You calm yourself by noting that he does not wear a belt with his coveralls.

"Daddy used to beat my tail good if he even *thought* that I wasn't doing my homework." He smiles at his near-empty plate, savoring the memory of pain. "I used to be mad because he would beat me all out in the yard. My friends who probably had did the same thing would be out laughing at me. They had daddies who didn't care enough to take a switch to them when they needed it." He wipes his plate with the last scrap of toast. "Today, somebody would call the police on Daddy and have him taken away for *child abuse.*" He smiles at you. Soft bread is lodged between his teeth.

You try to drink some Coke but your throat is shut. You hold the stinging bubbles in your mouth.

"But now, I thank him for it. Some of the fellas I grew up with ain't got half of what I got. Or even look at Joe. Daddy was too old when he was coming up to give him a good whipping when he needed it. What's Joe doing now? Picking up the garbage. If his boss decides to cut his wages, there ain't much that Joe can do. But me, I'm my own boss."

Father scoots back a little from the table, inviting you to take a long admiring look at him. "Your mama don't even have to work." He smiles. "You see what I mean?" Father leaves the kitchen. You go to the bathroom and vomit buttered toast and soda.

You're at school early again this morning. Wednesday is Mother's day to help prepare meals at church for the shut-ins. You are hungry as you wind through the corner store before the bell, but Mrs. Lewis's candies do not tempt you this morning. You tuck a pair of red lollipops in your pocket but they will not do for breakfast. Cherry candy, always improbably bright, never evokes the dark July sweetness of real fruit.

Turning the candy over in your pocket, you watch the breakfast kids through the narrow slit between the cafeteria doors. They eat with hungry appreciation but not with the starving abandon that you have envisioned. Octavia sits alone at an oval table absently eating eggs and cheese while reading a hardcover book. A chunk of egg falls on the page and she looks around her with darting eyes before wiping the book with her napkin. Leon tips a bowl of cereal to his mouth. Puffed corn and milk travel down his throat in waves.

You put your hand to the double doors and give a tentative shove. They yield easily and you walk inside. The room is much cleaner and quieter than it will be at twelve-twenty, lunchtime for fifth-graders. You make your way toward the serving line as a bell rings. A cafeteria lady is wiping down the counter with a stained rag.

"Can I help you?" She is eyeing your penny loafers suspiciously.

"I wanted to get some breakfast."

"Come again?" She plants her hands on her hips to brace herself against any foolishness of yours.

"I wanted to have some breakfast." You clear your throat and add, "Ma'am."

"Breakfast's over."

"Already?" There is a small lake of steaming water where vats of grits, eggs, and bacon had been warmed.

"Your mama didn't fix you nothing before you left the house?" Her eyes soften slightly.

You should be loyal to your mother and explain that you refused the meal she offered you. But to explain this rejection requires that you betray Father. You shrug.

"We got some toast left." She puts two slices on a plate. You do not reach for it.

"What? Ain't nothing wrong with that toast." She's looking at your loafers again.

You cry. Hard, shoulder-shaking sobs bring her from behind the serving bar. She kneels before you. Her uniform smells of fried food and fabric softener.

"What's wrong, baby?" She lifts your chin and dabs your face with a clean corner of apron. "What you crying for? You sick? You need to call your mama?"

You shake your head vigorously from side to side.

"It's alright," she says. "We don't have to call her." She hugs you, and you allow yourself to sink into the space between her arms. This is a guilty pleasure you have not enjoyed since before Sister was born. The cafeteria lady's body is as firm and comfortable as a good mattress. She rubs your hair in wide spirals. "Shh." Her kiss on the top of your head is as gentle as music.

Finally, you struggle in her embrace. You should tell her that you will be late for class. Embarrassment tangles your words like twine and you cannot speak.

"Better?" she asks, as if she has just adjusted the brakes on your bicycle.

You nod, glad to avoid words.

"Hold on," she says, disappearing momentarily behind a metal door. She returns and presses a banana into your hand. "You can't go all day without something on your stomach."

At recess you sit under the sliding board and carefully pull
back the yellow peel. The banana inside is the clean color
of eggshells and soft as a kiss. You hug your knees to warm
yourself after you eat. The slanted metal above you blocks
the wind. You pretend to be in a cozy attic room and fall
asleep.

You are shaken awake by a seventh-grader, Lumumba
Jones. His sister is in your class.

"You alright?" he asks.

You nod.

"He's okay," Lumumba says to Delvis Watson, another
older boy. "You in the fifth, right?"

Another nod.

"Man, you must have stayed up late last night to be sleep
all this time out here on the cold ground." He pulls you up.
"You got dirt all over your pants."

Delvis starts to laugh. "His name need to be Black Van
Winkle."

"Leave him alone," Lumumba says; he turns his head to
one side. "You sure you okay? You want us to take you to
the nurse?"

"Where's my class?" you croak.

"They just getting out of lunch. If you hurry up, you
might get to class before they notice you cut."

You thank him and run toward the building. You hear
Lumumba say to Delvis, "Little man sho do run flickted."

You are able to fall in with the rest of your class as they
leave the cafeteria. You file into the classroom and slide into
your desk. "Mr. Green," says Mr. Harrell. "Please step outside."

What does he want? Is he angry that you missed lunch?

You stand before his desk, waiting for him to rise and follow you beyond the trailer door.

"You have a question, Mr. Green?"

You shake your head no and leave the trailer alone.

Father stands on the covered walkway. His filthy coveralls stink of oil and anger.

"Sir?" You draw your cold hands up into the sleeves of your sweater.

He looks at you for a long appraising moment and then glances around as if searching for someplace to spit. "Virginia Lewis called me on my job today."

Your heart falls hard in your stomach like a missed pop fly tumbling past your glove to the ground.

"I don't know what your problem is." Father shakes his head in what seems to be genuine bewilderment.

"Did you hear one word I said to you this morning?" The outdoor air coaxes a thin transparent trickle from his nostril. "Do you think I take the time to tell you things just because I want to exercise my face?"

"No sir." But you have no idea why he says what he does.

"Virginia told me you been hanging with the wrong crowd. Coming in her store and stealing candy." He pauses.

"I didn't," you begin.

"Don't lie to me, boy. I didn't come way out here to listen to you lie. I came out here for you to listen." He takes a breath. "Then I call up to the school and they tell me you ain't where you supposed to be. I come running up here and then you seem to have found your way back." His voice rises in the damp air.

"But—"

"You can hang out with your friends when you supposed to be in school. You can hang out with the crowd and
steal from Virginia. But let me tell you this, the crowd aint
going to be there for you when it matters. When you have
to make something of yourself, you stand alone. You hear
me?" His stained index finger grazes your nose.

"Yes sir." But you have never been part of a crowd. It is
even difficult for you to recall being in the presence of more
than one kid at a time. "Can I—"

"What I just tell you?" Father says. "I didn't come here
to hear you lie. I came here to show you that *I* am your father and you do what *I* say do. Not what your friends want
you to do."

Now you notice the belt rolled tight and stashed in his
palm.

"We going to go in that classroom and I am going to
beat your behind. And you'll see that the crowd cant do
nothing to help you."

You are required to stand before Mr. Harrell's desk,
which he has cleared to accommodate the impending ritual
of humiliation. The room is silent as death when you lean
over the oak desk and grip its opposite edge with your quivering fingers. You are not the first child to be humiliated before his peers. Twice already this year, mothers on lunch
breaks have snatched unsuspecting youngsters from their
chairs, flogged them briefly, apologized to Mr. Harrell for
disrupting math lessons, and dashed off to work again while
the children sobbed and sucked snot.

But there had been no preamble to the other beatings.
No agonizing suspense. The mothers were not their own
bosses and would hardly waste hired minutes announcing

what would soon be apparent anyway. But Father has plenty of time.

"I'm sorry, sir, for disrupting your class," he says to Mr. Harrell. "But Rodney has got to learn not to go running off without no one knowing where's he's at. These days are too dangerous for that."

The class behind you emits a sudden murmur of comprehension. The tension in the room snaps in two like a pencil as the full import of Father's words settles. Everyone understands that he is punishing you for putting yourself in harm's way. You know this is a lie. You release the edge of the desk and fill your lungs to scream, "I stole!" but Father has begun swinging his belt.

The licks are not as hard as the ones last night, but the leather against your behind smarts. You open your mouth wide to shout above the whisk of the belt and Father's grunts, "I STOLE!"

"I," you say as loud as you have ever said anything.

Father interprets this utterance as a cry of pain or an admission of defeat. He stops whipping you.

"Stole," you finish, but Father speaks louder than you and the word is lost.

"Mr. Harrell, I hope this takes care of the problem. If there is any more trouble, just call me."

You walk back to your chair on legs as unsteady as spaghetti. Your classmates look at you with faces splashed with horror. "What he do?" someone asked. "He went off by hisself and almost got snatched." There were no clucks of sympathy. No one said, "He didn't have to whip him like that, all in front of everybody," like they had when the tired mothers invaded the classroom with their violence and fury.

You put your head on your desk and wrap your face with your bony forearms.

"Mr. Green, do you need to excuse yourself to the lavatory?"

You don't answer.

"He said no," Octavia says. "I heard him."

You are grateful but do not lift your head. With closed eyes you try to trace memory to its origin, to the instant you were born. And then maybe you could take your recollections back a single moment earlier to the place before. To the time when you weren't even thought about.

You are awakened by the final bell.

"Wake up, Rodney." Octavia pats your arms with hands that smell like lemons. "You alright?"

You open your eyes. Her face is dark as pencil lead and shiny as a new penny.

"I stole."

"You told?" she says. "Told what to who?"

"Never mind." You reach into your pockets and give her the two cherry lollipops.

You are cold without your tweed coat. You should return to the classroom and retrieve it from the coat rack. No one will be there. All the kids are gone. Sister will be ready to walk home now. You must turn back. Nothing you know is in the direction you're heading. Home is the other way. You keep moving, ignoring the blistering rub of your sock, which is twisted inside your loafer. There is the sting of rain in the air that beats you around the ears. You would be much warmer wearing your good tweed coat.

At Martin Luther King Drive, you dart across four lanes of traffic against the blinking warning of the cross signal. Car horns scream, but the drivers accelerate when you find yourself alive and disappointed on the north side of the road. Carillon bells sing from the college campus nearby and you walk toward downtown. Home is the other way.

A blue sedan pulls up beside you.

"Excuse me," says the driver, lowering the passenger-side window. "I'm a police officer. There has been a bank robbery in this area. We need to get all the civilians off the street." A tree-shaped air freshener swings back and forth from his mirror.

"You're not a real policeman."

"What did I just say? Hurry up, kid, and get in the car. I don't have all day." He produces a U-shaped piece of metal. You run your finger across the metal. It is as smooth as chocolate and fake as a glass eye.

The car burps sour exhaust onto the November day. You inhale deeply, tasting the gray poison. "Which way are you going?"

He points toward downtown. Against the overcast sky, you make out the lights rimming the Peachtree Plaza Hotel. When you enter the car, you press your eyelids against your eyes until you see only dancing spots the color of marigolds. The door shuts and the sedan vaults away in the direction opposite of home.

PART 3

Sweet Pea

My mother tells lies. She tells them all the time. For all kinds of reasons. Some of them make sense and other times it's like she lies just to hear herself talk. It gets tricky because she can mix a lie and the truth together so it ends up like Kool-Aid, and you can't really separate what's water, what's mix, and what's sugar. Like she told me there wasn't no such thing as a Easter Bunny, which is true. But then she turned around and told me that my daddy had sent me my Easter basket, which wasn't. She went out and bought the thing and put his name on it. I know this because I found out that my daddy doesn't go to church or celebrate any holidays that got to do with God. And also she told me the truth about Santa right up front. I heard her explaining to her best friend, Miss Darlene, my friend Delvis's mother. "I told Sweet Pea right up front that there wasn't a Santa Claus. Why should she think some white man sneaking in here to give her presents? I'm the one that working double shifts. And the sooner she know ain't no white man ever gonna give her nothing, the better." So that makes sense. But a whole bunch of other times, she told lies that I still can't understand why.

Like the time she told me that dope needles was the same as doctor needles. That was a lie she didn't have no reason to tell. I was little then, about six maybe seven. We were walking to the bus stop when I saw a needle hiding in the grass. I thought that it was a quarter at first so I bent down to get it.

"Don't touch that," Mama said.

I pulled my hand back. "I was just looking at it." It looked like a toy except that there was blood in the part where the medicine go.

"A doctor must've dropped it out of his bag on his way to the bus stop."

I believed her. Back then, I didn't have sense enough to know that doctors don't catch the bus. They ride around in big blue Cadillacs.

And she's a hypocrite. Tells me all the time to tell her the "whole truth." If she asks me if I did my homework and I say "yes" when I only did half of it, she has a fit and won't let me watch TV for a whole week.

"You didn't ask me if I did *all* of it," I said. "You said did I *do* it." She looked at me and said, "Octavia, you ain't crazy. You knew that was a lie as soon as you told it."

But when I came home from school today, what was she doing? Stomping on the electric bill to make it look like it got lost in the mail. I bet they go and cut our lights off anyway.

I opened the fridge to see what she had left out for my snack. On a little saucer was a plate of cheese squares and crackers. It's a good thing that I like cheese because we always have a lot of it.

I ate three or four crackers and went into the fridge again for juice.

"Stop opening the fridge. Decide what you want and

get it." Evidently, she had put too many footprints on the bill because now she was trying to smooth it out.

"We don't have no juice?" I had already had a bad day at school and I didn't need to add thirst to the list of things on my mind.

"Drink water. It's good for you."

Now, did I ask her what was good for me? All she had to say was that we were all out. "You'll go to the store tomorrow?"

"Friday." That's when she gets her check.

The phone rang and she picked it up on the first ring. "Hi, Mama," she said. It was Granny calling from Macon. Mama can be psychic like that. It's like she know the way Granny rings.

"Mama, I know what you saw on the news. How many times do I have to tell you that is not happening around here."

She was talking about the Missing and Murdered Children. That's all anybody want to talk about when they call long distance. But that right there that Mama said was a straight lie. It was happening all around here. Jashante Hamilton, who stay right next door, went to play basketball last October and never came back. His mama went and put extra locks on her doors but that's closing the barn after the cow done got out. The boy dead now. They ain't found a body yet but everybody know that's what happened to him. Last time anybody saw him, he was selling car air fresheners at the West End Mall.

I started chewing the crackers with my mouth open because I didn't want to hear her conversation. I don't like to think about nobody being dead. But she was getting mad at Granny and I could hear her over my crunching.

"I don't care what Kenny told you. We do not live in the projects."

Uncle Kenny is something else I didn't want to go into. I started to leave the room, but Mama motioned for me to stay. I don't know why she needs a witness for everything.

"Listen, Mama," she said. "Sweet Pea is *safe*. Atlanta is a very big city you know. Those kids getting killed are way on the other side of town."

Mama rolled her eyes and reached into her pocket for her cigarettes. She snapped her fingers at me and I handed her the lighter. She took a deep pull of her cig and then she blew it out hard so Granny could hear she was smoking. "Mama, you act like no black boy ever got killed in Macon, Georgia. At least here it's considered a crime."

I could hear Granny voice squawking out the phone like a hit dog. I don't know why Granny call so much if all the two of them do is fight. They get to talking about Atlanta and Macon like two kids saying who can run the fastest. If Granny saw on the news that we getting rain in the city, Mama will look out the window at the water dripping off the glass and say it's sunny. And then she'll turn around and tell Granny that a tornado is headed right for Macon City Hall.

All of a sudden Mama changed the subject. "Sweet Pea just got in from school. She brought her report card yesterday. All As *again*."

Now that there was a ball-face lie. I brought home my six-week assessment two days ago. I didn't make all As. I made some As but some Bs and Cs too. Now she made it seem like me and her was a lying tag team. Then she shoved the phone in my hand so I could talk to Granny. My mama is a trip.

"What's wrong with you?" Mama said, as soon as I had put the phone on the hook.

"Why you say that to Granny? About my grades?" I said.

She waved her hand at me like she was fanning my mad away with the smoke. "You know how Mama is." She smiled like we were sharing a secret joke. But I refused to show her tooth the first.

I didn't say nothing else about it. My mama don't believe in beating kids, but she got other ways of showing that she don't appreciate back talk. She don't tolerate eye-rolling either, so I squeezed them almost shut and gave her my evil eye.

"Why you sitting looking at me with your face all balled up?" Mama scooped up her cigarettes on her way to the table where I was sitting picking at my snack. "Something must have happened at school today."

Something did happen at school but I really didn't feel like telling her about it so I said, "Didn't nothing happen." I got up and opened the fridge like I thought some juice grew in there while I was on the phone.

"Sweet Pea, shut that fridge. Electric bill is high enough without you trying to cool the whole kitchen."

I closed it and sat down at the kitchen table. Mama had put a wad of paper under one leg to make it more steady, but it wobbled anyway. I rocked it back and forth like a loose tooth.

Mama took a couple of puffs. She had her eyes clamped

on me like two clothespins. She hates it when I have something on my mind and don't tell her about it. I think if we had the money she would go buy a X-ray machine so she could look inside my head a couple times a day and make sure I'm not thinking anything that she don't like.

"Did you get in trouble?" she asked. "Tell me the truth. I don't want no surprise phone calls."

She's always bringing that up. And it's not fair. Only one time did a teacher call over here to report me. And that wasn't really my fault. Somebody stole my spelling book.

"No, Mama," I said. "It wasn't me that was in trouble." She looked relaxed now. "It was my friend, Rodney." She tightened up again. I should have told her my friend was a girl. Now she was going to try to squeeze the whole story out of me.

"Who?" she said, with her eyebrows all up in the air.

"Rodney," I said. "This boy I know. Sit behind me. Remember I told you about him? Quiet and everything?"

She nodded her head like she knew what I was talking about, but I knew I had never said one word to her about him.

"What kind of trouble?"

"His daddy came up to the school and beat him in front of the class," I told her.

Mama got up and went to the cabinet and took down a blue glass. She rinsed it out before filling it with ice water. "His *daddy?*"

"That what I said. Whoever heard of a *man* coming up to the school in the middle of the day to whip somebody?" I had heard about people's fathers getting rough. And stepfathers supposed to be the worst one out of all of them.

My own daddy never got rough with me because I don't hardly know the man. He stay in South Carolina with his wife and they baby girl. And I had never seen a man raise his hand to a child out in the public. "Ain't a man supposed to be at work during the day?"

Mama said, "Well, the mothers that come up to the school have a job."

"Yeah," I said. "But daddies supposed to have the kind of job you can't just up and leave."

Mama drank some more of her water and shrugged her shoulders. "At least he was there." She got up from the table and poked around with frozen chicken soaking in a sink full of water.

Least he was there? She make it seem like any old daddy is better than none at all. Don't get me wrong. I sometimes wish that maybe my daddy, Ray, would be around here with us. And not just for TV-reasons like taking me to the park or letting me step on his shoes to learn how to dance. But also because when your daddy is not around, it look like you and your mama ran him off. Like he just couldn't stand to be around you no more.

But if I had a daddy like Rodney got, he would have been the one ran *me* off. For real. He took that strap to Rodney like he was enjoying it. And Rodney is so quiet that he couldn't even cry. When it was all over, I thought the man was going to take a bow while my stupid teacher, Mr. Harrell, clapped. Rodney walked back to his chair, but it seemed like he was crawling. Then he just stayed there, all crumpled up like a dirty napkin.

But Mama wouldn't understand so I didn't say nothing else about it. It was easy keeping it to myself after dinner because Mama don't talk much after the sun go down. This is because she is too busy being worried about me being home by myself at night while she's off at work.

She try to act like it's not a big deal, but I know different because I heard her lying to Granny saying there wasn't nothing to worry about. "Eleven-to-seven shift ain't that bad," she said. "It's better for me to be at work when she sleep than for me to be gone when she get home from school. The afternoon is when kids get into mess." She put the phone back on the hook and blew smoke out her mouth and sucked it back up through her nose. "Mama act like that white man *ask* me when I want to work." Then she mashed the cigarette out.

So what ends up happening is that I have two bedtimes. Nine o'clock is the first one. Mama makes me go to bed then so I can be good and sleep by the time she leave for the SunBeam Factory around ten-thirty. It mighta worked if I didn't know that she was leaving at eleven P.M. Then I could sleep as sound as I do on her off days. But I can't get locked good into a dream because I keep waking up looking at the clock to see how much longer before I'm by myself. It's like the men that's about to be put in the electric chair. They always ask them what they want to eat. But I bet they bring them the fried shrimp or whatever and the men can't even eat it because they so worked-up about what's going to happen next. That's how I am at night. My stomach get balled up in a gooey mess like chewing gum stuck in somebody's hair.

Before she leaves, Mama comes in my room to put an extra quilt on. She do that no matter what time of year it is. I always make little sleepy sounds when she kiss my forehead, but soon as the lock clicks, my eyes pop back open. I stay in the bed awhile longer to make sure she good and gone. I used to have my feet on the floor as soon as the door shut but one time she came back to get her sweater. It took some fancy dancing to get out of that one.

The first thing I do when I get out of bed is put on my shoes. I get nervous and I like to be ready to run if I have to. I ain't never had to, but it's good to be ready. The next thing I do is get my door key from my nightstand. I threaded a shoestring through the hole so I can put it around my neck. I've only had the key for about two years. Mama used to just lock me in the house and the door would stay closed until she came back. But three little kids who stay in the projects across the street got burned to death while they mama was at work. After that, we rode the bus to Kmart and got a key made just for me.

Once I got everything I need, I head to the living room to watch TV.

It was a regular night. I was wrapped up like a mummy in my quilt, with the TV turned to the eleven-o'clock news. I had watched at the six-o'clock show with Mama, but I like to watch it again at eleven to make sure that everything is still okay. Channel Two is the best channel because they got Monica Kaufman, a black lady, giving the report.

As soon as the theme music went off, and the camera zoomed in on Monica, I knew that somebody else was dead. Whenever there was bad news, she took a breath before she talked, like she was fixing to dive under water. I held my breath too and waited for her to tell us who it was. *Please, God, let it be far from here,* I prayed right quick. But I should have known that praying only makes thing worse. It gets God's attention like with Job. Right there in the middle of the screen was my friend Rodney.

Monica has this way of talking about everything like it was just a ribbon cutting downtown or something like that. "A twelfth child has been reported missing in Southwest Atlanta tonight. Police are looking for information regarding the disappearance of Rodney Green." On and on like that. She said almost the same thing when Jashante next door came up missing. It would seem like there should be some different words to talk about two people that were nothing alike. But all Monica had to say about both of them was that they were gone. Then they showed Rodney's mother and father. They both just said how much they wanted him back just like Miss Viola had said back in October.

And even I was almost the same. I was on the same couch in my same pajamas staring at this same TV like I had never seen one before. But last time, my mama was with me. We knew Jashante was missing because his mama had been all over the neighborhood looking for him. She knocked on our door twice. "You seen Shante?" she said. I had the door locked because my mama wasn't home. "No ma'am," I hollered. She came again and I said no. Mama came home before Miss Viola came back again.

Miss Viola had on a black skirt and a yellow-and-green top. Thick stockings the color of white ladies stretched up her legs and tied off at the knee. She sat down at our rickety table while Mama fixed her a cup of black coffee.

"When the last time you seen him?" Mama asked her.

"When he went off for school this morning."

Mama looked at the clock. It was nine o'clock at night.

She had only been looking for him since eight. I sat as quiet as I could so I wouldn't get sent to my room.

"You going to call the police now?"

"You think I should?"

"Yeah," Mama said. "They can help you look."

"But I got some hot checks at Big Star, some other places around town." Her voice faded out. "Sometimes the police pick people up for stuff like that."

"Viola," Mama said, "this ain't no time to be worried about no bad checks. This your *baby.*"

"You right," Miss Viola said. She pushed up on the table to get up.

"Wait a second." Mama put another cup in front of her. "You better get another cup of coffee in you before you go talking to the police."

Now, why she need to have coffee before she talked to the police, I don't know. She didn't look to me like she was about to fall asleep. Maybe coffee makes you brave. Granny say that it put hair on your chest. But Mama don't let me touch it because she believe it will stunt my growth.

So when they put Jashante on the eleven-o'clock news I was ready. But this Rodney thing caught me by surprise like a cheap trick. Like when Leon put vinegar in my thermos at school and I took a big gulp, setting my whole head on fire. I coughed so hard the vinegar came out my nose and all the kids laughed. When I saw Rodney's school picture on the screen with the task force number blinking under it, my crying came hard and sudden like a coughing fit. And the tears were hot as blood.

Then I had a stupid idea and I dried my tears up. Maybe he wasn't dead yet. Miss Camille Bell was on the TV a few weeks ago saying that her boy, Yusef, stayed alive almost a week before they killed him. When they found little Yusef he was clean looking, well-fed, she said. But he was still dead. Then I thought something even more crazy. Maybe Rodney was having a good time with those child murderers. They might be giving him Big Macs and strawberry shakes to keep him from hollering and running for the police. Like with Yusef. But like the man in the electric chair and the fried shrimp, Rodney would be too scared to enjoy himself.

They put a big clock on the screen. "It's eleven-fifteen. Do you know where your children are?"

Mama knew where I was and I knew that she was at the Sunbeam factory making bread and imitation Twinkies. But knowing don't mean nothing if you can't be there. And anyway, by the time a mama can figure out that she don't know where her child is, it's all over with anyway.

A commercial came blasting out of the TV. It was loud like somebody had snuck up behind me, screaming in my ear about washing powder. Two little white boys dropped blueberry pie all over their white shirts. "Uh-oh," one of them said. They mama said, "It's okay; we got All." The kids hollered, "Hoo Ray!" Uncle Kenny used to say, "Who is Ray anyway?" I would laugh because Ray is my daddy. "Nobody," I said. Uncle Kenny would be laughing too and bounced me on his lap hard and kissed the back of my neck. The TV showed how All can lift off any stain. "Hoo Ray!"

Rodney's picture was back on. Sometimes you can see a picture of somebody you know that don't really look like that person. Like a picture of Mama when she was a girl. It's her but then it ain't her. Her driver's license is like that too.

And the photo of Rodney hit me the same way. In the picture he looked like a regular boy from our class. He was by himself so you couldn't tell that he was shorter than most of them and just nicer and smarter than all of them put together. Kodak commercials say that a picture is worth a thousand words, but the one they showed of Rodney ain't worth more than three or four. Boy. Black. Dead. Rodney was what my mama call "good people." Nice for no reason at all. Sometimes he might leave a Blow Pop on my desk and not say nothing about it. He just wanted me to have it. I turned around one time and said *thank you* and he looked shocked like he didn't have nothing to do with it. But I know it was him because nobody else in our class say *hi* to me let alone give me nothing. And Rodney come from a family with a lot of money. He always had so much candy in his pockets like he must spend two, three dollars a day. But I said thank you to him anyway. My voice was always a little bit soft when I talk to him. It was because he speak almost like a whisper. Talking loud to Rodney Green would be like screaming at a librarian. But you couldn't see none of that in the picture up on the screen. I could tell it was Rodney, but the picture didn't show him good enough for someone to see him and know him.

But it don't matter anyway, I guess. Gone is gone.

My alarm clock scared the bejesus out of me. Mike Roberts said, "This is V One-o-three FM" and I like to had a nervous breakdown. It's been like this on and off ever since this first started happening with the kids. When the first kids got found, I was jumpy at night like after I seen *Night of the Living Dead*. Then I started getting over it. Then Yusef Bell who went to E. A. Ware Elementary got snatched. I didn't know him but I knew where that school was at and I got tied up all over again. When Jashante got took, I couldn't get no scareder. As a matter of fact, when he got killed it cooled me down a little bit. I was thinking that it couldn't happen in the same place twice. That's what they say about lightning. But now it seems like bad luck could be like chicken pox. You got to catch it from somebody. And if any-body could catch it from Rodney, it would be me. After all, I was the only one he talked to really.

When I looked over at the clock again, it was seven A.M. My mama probably was punching out at that very second. She told me that her and Miss Darlene be out the door by seven-o-two. Sometimes if I'm running late, I'll see her just as I'm heading out.

I went in my room to see what Mama had laid out for me to put on. "Man!" I said out loud. My green jeans were stretched across my chair. Why she feel like she have to pick out my clothes anyway? These pants were way too short for me, but she don't care. Now if they were too tight, she would get rid of them in a hot second. Last week, I had on my favorite jeans. They were kind of light blue with long legs rolled up into fat cuffs by my shoe. I was about to go out and Mama stopped me. She pulled at the back pocket.

"Take them off," she said.

"Why? These my favorite pants."

"They too close in the seat."

And I haven't seen them pants since. I bet she put them in a box to send to my cousin Kay-Kay in the country. It makes me mad to think that I'm going around with these in-the-water green pants and Kay-Kay having the only in-style thing I got. And Kay-Kay stay out in Macon where they don't even know what style is.

But there wasn't nothing I could do about it that morning. Once I had the outfit on, I went to the bathroom and stood on the commode so I could see how I looked in the mirror over the sink. "Man!" I said again. The pants were riding up my legs so high that my socks showed. Mama need to stop bragging to everybody that I'm growing like a weed if she don't want to buy me no new clothes. Now when I walk into class, everybody going to start singing "Wade in the Water."

But no, Rodney Green got snatched yesterday. I bet everybody in that whole class would be quiet and scared.

When I was headed out, I bumped into Delvis Watson. I was shocked to see him so early. Since his mama work eleven-to-seven with mine, he have to get his little brother and sister ready for school. The three of them was usually running late. Today they were out early, but they should have spent another minute or so in front of the mirror. I couldn't tell if Delvis had dressed the twins or if they had dressed themselves, but they looked a mess. Darlita's skirt was twisted and Donathan had a sock on his left hand and a glove on his right. His eyes were ringed around with a soft crust. I couldn't tell if it was from sleep or from tears.

"What's the matter, Little Man?" I asked him.

"Darlita bit me." He looked like just saying it was going to jump-start his crying.

"It was a accident," Darlita said.

I didn't see how you could bite somebody without

meaning to. Especially since both twins were missing their main biting teeth.

"You seen the eleven-o'clock news last night?" I asked Delvis.

"No. I was sleep. What they said?"

"Somebody in my class got snatched." I didn't like saying dead people's names.

"Who?"

I started describing Rodney.

"Just tell me the name." Delvis rolled his eyes.

"Can't," I said. "Bad luck."

"It's bad luck to say the name of *dead* people. When people just missing you can call them all you want."

"Rodney Green," I whispered, in case he was dead.

"For real?"

I nodded.

Delvis was real quiet. The sound of wind in the pecan trees was like girls giggling. He bobbed his head a little bit like an old man agreeing with the preacher. The twins stopped passing licks and followed him like quiet baby ducks.

"Get one of them so we can cross the street," he said. I took Darlita's cold hand. Her nails were colored with blue Magic Marker.

"Rodney Green," Delvis said all loud. He didn't let go of Donathan even though we had been gotten across the street. "He in your class; wear glasses?"

I nodded.

"Always be in Mrs. Lewis store stealing candy?"

I shook my head. "This boy I'm talking about not like that. He real quiet. Smart too."

"Got a blue book bag with a green stripe?"

"No. Not Rodney. He got money. Sometimes you see his mama bringing him to school in a long blue car with a tan top."

"That's him." Delvis brought his cheek low to scratch his face without having to let go of his brother. "His sister in the same class with the twins."

"Who?" they said at the same time. They know better than to get into big kids' conversations, but when somebody say their name they think they can join in.

"What's that girl name in your class who wear her hair curled like on *The Brady Bunch?*"

"Patricia Green," said Darlita.

"Her pencils got her name on them," Donathan added.

Rodney had the same kind of pencils when we were in the baby grades. I wish I could find one maybe under the radiator and take it home to remind me.

"See," Delvis said. "That's him."

"But he not roguish." Delvis needed to mind his own business. Calling up the dead is bad luck, but lying on them is just plain evil. And anyway, how he got all this time to be watching Rodney? He needed to be watching the twins. He let Darlita out the house with her plaits sticking out from the side of her head like a TV antenna.

"I seen him with my own eyes." Delvis looked at me like I had gone crazy in ten minutes flat. "Why you getting so mad? Y'all go together or something?"

"I'm mad because the boy got snatched and you all up in his business like the police." I licked my lips. Why he had to say something about going together? He bad as Mama.

All I got to do is say a boy name and she asking fifty million questions.

Darlita squeezed my hands, smashing two of my fingers together. "Patricia's brother got killed?"

"At school?" Donathan put his fingers in his mouth. He been looking for something to cry about all morning. "He gone to heaven with Jashante?"

Delvis gave me a ugly see-what-you-did look.

"I don't want to go to heaven," said Darlita, probably because somebody told them Jashante was there. All the little kids hated him because he liked to give them Indian burns and take their milk money.

"Well hurry up then." Delvis pulled hard on Donathan's arm. "We gonna miss breakfast." He turned around and said, "Come on Sweet Pea. I got a extra dime if you want to get chocolate milk."

Just as we got ready to cross Beckwith Street, we saw a white man standing on the corner wearing a red hat, kinda like a beanie, but baggy. Me and Delvis saw him at the same time.

"Where Miss Wilcox?" Delvis asked, looking for the regular crossing guard.

"It's too early. She don't be out here till seven-thirty."

"Well, who is the white man?" He took Darlita's right hand like me holding her left wasn't enough.

"He just one of the Guardian Angels. They from New York."

"How you know?"

I hate it when people act like I don't know what I'm talking about. I also hate standing out in the cold weather.

We were only about half a block from the warm school building. "I saw them on the news."

"How you know they okay?"

"I didn't say they was okay. I just said that I knew who they was." The Angel had his arms crossed in front of him like Superman.

"We need to cross someplace else," Delvis said, looking around.

"Let's just cross," I said. "That man ain't nothing to be scared of. He not even in a car. How he gonna kidnap somebody without a car?"

"But still," Delvis said.

"Oh come on. We look crazy standing out here in the cold." And my ears were starting to hurt from all the wind blowing up in them.

Delvis still didn't move. I was surprised because he is usually the one making other kids do things they know better than to do.

"Delvis, them Angels alright. When I saw them on the news they were with Miss Camille Bell. They work in the evenings with the Bat Patrollers."

"They didn't have no black Angels in New York that they could have sent down here?" He was steady complaining, but I know he felt better knowing that Miss Camille Bell be with the Angels. People say she stay around here somewhere. Over by Friendship Baptist Church. But I ain't never seen her, except on TV.

I called myself being cool, calm, and collected, but my stomach balled up and my legs got ready to run when we got to the side of the street where the Angel was. He didn't look dangerous. But if child murderers looked like child murderers, they wouldn't be able to drum up business.

"You kids alright?" he said.

"Yes sir," I said.

"Yeah," Delvis said. "But let me ask you something."

The Angel smiled and relaxed his Superman arms. He bent his knees a little bit. "Shoot."

"Y'all got any black Angels?"

I couldn't believe Delvis. Ten minutes ago, he was scared to cross the street, but now he got right in the man's face, asking him if he was prejudiced.

The Angel kept smiling. "That's a good question. Young people need to ask smart questions. The answer is *yes*. The Guardian Angels is a multiethnic organization."

"So y'all got black ones?"

Delvis was going to get himself in trouble mouthing off like this to this Angel. "We better hurry up," I said. "The twins are hungry." I jerked Darlita's arm a little bit trying to get her to whimper or something. But since we got to this side of the street the twins acted like they ain't got a tongue between them.

The Angel held his hand up. "Just a moment." He looked at Delvis in the face like man-to-man. "Yes, young man, there are a lot of black Guardian Angels."

"Well," Delvis said, "that's who I want to save me."

When we got to the cafeteria and got our trays, we split up. Delvis went to the back where the sixth- and seventh-grade boys would sit when they got here; the twins ate together at an oval table. Next year, they will sit apart, boys at one table and girls at another one. I sat by myself at a table by the window; I didn't care that the wind blew right in like it didn't see the big piece of glass trying to keep the air out. I pulled my coat around myself and looked out the window.

In front of me was a bowl of grits thick like white mud. I gave the cafeteria lady my bowl and asked her to fill it up with Froot Loops. She didn't smile or call me baby. Instead she looked at the wall above my head and gave me these nasty grits. I was surprised because the cafeteria ladies are most of the time nicer than teachers or kids.

"Scuze me," I said. "I asked for Froot Loops."

"Don't have none today," she said.

I saw a big ol box of them behind her, but I didn't want to get in a fight with a cafeteria lady. If you get on they bad side, you'll never get nothing decent on your tray. I looked at her again, but her mind was moved on to someplace else.

I couldn't decide to eat the grits or throw them away. I knew I would be starving like Marvin by noon. I scooped a chunk of grape jelly out of a little container. I stirred it into my grits and got ready to just choke it down. Nobody ever died from eating stiff grits, but hunger hurts and a growling stomach is embarrassing.

I managed to get three or four lumpy spoonfuls down, when I saw a pretty maroon Cadillac float into the parking lot. This is why I liked to sit by the window. I got up all my things, threw that ten-ton bowl of grits in the trash, and ran outside real fast before one of the hall monitors could ask where I was going.

"Mrs. Grier!" I hollered. "You want me to help you tote something?"

She smiled at me. "Good morning, Octavia."

"Morning," I said back to her. I love Mrs. Grier. For real.

I told Mama this when I was in the second grade and Mrs. Grier was my teacher. Mama said, "Does Mrs. Grier put food on this table?" Like somebody got to feed you for you to love them.

Mrs. Grier opened her trunk and gave me a spelling book. "You can carry this," she said, leaning on the word *carry* to let me know it was better than saying *tote*.

"I'll *carry* it for you," I said stretching the word out.

Mrs. Grier is one classy lady. She is tall and big, not fat, but big like she deserves the biggest room or the best plate of food. She brushes her hair to the back of her head and then she twists it into this pretty crisscross. But at the Spring Fashion Tea last year, she had it all fluffed out and I saw why they say old people's hair is silver. Hers caught the light and gleamed like a quarter do to just make you have to bend down and pick it up. But more than just being classy, Mrs. Grier is *right*. I won't say that she is nice because she isn't really. She don't play. If you don't have your spelling words, you going to be in the corner, no doubt about that. And if you do something real bad like talk back or fighting, she will take a ruler to your palm without even thinking about it. But I say she is *right* because she can know the truth from a lie just as soon as she hear it.

Like one time, a library book had got abused. Mrs. Grier held the book up where everybody could see that damage and asked who did it. (She always gave the misbehaver a chance to tell on hisself before she went to investigate.) Nobody said anything. I was staring at the book with my mouth hanging all the way open to my knees. One of the first things we learned way back in Pre-K is to respect library property.

Monica Fisher said, "I saw Octavia Fuller writing in that book."

I turned around and looked at that h-e-f-f-e-r. The ends of her ponytails were tied with smooth yellow ribbons. I couldn't believe that somebody could sit there and lie for no reason at all, and in front of the person they were lying on. Even in the second grade I knew about kids talking about people behind they back, but I didn't think somebody would do it right in front of my face. Mrs. Grier mashed her lips together and I knew that she was really mad. I opened my mouth right then to say my mama didn't allow people to beat me. But quick as a flash, Mrs. Grier said, "This is not Octavia's handwriting."

Now, see, that's what I'm talking about.

It was amazing for me to think that somebody could pay enough attention to me to know that I wrote my words in a certain way. And that thought made me feel good, but then my heart went in my stomach when I started picturing my letters. Sometime I crossed the Ts and sometime I didn't. I used to write real fast and sloppy. My Os looked like Us because I didn't take the time to close them off. But after then, I made sure that my penmanship was perfect, so somebody could know me for that.

After that, me and Mrs. Grier been friends. And that was good because after that day, I didn't have no more regular friends in school anyway. Before, people had picked on me. They said, *Octavia so black and ugly.* Or they said my hair is short and nappy. But not every day. The next day, they would be on to the next person. Maybe talking about Tayari Jones because her mama, president of the PTA, always came to the school wearing weird square shoes with laces up the

front. Sometimes, they laugh at Cassius and call him rac-
coon because he got circles around his eyes. But after that
day, Monica Fisher made it her business to mess with me
every day the Lord gave. And the Lord done gave a lot of
days since second grade.

We went in the classroom and Mrs. Grier shut the door
behind us. The desks were lined up in the same eight little
rows like when I was in the second grade. I wanted to sit in
my old desk for just a minute, but I couldn't remember
which one it was. I walked up in the rows, trying to think
like a second-grader, and hoped that my legs would stop in
the right place. I bent to sit; the chair was so low that I
thought that the school board had sent over littler chairs to
save money. But these desks were too beat-up to be new. I
squashed my big old self in anyway. The top of the desk was
all written on. TJ+AM and stuff like that. I ran my hand
under the desk top and felt wads of gum, dried hard. I
couldn't believe it. Little kids writing on school property?
Drawing little hearts talking about they going together?
When I was in the second grade, boys and girls didn't sit together in the cafeteria, let alone try to be a couple. And then
they have the nerve to chew gum in class and not even dis-
pose of it properly?

"Mrs. Grier," I called.

She looked up from her desk where she was situating
her teacher stuff. "Yes?"

I shook my head in a way that was a question.

"Wrong desk, Octavia. Move up one."

That meant that I was sitting in Rodney's chair then. He
always sat behind me because Fuller comes before Green in
the alphabet. I tried to remember him sitting back there

three years ago, but I couldn't see him. Why hadn't I talked to him before this year? Why was I sitting in his chair right now? The feeling was like the time I was halfway through brushing my teeth and I realized that I was using Uncle Kenny's toothbrush. I knocked the little seat over trying to unjam myself. My arms and legs were long and wobbly these days, like the bean plants growing in milk cartons on the windowsill.

Mrs. Grier came over to help me. She smelled nice always like talcum powder, cologne spray, and warm air. "Tell me what's on your mind," she said.

There was so much in my head that I couldn't get it all lined up to come out. I opened my mouth and moved my lips around trying out different words. Before I could pick out one, Mrs. Grier hugged me.

I wanted to hug her back. Her warm arms smelled so good. I looked at the little window in the closed door. What if someone saw me? Every time Mrs. Grier do something for me, kids go around saying it's because I can't get somebody to do it for me at home. One time, Mrs. Grier brushed my hair and the next thing I knew, people said, *Octavia so poor she ain't got a brush at home.* Mrs. Grier gave me some banana bread and they said my mama don't feed me. If they saw me now, what would they say—that my mama don't love me so Mrs. Grier have to hug me every day before class?

But after a second, I had to melt into her hug. I was tired from being up half the night crying for Rodney and sitting up listening for weird sounds. Her chest was a good place for me to take a little rest. I closed my eyes so if somebody could see me through the door-window, at least I didn't have to see them doing it. After a minute, she held me away from her and looked at me. She turned her face to the side. "You're friends with Rodney Green?"

"Kind of," I said. "He was nice to me, mostly he was."

"Always very mannerable," she agreed. I could tell that she was leaving words out so she wouldn't have to say *was* or *is*. *Was* would mean he was dead and *is* means he's coming back and I know Mrs. Grier don't like to lie.

"You think he dead?" I waited for her to say, *Heavens no, Octavia. Why would you even suggest something like that?* But she didn't open her mouth. After I sat there a little more, I got hungry to hear her say anything at all.

"Ma'am?" I said, as if she had called my name.

"I don't know," she said.

That was it? I didn't come all the way down here for her to say something I could have came up with by myself. I tried to pull my hands out of hers but she held on.

"You don't walk home alone, do you?" She was looking at my fingers. My nails were clipped short and the cuticle pushed back, just like she told me.

"No, ma'am," I said. "I walk with Delvis and the twins. On Wednesdays, though, I stay late for chorus."

She nodded. "Are there patrols in your community?"

"Like the Bat Patrol? No. They all stay out in Techwood homes. We got Muslims, but Delvis say they can't save nobody all dressed up in suits and church shoes."

"Delvis is wise beyond his years." Mrs. Grier laughed a little bit. "I never thought of it that way."

"We saw a Guardian Angel this morning, but I wish we could get some Bat Patrollers over here."

"I don't know about that," Mrs. Grier said. "I'm not sure

that I like the idea of angry men roaming the streets with baseball bats. That seems like conflict just waiting to happen."

"But at least they'll be able to do something if they see somebody messing with a kid. What the Angels going to? Tell them to stop?" I heard myself shouting and I lowered my voice. Miss Russell the white art teacher walked down the hall with her brushes. "And anyway, at least the Bat Patrollers is black."

"Calm down, Octavia. I was just thinking aloud."

She wouldn't be calm if she was the one people was trying to kill.

"I bet Rodney Green wish he had a Bat Patroller with him yesterday." I couldn't help saying one last thing.

"That's enough, Octavia," Mrs. Grier said. She looked back at my hands. Now I wished that I hadn't groomed them like she said. She touched her lips together. "Make sure Delvis walks you all the way to your door, hear?"

She looked worried like Mama did that time I had a fever so bad that my lips chapped and the skin pulled back. Mrs. Grier's mouth, pretty with lipstick, shrunk a little bit.

"My mama be there when I get home." I said it to make her not worry, but her eyebrows shot up.

"Your mother is not working?"

Now what to do? Mama told me not to tell any of the school people that she was working the eleven to seven. Sometimes when they find out kids stay alone, they call the State and that's how kids get took away to live with foster families that beat them.

"Oh, she still work at the bread factory. She just get off before I get home." That wasn't a lie but it tasted like one.

The bell rang in the hallway and I was glad. "Have you eaten breakfast?"

"Sort of," I said, thinking about the gummy grits.

"*Sort of* is not a complete sentence, or a balanced meal." She went into her drawer and gave me a package of orange crackers with peanut butter in between. "You can't concentrate with an empty stomach."

Some of the second-graders were coming in the room now. It was time for me to leave. "Have a nice day," I said to her, but she was helping one of the little kids get his scarf untangled before he choked himself to death.

To get to the fifth-grade class, I had to walk all the way down the hall, past the girls' room, then outside through the double door. Over the summer, they put trailers out back to make room for all of us. A lot of people complain about being out there, saying it's too hot in the summer and all of that, but I don't mind it. Being out back means that you get to keep the hall pass longer when you say you have to go to the girls' room. I'm always trying to think of reasons not to have to be in class. Sometimes I'll ask to go to the nurse, or something like that. Last year, I used to go out in the hall with Fanon Robinson and Malcolm Smith when everybody was saying the Pledge. The two of them had letters from their parents saying they didn't believe in the flag. I said I didn't believe in it either so I could be out of the classroom. But this year, Malcolm and Fanon both got tired of being so different. They stand up with everybody else and put their hand over their heart. I'm not bold enough to not-believe by myself.

I stood outside the trailer door a second before I pushed it open and went inside. Two things I noticed right off the bat. One, was that a lot of people was absent that day. Every single row almost had one empty chair in it. And second was the noise. Whispering really. But when a clump of people get to whispering at the same time, it make a rumbling sound like on TV when Perry Mason call somebody a liar. At first I didn't notice what had happened to my row. It had one empty seat, like most of the other rows. But when I sat down, I sat in the empty seat. So then my row was full. But how could that be? Rodney was absent, for sure. Stanley Halliday was right behind me in his seat.

I turned and looked Stanley right in his fat face. He was almost all cheeks.

"You sitting in his seat?" It wasn't a question. It was like when Mama stood in the doorway of my room and said, "You didn't make up your bed?"

Stanley looked shocked. Probably because I ain't said two words to him since we been in school together. "No," he said. "You the one."

"Uh-uh. I sit one seat from the front."

"Well I sit one from the back. *He* sat three from the back and that's just where you at."

"But—" I was about to tell that fool that the same was true if you counted the other way. Rodney sat three from the front and that's where Stanley had his big behind. I can't stand him. But I let it go because the problem was that Mr. Harrell had took Rodney's chair right out of this row. Like he was never there. That wasn't right. When my granddaddy died, Granny didn't go and move his chair from the head of the table. When we went there for Thanksgiving, his place was just empty. So when we got to remembering how much he used to love sweet potato pie, we could look at his place, shake our heads and say, "Sho do miss him."

Moving Rodney's chair was just plain disrespectful.

Mr. Harrell tapped his ruler on the desk to get people to cut out all the whispering. He cleared his throat like he was about to say something big. But he just sat down at his desk and pulled out his roll book.

"Angelite Armstrong."

"Here," Angelite said.

"LaTasha Baxter."

"Absent," somebody said from the back.

I got this nasty feeling in the bottom of my stomach. What was he going to do when he got to Rodney? Was somebody going to say, "Dead"? Or should I say, "Absent"? Somebody should stand up and say, "Missing, like his chair!" Maybe I would do that. Everybody would just about have a heart attack because I'm just about as quiet as Rodney was. I hardly open my mouth unless somebody is messing with me. Like Mama say, I stay to myself.

Denise Daniels said, "Here."

I had to hurry up and make up my mind. When Mr. Harrell called Rodney's name, I had to say something good to let him know I didn't appreciate what happened with the chairs. Maybe I could say, "He not here, but who ever took his chair better have it right back by recess." But if I said that, I would get sent to the principal's office. Then I got a better idea. I wouldn't say anything at all and it could be like a moment of silence for him.

Monica Fisher said, "Here."

And then Mr. Harrell called my name. "Octavia Fuller."

I said, "Here," and then bowed my head to get ready for the memorial.

There was a quiet second while he wrote a little check in his book, but then he went on to Stanley Halliday. I snapped my chin up and looked at Mr. Harrell like he had lost his mind. He was supposed to call Rodney's name and we could do our moment. But he just went on like our class was a creek and Rodney was just a cup of water that somebody dipped out.

I twised around completely in my chair and looked right in Stanley Halliday's fat face. "You better not say nothing," I said under my breath, quiet but mean.

His eyes got kind of big and he looked over at Mr. Harrell like he wanted the teacher to tell him what to do.

Mr. Harrell just called Stanley's name again, with a little edge on it like all this was trying his patience.

Stanley looked at me and I said, "I ain't playing with you." And I wasn't. So many times, I seen him cheat off of Rodney's spelling test and neither me or Rodney said anything. Now it was Stanley's turn to keep his mouth shut. I could almost hear his brain sloshing around in his big ol water head, trying to decide if he should be scared of me. Finally, his voice came out loud and on purpose like he was saying something in a play. "Present."

I hate Stanley Halliday and every single person in that class.

I never said *here* for Mr. Harrell again. After a couple of days, he stopped calling my name and the fifth-grade creek just kept on going.

———

Recess is the part of the day that I hate. I know that sounds crazy since I am always trying to think of ways to get out of class. But it's not the class *room* I be trying to get away from. It's the people in it. So recess is the same as being in class except we don't got no lesson and Mr. Harrell not telling everybody to shut up when they start talking. That's what makes it such a bad time. I generally hang by myself hoping nobody won't say nothing to me.

Mrs. Grier say that's my problem. I need to go out and make friends with people. "Octavia," she told me one time, "just go up to a nice young lady and tell her that you would like her to be your playmate." I like Mrs. Grier a lot, don't get me wrong. But sometimes I think that she been reading too many primary readers. I can just see myself going up to Trina Littlejohn and asking her to "be my playmate." The only time I ever heard anybody use that word was in that clapping rhyme, "Say say my playmate. Come out and play with me." That was always my favorite. I like the sound of the word. *Playmate* sounds more special than *friend*. Socks have mates when they are just alike.

But in real life, there ain't no playmates. Lots of kids go around together but they not mates, really. They get mad over stupid stuff and don't talk to each other for a couple of days. People think it's just girls that be like that, but boys are messy too. But it's the girls that be on my mind because I don't like to fool with boys no way.

If a girl wants you to be her friend, she will ask you to sit with her and her other friends at lunch. It's the one with the friends that get to do the asking. I generally sit alone and once or twice I have asked some girl to my table. She will say yes only if her other friends are mad about something.

But when they get back together, she will never ask me to sit at the big table with all of them. That's just the way it is, Mama says. I don't need to worry about it. I asked Mama if she ever got invited to a pajama party. She says when she was coming up, black folks didn't do stuff like that. Well they do now and I would like to get a invitation just one time.

I was sitting by myself reading my Judy Blume book. I had read it before but I had to read it again because I didn't have nothing else. I used to have a library card and could get a new book every week, but I accidentally dropped a hardback book in the bathtub. I went to the librarian and told her I was sorry. She wasn't mad at me, but she said that I would have to pay for the book before I could borrow another one. Mama came to pay, but when they told her that it costs seventeen dollars, she told them they must be crazy. So now I have to read what I have.

I heard somebody say, "On your marks, get set, go," and a few boys started running but nobody was much paying attention to them. People had things on their mind: Rodney.

Well, not really thinking about him like Mama think about Granddaddy and tell me how he used to sing "Hush Little Baby" to her when she was a girl. Or how he brushed his teeth with baking soda. They didn't know Rodney well enough to look back on him like that. But they knew he was gone and they wondered where he was at and would whoever got him come back to this school to get somebody else. Oglethorpe is the only school where two people got snatched from. Three if you count Yusef Bell, who came once a week for gifted classes.

But I didn't talk to nobody. I just minded my own business and tried not to be too cold. Warm is a state of mind,

Delvis say. I don't know if I agree with him all the way, but I do know that thinking about a thing makes it feel stronger. So my mind had its hands full thinking about staying warm and the book in my hand. When somebody said to me, "Hey, Octavia," I thought it was my imagination.

I looked up and saw LaTasha Baxter standing in front of me. She had on a fancy pink coat with fur around the hood and even this little fur pouch thing to keep her hands warm. I seen the whole getup in the Sears catalog. That's how I know that little fur thing had to be bought separate. Her parents must got some serious money.

"Hey," I said, putting my hand without the mitten behind me. Tasha rubbed her lips together a couple of times. What did she want? Tasha's one of those girls that don't talk to you unless her other friends is mad with her. But she was nicer than some of them. She never called me "Watusi" or pinched her nose when I walked by.

"Sad what happened to Rodney," she said.

"Yeah," I said, wondering why she was coming to me with this. She looked over her shoulder every few seconds, over to where her friends jumped rope. They would be talking about her like a dog by the time she get back there.

"You think they going to find him?" She said it in a soft whisper. The wind pressed her fur trim against her face.

"No." I felt like I was a grown-up talking to a little kid. Hadn't she noticed that none of the kids who were *missing* never got un-missing? All *missing* meant was they didn't find the body yet. All the search parties that went out on Saturdays and Sundays were looking for dead bodies, not live children.

"Jashante neither?" she said.

Then I knew why she came over here in the first place. Her and Jashante had this kind of thing going on right before he got snatched. He sat with her at lunch a couple of times, I thought. I couldn't quite remember because I don't like to be up in people's business. But evidently she was up in mine because she knew that me and Rodney had been friends too. And to tell the truth, I didn't mind it so much. It was like me and her were mates, having the same problem and everything.

"No," I told her. "Me and my mama gave Jashante's family a pound cake and everything." I almost said "like he was dead," but I bit my tongue.

Tasha maybe got the message. She nodded.

"Your mama going to carry something over to Rodney people?" I asked her. I figured that all the money-people live nearby to each other.

She shook her head. "Our parents don't know each other."

"Oh," I said.

She kept looking back at her friends. One of them said her name.

"You better get back over there," I said, like I was tired of talking to her. I wanted to send her away before she could say "I gotta go," and run off with her siditty girlfriends.

"Well, if you hear something about Jashante. Either one of them. Would you tell me?"

"Anything happen like that, be on the news," I said. "You don't need me to tell you nothing."

She looked like her feelings was hurt a little bit. But I didn't have time to be worried about her feelings. At lunchtime she wasn't going to be worried none about mine.

Mrs. Grier would say, "Now, Octavia, don't assume the worst." But at lunchtime, that girl didn't even look at me when I was trying to find a seat. I stood in the middle of the cafeteria for a second, craning my neck all around so somebody could invite me to sit down if they wanted. Nobody said anything, and I sat at the little oval table where I always sit, always by myself.

———

I think that it might be nice to go to Chicago. I never been there. I never been anywhere really. Just to Macon to see my Grandmama and one time we went down to Savannah to see the old houses and the beach. I can't remember the Savannah trip, but we got pictures to prove it really happened. Me and Mama sitting on the sand with our legs crossed in front of us and our arms behind us like a couple of movie stars. I wish that I could remember it, because it might be the most fun I ever had. Even now, when I'm doing something and kind of enjoying myself, I say, *Is this better than Savannah?* And I can't know. I just have to trust what the picture say.

But Chicago is even better than Savannah. We got family up there. My mama's cousin Elaine moved up there right after I was born. She got a daughter named Nikky who is about three years older than me. I can't remember Nikky, but Mama got a picture of me laying on the couch and Nikky looking at me like she never seen a baby before. Even back then, Nikky was a sharp dresser. Since I was just born, I only got on a Pamper. Nikky got on a green-and-yellow dress with bows all over the place. And right on the top of her head was a yellow ribbon edged in white. Cousin Elaine got good taste.

Once a year, or thereabouts, Nikky sends me all her clothes that she got too big for. Pretty things. Velvet dresses with lace collars. Or cotton ones with flowers. Some long to the ground and others just before the knee. But all of them have big ribbons around the waist that tie in the back. That must be the style in Chicago. The Windy City. I can see all those girls walking through the streets with their satin sashes flapping behind them. That's where I want to go next time I get to go someplace. Forget the beach; I don't need to be sitting out in the sun getting no blacker anyway.

The mailman knocked on the door this afternoon, right after *The Flintstones*. I turned the TV down and looked through the peephole. Mama wasn't home and I didn't have no business answering the door.

"Who is it?" I asked, trying to waste a few seconds so maybe Mama would come up just in the nick of time.

"Mailman," he said.

Everybody been saying the child killer probably going around dressed up like the police or a fireman or somebody. I shouldn't believe that nobody is what they say they is. But I could see the box through the peephole. I opened the door but left the chain on. I saw my name.

"Could you leave the package? My mama not home."

"No, I need a signature."

"What happen if you don't get one?" Where was Mama? This man wasn't going to stay out here all day jawing with me. I could see already that he was ready to leave.

"I'll have to take it back to the post office and your mother can pick it up from there."

"Later on today?"

"No, tomorrow."

That was too long. The best thing about Nikky Day is I never knew when it was coming. I didn't end up awake all night with grasshoppers in my stomach like on Christmas Eve. Nikky Day was a surprise holiday.

"Could I sign for it?"

"How old are you?"

"Fourteen." I was glad the chain was on the door and he couldn't get a good look at me. I wasn't even a real grown-looking eleven.

"Fine," he said.

"Slide it through the door."

He blew air out like *I don't get paid enough for this.*

I wrote my name on the line in my best cursive. It was the first time anybody ever asked me to sign something. I looked it over carefully to make sure that all the letters were right and slanted to the side. The mailman knocked again.

I put the paper through the crack. He glanced at it and stuffed it in his bag.

After I was sure he was gone, I opened the door and slid the box inside. It was wrapped up with brown paper sacks cut open and turned outside in so I couldn't see the name of the grocery store. Should I open it when Mama wasn't there? How was I going to explain to her how I got it in the house? She said "Don't open the door for nobody." I was going to have to slide it back in the hall. It was just that simple. But first, I wanted to at least *look* at it. My name was across the front. Miss Octavia Yvette Fuller. I wondered did Nikky write it or her mother. Nikky was fourteen herself and old enough to have a nice script. Whoever wrote my name didn't take pride in they letters. The O on my first name wasn't closed all the way and looked something like a U. The t was crossed but the i had no dot. It must have been Cousin Elaine that wrote this. Pretty Nikky in her dress with a sash would take time for proper penmanship.

Finally I scooted the box back in the hallway and locked the door again. I couldn't see it through the peephole. What if somebody came by and stole it? This not the projects, but still people can be roguish over here. I kept my eye pressed to the peephole anyway; even if I couldn't see the box itself, I could see somebody if they came to mess with it.

The box was every bit worth the wait. Last year must have been a good year for Nikky. She had two long dresses. One pure white and the other one blue velvet.

"Where she be going in these dresses?" I asked Mama.

"I don't know," she said, pinching the fabric in at the waist to see how much it would have to be took in to fit me. "I think Elaine have her in pageants and stuff."

"Like Miss America?"

"I don't know. Never been."

"You ever been to Chicago?" I asked.

"I had a chance to go one time." Mama tucked the bottom of the skirt under and put straight pins to hold it there.

"For real?" She never told me this.

"I was about to finish high school. My aunt and uncle promised me a bus ticket up there. I was supposed to get a job working with the phone company." She smiled a little bit. "It was going to be my graduation present. Back then, everybody wanted to work for Ma Bell or for the post office. Benefits and stuff."

"And everybody wants to go to Chicago. Especially me," I said.

Mama stopped fooling with my dress. I wanted to go look in the mirror and see myself, but there were straight pins all around and I didn't have my shoes on.

"Sweet Pea, hold still," Mama said, with pins between her teeth. "My mama was so excited. She took four weeks getting my stuff together for my trip. New clothes, new hairbrushes, even luggage from Sears and Roebuck."

"So why you didn't go?"

"I'm getting there," Mama said. "One morning, Mama came in my room to tell me that we were going to walk into town to get me a hat. She wanted to get a early start. It was just April but it was plenty hot already. And I think she wanted to get it over with. Mama hated shopping."

"How come? I thought everybody like to go to the mall." At least, I know that I like to go when I know for sure I'm going to get something. When I go and just have to look at things I can't have, I get grouchy and be ready to go on home.

"Well," Mama said, taking out some of the pins in the waist and putting them back in looser.

"You making it too big."

"You don't need your clothes all tight up on you," she said. "But anyway, Mama didn't like going into town because white folks were so mean back then. We couldn't try on the dresses or hats. You just had to pick one out and pray that it fit when you got home. And you know if we couldn't try nothing, they wouldn't let us *return* it. Well, I take that back. You could try on a hat, but first you had to put this stocking thing on your head.

"But even knowing what was ahead of us in town, she was in a good mood. But I was feeling sick that morning. I was talking to her as normal as I could, then I ran to the rest room and threw up. When I came back into the bedroom, she had took off her hat and shoes.

" 'You ain't going to Chicago,' she said to me, just like that."

"Because you was sick? You was too sick to go?" Poor Mama.

"Yeah, I was sick alright." She shook her head from side to side.

"So how come you didn't go when you got better?"

"I had you," she said, like they don't let people have babies in Chicago.

"I coulda went," I said.

"Well, Auntie and Uncle never asked me again." She patted my behind. "Go look in the mirror and see how you like it," she said, picking up the pins off the floor.

When I got back from the bathroom, she had hung up the other dresses, pins and all. Mama never went to the trouble of sewing them in place until I had someplace to go to wear the dresses. Now that the box was empty, she started loading in the dresses from Nikky Day two years back. She folded them, and wrapped each dress in tissue paper. We were going to send them to my cousin Kay-Kay, in Macon.

Mama was in my closet taking the pins out of the dresses from last year. I could fit them now without her taking them in. All of a sudden I started laughing. It was like when somebody tell you a joke and you don't get it till half a day later. Kay-Kay probably think that I get to wear these dresses all the time. What if she call it "Sweet Pea Day"?

Chicago is the windy city, but what is Atlanta? I asked Miss Grier one time and she say, "Atlanta is the city too busy to hate." Mama say it's the "Chocolate City." Kay-Kay probably think everybody up here smile all the time and eat Hershey Kisses wearing velvet dresses.

———

The phone rang just after Mama left for work. I hate it when that happens. I never know what to do. If the person on the phone is somebody that want to rob us, or something, it's good for me to pick up so they will know that somebody is here. That way, they will go and rob somebody else. But if the person on the phone is a murderer, then it would be better for him to think that nobody is home for him to kill. I went ahead and answered it because only one of the kids that got killed got killed at home. There was one little girl who got carried out her window. My room is too high up for all of that.

"Hello," I said.

"Sweet Pea."

"Uncle Kenny?" I said loud at first. Then I lowered my voice even though I was home by myself. "Kenny?"

"Yeah, it's me," he said. "My sister there?"

I didn't know what to do, again. Mama say that I'm not supposed to tell nobody that I'm home by myself. Except family. And except Ray. But when she threw Uncle Kenny out, she wasn't acting like he was family.

"Yvonne there?" he said again.

He didn't sound mad at me. And I was grateful about

that since I'm the one that got him put out in the first place.
But I didn't want to get on Mama's bad side either.

"She at work, but she'll be right back." That was a half
lie.

"I thought she was working eleven to seven," he said.

If he knew that, why was he calling right now? "I don't
know," I said.

"How you doing Sweet Pea?" he said.

"I'm alright."

"You being safe with all that going on down there?"

"Yeah," I said. His voice wasn't as nice as it was a few
minutes ago. I should have told him Mama was here.

"I miss Atlanta," he said. "Miss seeing you. My friends.
Ain't nothing going on here in Macon. Nothing at all. No
jobs, no clubs, no nothing."

I didn't speak. It was my fault that he wasn't still here.
But it was a accident. And in a way it was more Mama's
fault than mine. She the one told me the lie in the first place.
She the one gathered up all his stuff in black garbage bags
and put them by the door. I was just trying to help.

"You there?" he said.

"Yeah."

He didn't say nothing. I heard a soda can open.

"Where you at, Kenny?" I asked.

"At Mama house. Where you think?"

"We better get off the phone then. You know Granny
get mad when people run her bill up."

"So you don't want to talk to me either?" he said. His
voice was getting a little meaner.

"Granny there?"

"I'm not going to hurt you over the phone, Octavia."

He said my given name slow. Like he thought it was a stupid name.

"I'm sorry," I told him. "I didn't mean to get you in trouble that time."

"Sorry ain't nothing but a word," he said.

"But I'm still sorry."

"I gotta go. You know I can't be running up Mama phone bill. Bye."

"Bye," I said. He didn't believe me, but what I said was the truth. He should know already that I didn't mean to give away his secret. When Mama put him out, I was the one that suffered the most. When he was around, everything was fun like a day at Six Flags. He had came to stay with us three years ago, right when he got through graduating from high school. Mama and me went to Macon to see him in his blue cap and gown and he came right back home with us on the Greyhound.

We didn't have an extra room for him to have, so he slept in the living room on the divan. When I was in my bed, I could hear him breathing in like a horn and blowing out with a whistle. When he was awake, Uncle Kenny was more fun than television. He used to say, "Who knows what the nose knows?" And then in a squeaky voice he'd say, "Speak Beak," holding his hand out to me like it was a microphone. Sometimes, when I was at school and people mess with me, I could say in my head, "Speak Beak" and almost start laughing.

But now when I think about him, I feel like crying. I hate the way things can just be not fair and there ain't nothing you can really do about it. It wasn't my fault that my mama like to tell lies. She told me that dope needles was the same as doctor needles. But I guess it was my fault for believing her.

The thing that's so wrong about it is that I called myself helping him. See, Mama had told me never to touch a needle laying on the ground because a doctor would come back looking for it. A lie ain't nothing for her to tell.

"How come we don't just pick it up and carry it to the doctor?" I asked.

She made a face like she was thinking it over, but then she shook her head. "Doctors don't like people messing with they stuff."

"What he'll do if he catch somebody?" Doctors were scary enough even when they smiled and gave out lollipops.

"He won't help you when you sick and just let you die."

So I was just trying to be helpful when I said, "Mama, the doctor is going to get Uncle Kenny because he got them needles off in his bag."

"Where?" Mama said quick, looking up from the cornbread she was stirring in a plastic bowl. "Show me." Worry beaded up on her face like she was scared what would happen when the doctor came back looking for his needles.

I showed her Kenny's black bag with the zip. I thought that she was going to ask me what I was looking in there for in the first place, but she didn't.

"Get back," she said, like it was going to explode. She looked in the bag and saw the needles. She took out a spoon, burned and bent up, and held it up to the light. Then, she cussed. I don't mean those little cusses like "hell" and "damn" that are in the Bible. But a true cuss word.

"That motherfucker." She said it slow and quiet like she was amazed.

"It wasn't one of the good spoons." She acted like she didn't hear me.

"Sweet Pea," she said. "You missing anything?"

I shook my head.

She went in her room and yanked at her top dresser drawer. It was stuck. Mama pulled at it softer, whispering sweet talk as she eased the wood back and forth. Finally, it opened far enough for her to slide her hand up under her stack of nightgowns and get out a fuzzy little box. Inside was her ring with all the little diamonds in the shape of a heart. She say she's going to give that to me when I finish college. She pressed it to her chest.

"Where's your bank?" she asked, reaching for cigarettes.

We went into my room and got the smiley-face bank down from the shelf. It was empty.

"Did you have some money in here?" She tried the lighter twice before she got a tired little flame.

I shook my head no so I wouldn't have to tell a lie with my mouth. There had been almost three dollars in that bank that I was saving for the book fair at school. I earned it doing little things for old people for maybe a quarter. Sometimes just a dime. I couldn't tell this to Mama because she didn't like for me to go into people's homes or to take money.

"What about the five dollars Granny sent you for your school supplies?"

That money had been a long time gone, but I nodded my head. "I had three dollars left."

Mama sat on my bed and put her hand to her forehead like she was trying to keep her face from falling off. She put her cigarette to her lips and let it go with a sound like a small kiss. The Hamiltons next door had their TV up too loud and I heard fake laughing. I leaned my face on Mama's cool arm.

"I'll give you the three dollars back on Friday."

"But what about Uncle Kenny? Is the doctor going to let him die?"

Mama breathed out hard. "That fool boy going to let himself die."

Kenny stayed gone till after the late news. Mama turned off the TV, but she didn't go to bed. In the mirror over my dresser, I watched the picture shrink to a white dot. Mama sat in the dark for a few minutes flicking her lighter on and off. I couldn't see the little blue sparks but I heard the scratchy sound. Then I heard Uncle Kenny's key in the door.

"Yvonne," he said. "What you doing up?"

"Where you been?"

"What?"

"Where you been, Kenny?"

"Why you talking to me like that?" he said. "I left my mother in Macon."

"I believe you left your common sense there too."

"What's wrong with you?" He switched on the TV. The room went purple, then blue.

"Kenny." Mama had to talk loud over Johnny Carson. "You said you wanted to come to Atlanta to try and get yourself a better job than you could get at home."

"I'm looking! You see me with the paper every day." Kenny's voice rose high like a girl.

"You come into my house. Take advantage of my child."

"What? I didn't touch Sweet Pea."

My stomach clenched up. The beans and rice that I had

for dinner pushed up like I was going to vomit, but it just stayed in my chest and burned.

"You stole from her. What kind of grown-ass man would take three fucking dollars out of a child piggy bank?"

"I didn't even know she had a bank."

"Don't lie to me," Mama snapped. "You the one said you left your mama in Macon. You in *my* house now. *I* don't think you're handsome. *I'm* not the one who thinks you can do no wrong. Now I'm wondering what you can do right."

"Yvonne, what's wrong with you?"

The TV colored the dark room like nighttime lightning.

"Kenny, what's wrong with *you?*"

"I'm getting tired of these mind games." He wanted to sound tough but his voice was wobbly. "You need to tell me what's on your mind or get out of my face."

"Oh!" Mama said with a little laugh that sounded like a bark. "*I'm* the one playing games. *You* the one acting like you want to make something out yourself while being a undercover junkie."

"You went in my bag?" Uncle Kenny shouted. "I don't believe you."

"*You* don't believe *me?*"

Every time he said something, she threw it back on him. I felt bad for him. He sounded like he was going to cry.

"You brought dope needles into my house where Sweet Pea could get them."

"Sweet Pea saw?"

"She was a mess." Her voice went high like she was mocking me. "So in love with her Uncle Kenny." Now her voice went nasty. "But now she know you ain't nothing."

"What you tell her?"

"She was crying like the world was over."

"What else she say?"

I curled myself into a little knot because I didn't want to hear Mama lying on me and I couldn't take it if Uncle Kenny told her the truth.

The next morning Mama didn't go to work. She was at the table having Kools and coffee for breakfast. She told me that Kenny went back to Macon because he missed Granny.

Mama said that he is a junkie. She said that to Granny and they didn't talk again for two weeks. It's a stupid word. Junkie. Sounds like he didn't put his things back in their proper place. Delvis say he hate junkies too. When we see a needle on the sidewalk, he kick it in the street, then wipe his shoe off like he just got through stepping in some dog doo-doo. I don't kick the needles when I see them because the junkie might come back looking for it and junkies don't like people messing with they stuff.

———

Then I got my period. It wasn't a big deal. I had a box of supplies at home and a little pink book explaining what was what, so I was ready. But I wasn't ready *today*. Talk about the wrong thing happening at the wrong time. Not only was I wearing a nice dress, but my supplies was at home. I made do with some toilet tissue folded up until I could go see Mrs. Grier after school.

After the bell, I baby-stepped all the way to the second-grade class; all the kids was gone except for one little boy. Mrs. Grier was giving him a small plastic bag with his tooth in it. "Now, Turner," she told him, "when you get home, rinse your mouth with salty water."

"Okay," he said.

She looked hard at him from the corner of her eyes and he corrected himself. "Yes, ma'am."

"That's better." She smiled. "Put the tooth under your pillow. If the tooth fairy doesn't leave you anything, tell me in the morning. Sometimes the treats are delivered to my door instead."

Turner nodded his head and left.

Crazy as it sounds, I was kind of mad at Mrs. Grier. She had told me the same thing when I was in her class. The only difference was that she gave me some Girl Scout cookies because my tooth didn't just *fall* out. It got *knocked* out when Lucius Petty put his leg out to trip me. But still, I didn't like to think of her being so nice to everybody like it was her job or something.

She looked up and saw me in the doorway. "Hello, Octavia," she said, still smiling the smile she had left over from Turner.

I didn't say anything.

"Remember when you lost your tooth?" she said like to let me know she didn't care that I heard what she said to little snot-nosed Turner.

"But mine didn't fall out. It got knocked out." Why was I acting like such a baby? Sometimes I know I'm being stupid but I can't help myself.

"If I recall, that tooth was already a little loose." She was still smiling like she couldn't tell I was seriously upset.

I started to walk away, but my homemade Kotex moved a little bit to the left. I decided to get what I came for.

"Mrs. Grier, I need something."

"What's wrong?" Her eyebrows went up and her face was interested and worried at the same time. She forgot about that Turnip Green and his tooth.

I came up close to her desk and whispered. "I got my period today."

"Already? Are you sure?"

"Yes'm," I said. "It's just like the book you gave me."

"Do you have supplies?"

"No'm. I just used toilet tissue."

"That was very resourceful," she said, patting me on my head.

Mrs. Grier went into her cabinet and put some things into a paper bag. Then she took me by the hand and took me into the teacher's lounge. It smelled like cigarettes and coffee.

Mrs. Grier opened her sack and took out a cardboard box about the size of my palm but thick as my math book. Inside was a Kotex folded in half.

"Do you know how to put it on?"

"Yes ma'am. From the book."

She pointed to a small door that looked like a closet. "Go take care of yourself. I'll be out here if you need me."

When I came out of the little rest room, she said, "Any questions?"

"Am I ever going to get some titties?"

"Bosom," she corrected.

"Am I ever going to get some bosoms?"

She looked at me like I was crazy, so I started over. "The book said you get bosoms first. But now I got my period."

"You've *reached your maturity*," she said. I guessed *period* must not be a nice word either. But I wished she would let me finish what I had to say and stop butting in.

"Well I reached my maturity without no bosoms; does that mean this is all I'm going to get?"

She looked at my chest and my little titties like the little humps on the top of an orange.

"Every woman is different," she said. "I can't say for sure, but you'll probably get at least a little more."

That didn't sound like good news to me.

When I came out of the building, Delvis was leaning against a big white pole in front of the door. The paint had chipped off and sat on the top of his hair like snowflakes.

"Hey!" I said. "You waiting for me?" I was trying not to act no different than normal. But soon as I said it I wanted to take the words back. I should have said, "What you waiting out here for?"

"Yeah," he said. "Where you been?"

"You got paint in your hair. On your clothes too."

"Man," he said, cleaning himself off with little slaps.

"Where the twins?"

"They went on with my cousin after you was taking so long." He waited for me to say where I had been.

I walked straight as possible. "I had to stay after for Mrs. Grier to help me with my word problems."

"Why you always going down to the second-grade room for? You too old for that."

I looked at his whole face to see did he mean I was too old after what happened today or just too old anyway.

"What you got in that sack?" he asked, all nosy.

People said boys had ESP about girls and their periods. Demetria said they could take one look and one sniff and tell who had their cycle. But if he could tell already, then why was he asking me so many stupid questions? I knew he didn't want me to come out and say what was in my bag. All the boys start freaking out if they just hear the word *Kotex*.

"Mrs. Grier gave me some extra workbooks to practice."

"Well she need to give them to you at lunchtime or something," he said, kicking a pebble down the sidewalk. It got stuck in a crack. "Had me sitting out here half the afternoon waiting on you."

"Didn't nobody tell you to wait." This was true, but I was so glad to see him leaning on that pole with snowflakes in his hair.

"My mama made me wait on you. And then you went and took so long that I'm going to miss *Happy Days*." He tried to kick the rock but ended up ramming his toe on a piece of broken sidewalk sticking out. "Man!"

I didn't say nothing. I just kept walking in little baby steps. I was worried about losing my Kotex. I didn't trust that sticky stuff to hold it on. Next time I was going to use safety pins.

Delvis was in a evil mood. "I don't know why she wanted me to wait for you."

I was surprised. "Because of—" I started but didn't finish. I didn't want to say *child murders*. Didn't Delvis care that I made it home alive? "You know kids not supposed to be out walking alone," I said.

"That's just boys that got to worry about getting snatched, stupid," he said.

"But what about them two girls?" I asked him. "Idiot," I added, to make us even.

"They the exception that proves the rule," he said, like he was God up in heaven and know everything.

"Says who?"

"My barber," Delvis said. He did have a fresh haircut, but that didn't mean he was right. And anyway, his part was cut in crooked.

We walked a little more without talking. The wind had picked up and it was too cold to be running our mouths. My socks were pulled all the way up to my knees but the air was turning my legs into chocolate Popsicles. It was getting to Delvis too because he started moving faster. I kept on with my baby steps.

"Why you walking so slow?" Delvis asked. "It's freezing out here, and *Happy Days* on too."

"What your barber said?" I asked him to get his mind off my turtle walking.

"He say that it's the boys they want. Because we going to get to be black men pretty soon and if it's one thing the white man scared of it's a black man."

His face looked mad but his voice sounded proud. Like girls wasn't worth killing. The wind blew some more and a tree dumped brown leaves on us.

"Well if they hate the men, how come they don't just kill them direct?"

"Cause they *scared* of the men."

I thought about the men that I knew. It was weird, but I didn't know too many. There was Granddaddy. He was old and thin even before his stroke. He might have been bad back in the day, though. My own daddy wasn't what you would call scary. Ray's skinny as a teenager. Last I went to Uncle Kenny. He seemed mean to me now. When he called on the phone. But not before. Not before I was messing with his stuff.

I carefully stepped up on a curb, trying not to gap my legs too wide.

"See," Delvis went on, "them boys—Jashante and them—not one of them had a daddy to run the white man off. And you see what happened."

"But what about you-know-who?" Rodney had a daddy that anybody could be scared of. Even Rodney himself.

"Exception that proves the rule."

"But you said that about the girls."

"Different exception, different rule."

We were passing through a neighborhood folks called the Bottom. When I walk by myself I take the long way home to keep from passing through there. There was a liquor store every ten feet seemed like.

"This is the thing with the girls," Delvis said. "They just snatched a couple of them so people wouldn't catch on that it's really the boys that they after."

I walked in the street to get around a man laying on the sidewalk. Delvis stepped right over him.

"Drunks are a disgrace to the race," he said.

We went along quietly for a while. The wind wasn't playing around. I had to worry about my dress blowing up.

Delvis bent down and picked up some magnolia cones in case we see a dog or something.

"Sweet Pea, get you some cones too," he said.

There wasn't no way I was bending down.

"We almost home," I said. "And anyway, I don't want to be late."

"You wasn't worried about being late all the rest of this time. I saw you over there trying to see how slow you could walk without stopping." Delvis shook his head like I was just too stupid for him to believe.

I tried to speed up a little.

"Girls, y'all got it made in the shade," Delvis said, tossing a cone at a small white dog that wasn't even barking. I was glad he missed.

Finally, we were in front of my building. "Run on in the house. Mama say I got to wait for you to get inside before I can leave." He looked at his bare arm. Skin time, kids say. "I know I missed half of *Happy Days* by now."

I kept moving slow but steady.

"Look at you taking your own sweet time," he hollered up at me while I was climbing the steps. "You a trip."

"Back to you," I hollered over my shoulder while I fitted my key in the door.

When I opened the door, Mama and Miss Darlene were sitting at the kitchen table shelling the pecans we had picked the week before. They were off today so they had little glasses of gin and tonic next to their ashtrays. The gin bottle was bumpy like it was allergic to something.

"Hey, baby," Mama said to me.

"Hey, Mama. Hey, Miss Darlene."

"Delvis walk you home?" Miss Darlene wanted to know. "I told him to come with you right to the door."

"Yes, ma'am. He came to the bottom of the stairs, but he watched till I got in." Delvis might have been talking stupid, but I didn't want to get him in trouble with his mama. Miss Darlene didn't have nothing against beating kids.

I started heading back to my room. I wanted to wait for Miss Darlene to go home before I told Mama my news. I hadn't gone two steps before Mama looked up from the bowl of nuts.

"Why you walking like that?" Mama's voice was sterner than just for a regular question but it didn't rise up like it did when she was mad.

"Girl, what you been doing?" Miss Darlene asked. Then, she put her hand on her hip like she was fixing to give me a little piece of her mind. See, that's why I wanted to wait for her to leave. Sometimes she act like she forget which children are hers.

Mama got up from the table fast like lightning and put her hands on my shoulders. "Sweet Pea, what happened?"

Miss Darlene made a sound like "Ump." I don't know what that was supposed to mean.

Mama said, "Darlene, hush for a minute." Then she look at me. "What is it, sugar?"

"I got my maturity today, that's all."

Her face went puzzled. "What?"

"My maturity," I said again.

"Her period," Miss Darlene said. "She just trying to talk proper." She picked up a pecan and broke it with her back teeth.

I nodded my head to the period part and ignored the proper part. Mrs. Grier said there is nothing wrong with speaking correctly.

Mama hugged me and kissed my face. "Already?" she asked.

"I guess so."

She smiled quiet and kissed me again.

"Don't be spoiling her like that, Yvonne," Miss Darlene said. "Now is the time to tighten up on her." She took a deep drink from her glass. "Watch out for boys now," she said to me. "They can tell you ready now. They can smell it."

"Darlene, you need to take that nasty mess on back home with you," Mama said.

Miss Darlene didn't move. She smiled at Mama like she thought she was kidding. She took a swig off her drink and opened her big mouth again. "You can get pregnant now and the last thing your mama needs is another baby. Ain't that right, Yvonne?"

"Darlene, didn't you hear me tell you to take that mess on across the way?"

This time she could tell Mama was serious as a heart attack. "Well give me a paper cup to put my drink in before I go." She pushed back from the table.

The door shut hard behind Miss Darlene. Me and Mama looked at each other and started cracking up, but I didn't know for sure what was so funny. Mama said, "Young girls got enough to worry about without people telling them lies." Then she stopped laughing and shook her head from side to side like *ain't that a shame.* "Go hop in the tub Sweet Pea."

"What?" I was whispering even though it was just the two of us in the house. "I don't smell alright?"

"No, baby. I want you to hop in the tub because me and you fixing to go out to dinner."

Our bathtub is white, like most bathtubs, I guess. But there is a spot on the right-hand wall of it where the white chipped off, showing black underneath. It looks almost like a scab. When I got in the tub, I covered the black part with my toe and pretended it wasn't there. I was covered all over with sweet-smelling soap when Mama knocked on the door and opened it. What's the point of knocking if you going to come right in anyway?

She sat on the closed toilet seat like me bathing was a movie she wanted to see. I wished I had put some Palmolive in the water so I could be all hidden by bubbles the way ladies was on TV.

"How you feel?" Mama said.

"Okay."

"No cramps?"

"What they feel like?" I asked. I did feel something in my stomach, but I thought that was just being hungry.

"Oh, if you had them, you would know." She smiled. "I want to talk to you." She was looking right at my chest.

"Now?" I said. She was my mama; everything I got, she had seen before. Still, I didn't really want to be having a conversation without my clothes on.

"Don't listen to Darlene," she started. Then she backed up. "Listen to her, but don't really listen to her. You *can* get a baby now. But you know that from your book, right?"

I nodded. I rubbed the soap between my hands. Maybe I could work up enough bubbles to cover my good parts.

"Just be careful," she said.

I was really tired of people telling me to be careful. How much more careful could I get? I was already half scared to answer the phone. I couldn't even look outside after the streetlights come on. I never was one to be talking to strangers, but now, I don't even open doors for old ladies I don't know. "I'm already careful." My voice came out madder than I meant to show her. "You know, with everything going on," I added softly.

"Not that kind of careful," Mama said. "I mean you right to be careful of strangers and all of that. But now I'm talking about being careful with the people that not strangers."

"Like who?" I spread lather over my chest.

"Like boys. Like men."

"I don't know no men." I put another layer of soap on my chest but the little humps still showed.

"Just listen to me, Sweet Pea." Mama was so serious that her voice sank down low and husky. "I'm just saying to watch yourself around the fellas. Don't talk to them unless you want to. And don't let them touch you even if you do want to. Understand?"

"Mama, you know I don't be messing with boys like that." I floated globs of soap in the water around my waist, hiding me like a little skirt.

"I didn't come in here to make you mad. I just came to tell you that. Now rinse so we can get ready to catch the five-fifteen bus." She went toward the door and looked over her shoulder. "You might have to run the shower to get all that soap off."

Red Lobster is my favorite restaurant; it's better than Piccadilly and Shoney's put together. When we got there, the lady told us that we would have to wait fifteen minutes for a booth. Mama said that was fine, but we wouldn't wait at the bar. We sat on a bench in the lobby in front of a big fish tank. There were lobsters in murky water with their hands taped together.

"Mama, I feel sorry for the lobsters." I looked into the bar where people drank colorful drinks.

"You don't need to," she said. "Can't nobody over here afford to eat them. Lobsters downtown got to watch out, but these here on Campbelton Road got it made in the shade."

I smelled my wrists with my eyes closed while we waited. Mama had sprayed Youth Dew right at the base of my hands. I wanted some on the backside of my knees like Mama, but she wouldn't let me.

We were the most dressed up of anybody in the whole Red Lobster. Folks were watching us as we followed the lady to our seats. I had on the best one of Nikky's dresses— one so blue that it was black with white lace under my chin, tied behind with a shiny white bow. Mama didn't wear her gray church dress. Instead, she put on the one for when her and Miss Darlene go to The Living Room Lounge, a black one with sparklies in the front and the back opened like a V below her shoulder blades. My mama is foxy.

The lady gave me a regular menu and a kiddie one. Both of them had popcorn shrimp, but for the grown people it cost a lot more.

"Mama?" I held up the two menus.

"Order from the kids' menu," she said. "If you want more, I'll give you some from my plate."

"May I take your order?" Our waiter was good-looking. Light-skinned with pretty eyes. His voice made me think of ice cream.

I couldn't hardly say *popcorn shrimp* for looking at his

pretty dimples. He couldn't hardly write it down for looking at Mama.

I got the child's portion but I made it last. First the
shrimp, then the french fries, chewing each bite thirty-two
times. When I got through, my plate was stone-cold empty
except for the parsley. I would have ate that too to keep it
from being over, but I didn't want to act like I never been
in a restaurant before, eating stuff that's just for decoration.

"Finished?" Mama said.

"Yes ma'am."

"Finally." She wiggled her finger at the waiter.

He smiled and trotted over.

"All finished, ma'am?" he said to *me*. Here I was, just
reached my maturity that afternoon and already people calling me *ma'am*.

All I could do was grin like a jack-o'-lantern.

"He cute, ain't he," Mama said.

"A little bit," I said. "I didn't really look at him."

Just then Mr. Cutie-Pie Waiter looked back like he heard
me. He raised his eyebrows up at Mama and she held up
one finger.

"What did that mean?" I asked her.

"What did *what* mean?"

I couldn't swallow another sip of my Shirley Temple. My
mama is the kind of person that you had to watch. I had
been to the bathroom twice to check on things. Who knew
what she did when I was gone? No telling.

Mr. Cutie came over to our booth with three other Red
Lobster guys. Two of them were looking at me smiling so
hard I could see their back teeth. The other one was smiling just as hard but he was checking Mama out.

"We have a celebration today," Mr. Cutie shouted to the entire Red Lobster.

I looked at Mama but she had her eyes on Mr. Cutie. Why did she have to front on me like this? Some things not for *everybody* to know. I looked around and saw that everybody in the whole Red Lobster was staring at our table. Did all of them know about my period? They all looked like they were just a giggle away from busting out laughing. And Mama was the worst one. Her hands were clamped together under her chin like she was so tickled she couldn't take it another second.

The fellas started clapping and Mama clapped right along with them. I kicked around under the table hoping to knock her knee and at least ruin her stocking. But it was a big booth and I couldn't reach. I ended up banging my own knee and my eyes filled up with tears. Why did she have to go and ruin my special dinner? I knew Mama told lies, but never knew her to be mean. This was worse than school.

People from other tables had put down their forks to watch us like a movie. I felt like I was in the school cafeteria. Cutie Pie opened his mouth and I put my hands over my eyes.

"Happy, happy birthday!" he sang.

I jammed my hands in my mouth, hurting my lip, to keep from hollering out with relief. To all those people staring I must have looked like a winner on *The Price is Right.*

When they left, Mama whispered, "I told them it was your birthday so you could get a free cake." She winked, flashing her soft green eye shadow.

I blew out the candle on the little white cupcake with

my eyes closed like I was making a wish. But for real, I couldn't think of anything to ask for.

———————

Just as soon as Mama had got out the door good, the phone rang. Girls are supposed to love the telephone, but I hate the thing. It sits on the hall table with the cords curled up next to it like a tail. Just ringing. It's scary how any fool with a dime can get right in your house with you. It could be some crazy like in that movie *He Knows You're Alone*. I didn't go see it, but the commercial by itself did things to my stomach.

"Hello," I said.

"Yes, may I speak to Yvonne please?"

It was a black man on the phone. But it wasn't Uncle Kenny. The only other men that be calling over here are bill collectors, and all of them is white.

"She can't come to the phone right now." I wonder if people know that when a kid say that, it means they home alone. Maybe I should get a new lie.

"Is this Octavia?"

Who was this man calling me by my given name?

"Hello?" he said. "Octavia?"

When I get scared, it feels like somebody tried to pull all my guts out through my belly button. "No sir," I said at last. "This is somebody else."

"I see," he said, with a smile in his voice. "Can you give Yvonne a message?"

"Yes sir."

"Please tell her Ray called. She has the number."

As soon as my ears told my heart who was on the phone, it started beating a thousand miles an hour and I had to work to get my air.

"Hello?" my daddy said, like a little question.

"I'll tell her," I said, and hung up.

I get to see my daddy once a year in the summertime when I'm in Macon staying with my granny and Ray is in town visiting his mother. When Ray call Granny and say he want to see me, she makes me get a bath and put on a Sunday dress, no matter what time of the day or what day of the week it is. The last time he came, he was wearing a pair of brown shorts and a shirt the color of eggshells. When he sat on Granny's brown-and-white couch it looked like he was trying to hide on there like a caterpillar on a green leaf.

"So," he said. Ray always starts things off like that. "So. What grade are you in?"

"Going to the fifth." He had asked me the same question last year. Did he forget or was he trying to make sure I didn't get kept back?

"You like school?"

"Yes sir." I don't know what else I could have said. What he would say if I got up, put my hand on my hip, and said, "What you think? Would you like school if everybody called you Watusi because you so dark and your hair so nappy?" I looked over at him and for the first time I noticed that me and him had the very same hair. I cut my eyes at him like he did it on purpose. But it's funny. Black and nappy look different on a man than on a girl. When a man is real black it make him look like he's all there. Like you better not mess with him.

"So," Ray said again. He so tall and skinny that when he

sat down, his legs almost folded double. If he tried to get up in a hurry, he might knee himself in the nose. "So," he started again.

Granny came out the kitchen and gave him a glass of Kool-Aid he didn't even ask for. She didn't bring nothing for me. Ray took two big swallows. "Ahh," he said, like a commercial.

Granny smiled. She liked to say that Ray is a good man. Fine man. She said it right before he got here and I knew she was going to say it again once he was gone. And if he go up to use the commode, she was going to say it once in between while we waited for him to flush. That's just how Granny is.

"So. What do you think about having a little sister?"

He was talking about his daughter he got with his wife. Granny sat the little girl's picture on the coffee table so Ray could see it. I looked at the picture. The baby was nine months old, he said. I had to admit that she was kind of cute. She was as black as me and Ray, but it looked sweet on her too. It seems like my black is the only one that don't quite lay right.

"She cute," I said.

Ray smiled and picked the picture up. "Kiyana," he said. "She's pretty like you."

I looked at him crazy. I almost corrected him and said, *I'm not pretty.* But that would have been rude. You supposed to say *thank you* when people give you a compliment.

His eyes were still all up in that picture. "I want the two of you to get to know each other," he said, like somebody could actually *know* a baby.

"Yes sir," I said.

He sat still a little longer, staring at me while he finished his Kool-Aid. He wiped his mouth with his hand. "You don't have to call me sir."

"Yes sir." I felt stupid as soon as the words came out. I should have just said plain *yes*.

He smiled. "You can call me—" He looked at the ceiling. Then he smiled harder. His teeth were small with a lot of space in between. "You can call me Ray, if you like."

He must be crazy. Granny would have three kinds of fits if I fixed my mouth to call my daddy by his first name. I wondered would he think it was funny if he knew that I always think of him in my head as *Ray*. I just say *sir* to be polite.

I must have been giving him a strange look because he changed the subject right quick. "Gloria and me bought you some things for school," he said. Gloria is his wife. Delvis said that meant she was my stepmother, but I don't think that a lady can be your stepmother until you have to live with her.

Ray went out to his car and got three shopping bags. "I hope you like it," he said.

"Yes sir. Thank you," I said.

Granny popped out of nowhere, smiling like she was trying to show off every tooth in her head. "Did you say thank you?" Granny said. She was so excited like the stuff in the bags was for her.

"Yes'm."

"I didn't hear you," she said, still grinning, but I could hear the warning in her voice. Mama didn't believe in beating children, but Granny didn't have no problem with it. I looked at Ray with my eyebrows in the air so he could tell her that I did too say *thank you*. He just stood there stupid.

"Thank you," I said.

It wasn't enough for Granny.

"Thank you, Daddy," I said.

He smiled back like this is what he came for. Granny relaxed. Ray kissed me on the forehead and left.

I stood on the porch while he got to his car. It took him a while to actually leave because everybody kept hollering at him from they porches.

"How you doing, Dr. Ray?" old people said. They like to call him that, but he's not a doctor. He's a teacher.

"I'm just fine, Mr. Holmes," he said. "Good to see you."

The way people carry on about him, I wouldn't be surprised at all if somebody asked him for his autograph.

The shopping bags had school stuff in them just like he said. Notebook paper and erasable ink pens. There was a pencil sharpener like the one at school. I liked that and also some letter writing paper with pink ducks on it. The last bag had two pairs of jeans and a regular shirt and a green sweater that seemed like it would itch when I put it on. All of it was too little.

Good thing he left the tags on. He always did. Me and Mama end up carrying it all right back to Rich's and got everything in a bigger size. But she never lets me switch the clothes out for a better color. I had to wear his clothes for my school picture so Mama could send him a five-by-seven.

Granny held the green sweater out in front of her. "This is nice," she said.

"Scratchy," I told her.

"I bet his wife picked it out. Quality."

It didn't look all that special to me. "How you know it's quality?" I asked. I get tired of Granny acting like Ray the president of the USA.

"She waited until she was married to have her babies," Granny said, folding the sweater neat like in a store.

I was confused at first, until I figured out that she was saying that Gloria was quality. I didn't care if she was quality or not, but I didn't appreciate what Granny was trying to say about my mama.

"You don't even know her," I mumbled.

"Did you say something to me?" Granny said.

"No."

"Beg your pardon?"

"No ma'am," I said.

I picked the phone up and put it to my ear. The dial tone made me feel stupid but I felt better at the same time. Better because Ray wasn't still on the line some kind of way, hearing me trying to think. But stupid because any idiot knows that's not how phones work.

But why was Ray calling over here in the first place? It wasn't my birthday. And he didn't ask for me. He wanted to talk to Mama. I wondered what for. Maybe they were getting back together. Like on *The Parent Trap*. But I can't remember them ever being together. They not divorced. And he got a wife anyway. Gloria. Quality. Well, he got another daughter too, but that don't mean he not still my daddy. His high-quality wife meant that the new daughter, Kiyana, was quality too. I wondered if somebody can be half quality. Like Patrick Fletcher in my class who is half white. But that's

the same as being black. He just light skinned. So am I quality too? Or does it work the other way around?

I went to the bathroom and looked at myself in the mirror. I didn't look like much quality. Why my teeth have to
be so crooked? Mama got a nice smile and Ray teeth may
be little and spread out, but they straight. And my hair. Even
if Mama was to let me get it pressed, it would take a lot before we got to quality.

———

Something was up and I needed some time to think
about it. I couldn't think about it at home because the phone
was there and I kept staring at it thinking Ray was about to
call at any second. He had called three times in one week.
He normally calls that many times in a year. One for Christmas. One on my birthday. And one more time when Mama
asks him for some extra cash.

One time, when he called, I answered; the other two,
Mama picked up. She tried to play it off, but I knew who it
was.

I needed someplace to go, but when you don't got no car
and ain't got no money, you can't be all that choosy. I decided to go to the park next to our church, Flipper Temple.
I could have some privacy there because hardly no kids hang
out at the park ever since children started getting disappeared.

It wasn't so far from school to the park, but by the time
I got to the top of that steep hill, I was panting. I sat on a
hard plastic swing to rest. Even with my gloves on, I could
feel the cold chain in my hands. In my pocket I had a sharp

pencil so I could stick it in the eye of anyone that might try and snatch me.

I pumped my legs back and forth to get the swing going. I was too tall for this baby swing; my toes kept scraping the ground and slowing me down. I tucked my legs tight under my behind and the swing went from front to back. I felt like a baby rocking itself in a cradle.

When I was little and my Uncle Kenny was staying with us, he used to take me to this park. Sometimes we went to Burger King across the street and got a large shake and two straws. I wish he was like he was and that he was here now.

I aint seen Kenny since two years ago at Christmastime when me and Mama was riding the bus going to Downtown Rich's. I sat by the window because I liked to see people Christmas decorations when we passed by. I was straining to see if a Santa's sleigh had all eight reindeer plus Rudolph when I saw Uncle Kenny sitting on the ground up against a rusted-out car. He was sleeping like people do in church, with his head bobbing up and down.

"Look, Mama!" I hollered, so that everybody on the sixty-six Five Points turned. "There go Uncle Kenny!"

Mama didn't look. "No, it's not."

"Look, Mama." The bus was stopped at a light. We had passed Kenny, but if she tried real hard she would still see him. "That's him in the blue."

But Mama still didn't turn around. By the time she even looked at me, I couldn't see nothing behind me but buildings.

"Your uncle is in Macon," she said.

"But you didn't even look." I kept my voice low. Mama can't stand to see kids cut up in public.

"Why I need to look out when I know what I know?"

When we got closer to downtown, Mama was the one looking out the window. "Sweet Pea, look at the Pink Pig."

I didn't turn around.

The Pink Pig is a roller coaster that they only bring out at Christmastime. It rides around the giant Christmas tree on the top of Rich's. From the bus stop, Mama pointed again. "There it is."

We went inside and took an elevator to the roof. I gave this white man the pink ticket I got at school for having perfect attendance. He fastened me in a little car built for two kids. Some other cars were filled up because a lot of kids came together. Right before we were ready to get moving, a little white boy came up with his perfect attendance ticket. The white man looked at the empty seat next to me. After a second he said, "Wait for the next trip." Then he pressed some buttons and the pig started inching up the track with little clicks.

I'm not scared of heights. Never have been. I have rode on the Scream Machine at Six Flags and that's ten times bigger and faster than the Pink Pig. But from the roof of Rich's downtown I saw the whole entire city except everything was too little to really see. One of the little spots out there had to be my Uncle Kenny. If he was to wake up he might see a little spot way up here and not even know it was me.

The only thing I could get a real good look at was the Big Tree itself, and it was ugly up close. The red, green, and gold decorations were as big as baby heads cut off and hung upside down by a hook where the neck used to be. Lights flashed in between the branches and I saw my face all pulled out of shape in the shiny sides of the baby-head ornaments.

When I got off, my legs were weak as matchsticks.

"Wanna ride again?" Mama had another pink ticket in her hand. "Look what I found. We can wait a minute till the man forget you, and you can go again."

"I don't feel like it."

She was looking up at the tree. "That tree is something, huh? I think it's a hundred feet tall. I wish grown folks could ride. Was it fun, Sweet Pea?"

I nodded my head.

"I never been on a roller coaster before," she said. "There wasn't no Rich's in Macon. And even if there was, black folks wouldn't have been allowed to ride. We couldn't even use the rest rooms in town. Did you know that?"

I nodded.

"So now that we can get on, I'm too old." She laughed. "That's a shame, huh?"

"Yes'm."

"So you want to ride again?" It was like she was asking me for a favor.

I rode again. But when the Pig started clicking up the track I closed my eyes and refused to see the city or my face in the baby heads.

I pumped my legs on the swing. The cold air dried out my wide-open eyes but I tried not to blink. I watched everything get small then big again. I swung up so high that the chain gave a little jump every time I went out. Some people walking by turned to look at me. They was wondering who is this big ol girl riding that baby swing like it's going to take her someplace. I stuck my tongue out and the air dried it too, like a towel on the line. I kept pumping my legs thinking about what I could see and what I already knew.

The swing couldn't get me high enough. I pushed with all I had, but I couldn't see no farther than the bread factory. I saw the tops of the soft-color projects near to where I stay at, but I couldn't get so high that I could see the people turn into ants and teach myself not be scared.

I kept pumping anyway like it was going out of style. Then I saw a man walking by. His hair and skin was the same brown-on-brown as Uncle Kenny. He walked with a little dip when he stepped, just like Kenny, except I thought that Uncle Kenny did his pimp on the other side. But maybe I was wrong and this man was walking just like Kenny. He kept walking and popping his fingers to some music playing in his head. Maybe it was him.

"Hey!" The swing chain jerked. "Kenny!" He didn't turn around. I pushed my legs back and forth racing to catch up with him. Then it was like my brain said to my body, *You still on the swing, fool.* And my hands, embarrassed, let go. For a second, I felt myself in the air with my legs moving like a cartoon. "Kenny," I said, but I was on my way down. I called him again with all the air in my chest.

My face hit the concrete but the rest of me landed in the grass. My lip was busted open. Blood on my chin. The man stopped popping his fingers and looked over my way. He turned his head to one side like he was trying to figure out exactly what it was he was looking at. He took a couple steps over with that wrong-side pimp. I looked up over my head and a streetlight was shining on me like on a stage.

I picked myself up and he stepped back one step. I

looked around me. It was getting dark. Even when kids wasn't getting killed, Mama said it wasn't safe to be out when the streetlights was on.

I grabbed my book bag with one hand. My knuckles were getting blood everywhere but I didn't care.

He took another step my way, looking around. I looked around too and didn't see nobody. Was this Uncle Kenny? I needed to tell him that it wasn't really my fault that Mama put him out. And that I didn't tell her that he was looking at me in the bathtub that time because it was an accident, like it was an accident that I told her about the dope needles. I breathed hard out my mouth. If he would come one step closer, I could see if it was him. But if it wasn't him, another step or two could be close enough for him to get me. My heart was going hard in my chest like when me and Delvis knocked over a wasp nest with a stick and took off running. The man stood stock-still like he was the one scared of me.

I couldn't take it.

Counting three in my head, I got my hurt arms and legs together and ran down the hill toward home. I was booking, jumping over stuff like Carl Lewis and Wilma Rudolph put together. Cold air was freezing my chest together, but I kept running, forcing the wind into me and out again.

When I got to the sidewalk in front of my house, Donathan and Darlita were standing out front shaking their little fingers at me.

"Ooh, Sweet Pea, you in trouble!"

Donathan reached up toward my face. "What happened? Somebody try to snatch you?" He crumpled his face up.

"No," I said. "But you better get yourself in the house. Streetlights on already."

Then Delvis came running out from behind the pecan trees, scaring the mess out of all three of us. "Sweet Pea," he said, like he had found the Easter egg with the foil on it. "People been looking for you." He put his hand out like he was going to shake my hand or give me a one-arm hug. "What happened to your face? Did somebody—"

"Where my mama?"

"Up in y'all's place. She was down here a little while ago, cussing people out. She said she was fixing to call the police."

I ran toward the building. Everything hurt. I tripped up the stairs. I felt the skin on my lip pull apart and the bleeding started again. Our door was half open; I pushed it in.

"Mama, I'm okay."

She put the telephone down. "Octavia Yvette Fuller, where the hell have you been?"

Whatever words I had disappeared because my mama didn't cuss at me.

"I was at the park," I said, but that was only half of it.

"What happened to your face?" Mama's voice was high like Darlita's.

"Nothing," I told her fast. "I just fell; that's all. I was up at the park."

"*At the park?*" Mama grabbed me by my shoulders and shook me hard. "Don't you ever go off like that again. I work too hard to have to be worrying about you. I didn't know if you were kidnapped, somewhere raped, laying dead in a ditch." Her fingers mashed my skin like dough. "Or with some boy."

"But, Mama, it wasn't like that."

Then she hit me cross the face.

I tried to pull away, but she still had me hard by the shoulders. She put her face right up to mine. The white part of her eyes was crisscrossed with red. Mama's breath in my face was strong like a whole pack of Kools. She shook me again and my head flopped back and forth like I was made of rubber.

"How many children got to die before you learn to bring your ass home?"

She slapped me again and had her hand back to give me another one. I opened my mouth to holler so maybe somebody might hear me and save me, but Miss Darlene came busting in, turning on the light.

"Yvonne! What you trying to do? Beat the child half to death?" She was looking at my face. Her eyes stopped on my chin. The blood drying there made my skin tight.

"Somebody see this girl and they'll call the county on you. That what you want?" Miss Darlene shut our door.

Mama let go of my shoulders and put her hands on the side of my face. I was scared she was still crazy. But at least she was moving slow. Miss Darlene was shaking her head like me and Mama both need to be shamed. I didn't really want Mama touching me, but I didn't want Miss Darlene to see me scared of my own mama. So I stood stiff and pretended that I was on the roof of Rich's and Mama was a little speck that couldn't hurt me.

Mama touched my chin with her finger. "Sweet Pea."

Miss Darlene gave a couple of clicks with her tongue like she was God's secretary writing all of this down.

"I was already hurt. I fell on my face in the park." And that was the truth.

Miss Darlene made the sound again like she was adding *lying* to her little list.

"For real," I said.

Mama was looking at her hands like she never seen them before.

"You want Sweet Pea to stay over to my place till you get your act together?" Miss Darlene said. "What's the point of carrying a child for nine months just to kill them when they get here?"

"Get out of here," I said.

"Watch your mouth; I'm the one trying to help you."

"I don't need nothing from you. I told you my mouth was cut when I got home so get out."

"Yvonne." Miss Darlene looked at Mama, who was sitting on her knees on the carpet. Her head came up as high as my chest.

I kept my eyes on Mama too. I never talked crazy to a grown person before and I didn't know what she was going to do. I ducked my head in case she was going to up and slap me again. But Mama just waved her hand like me and Miss Darlene was a couple of flies trying to spoil her picnic.

"If you need something," Miss Darlene said, "you know where I'm at."

I didn't know which one of us she was talking to, but neither one of us said anything to her.

Mama pushed herself off the carpet holding her hands out in front of her like she had on wet fingernail polish. I wasn't scared of her no more. I could see tears all over her like a hidden picture. Tears in her face, on her hands, swirled

in her legs. Whatever had rose up in her was back down
now. I couldn't say that it was gone forever. She sat on the
couch and I sat at the kitchen table.

The blood on my face was drying up. I picked at my
chin and brown flakes fell to the table. I brushed them away
and the table wobbled on its short leg. Mama hadn't said
anything to me since she tried to slap my face right off my
head. To tell the truth, I really didn't want her to. She the
one always talking about she don't believe in beating children. And then she didn't even give me a chance to explain.

The phone rang. Mama didn't move. It rang again.

"Want me to get it?" I said.

"Yeah," she said. Her voice was as faded as her blue
jeans.

"Hello," I said.

"You back! Praise God!"

"Yes ma'am, Granny," I said looking over to Mama to
see what I was supposed to do. But she didn't look up.

"You scared your mama half to death. And your granny
too. I was fixing to hop on the Greyhound and find you
myself. I need to call Ray and tell him you alright. Where
were you?"

"I was at school doing extra work. I forgot to tell
Mama."

"That's a shame," Granny said. "That's why Yvonne
need to get you out of that city. People like to talk about us
living in the country, but at least we don't have to call the
National Guard when a child stay a little while after to get
her lesson."

"Yes'm."

"Now let me talk to Yvonne."

Mama was still froze in her place on the couch.

"She in the rest room," I said. "Want me to tell her to call you back?"

"Tell her she can call me collect."

"Yes'm." I wonder if Granny know she wasting her time every time she call this house. She can probably count every true word we ever said on one hand.

I hung up the phone and went back to the table. I kept rocking it back and forth like a loose tooth. The little taps it made was like a clock. It was about seven o'clock. I hadn't had nothing to eat since lunchtime. Mama was still on the couch like a magician had hypnotized her and told her she was a rock.

She was still sitting out there when I came out the bathroom. Once I wiped off all the blood, I looked a lot better. My lip was split and meat was showing, but the rest of my face looked okay. Thank God, I'm dark. Light-skinned people are soft and show bruises easy. If a child go to school bruised, the teacher could call the county.

"Mama," I said, hoping my new and improved face would make her snap out of it. The word came out funny because it hurt to touch my lips together. Mama turned in my direction and I hurried over the couch. "See, it's better."

"Sweet Pea, I'm sorry, baby." She kept her hand in her lap. "Oh, look at your lip." Then tears started rolling down her face. They kept running into each other and getting bigger and bigger.

I got mad again. I'm the one got pimp-slapped twice. My lip was swollen up bigger than JJ. I'm the one who didn't have no dinner. And *she* sitting here crying like her feelings hurt?

She reached her hand out like she was going to touch my face. I jerked back. "Don't touch me." She snatched her hand back and I felt guilty. "It's too sore."

"I'm so sorry, baby."

"You said you don't believe in beating children."

She let the air out through her nose. "I know." She shook her head. "You scared me so bad."

"But you didn't let me tell my side. You just started shaking me and stuff." Then out of nowhere my tears found their way out.

Mama put her arms around me and hugged me to her chest. Her body smelled like talcum powder. I took a deep breath of it before I pushed her way.

"You mashing my face. It hurts."

She drew back and we did our crying on opposite sides of our couch.

When I got home from school, Mama had put the Christmas tree up. I know my life ain't a TV show where they go out in the woods and chop down a tree and they put the ornaments on one by one saying "This one from Granny" and "Remember this special angel we got in Paris?" But still, me and Mama have this little thing we do. She is the one who puts the tree together, but I hand her the branches one by one and she lets me do the ornaments however I like.

But she snuck and did it by herself while I was gone to school. I opened up the door and it was standing in the corner flashing on and off like the lights in a liquor-store window.

Mama was sitting at the kitchen table smoking cigarettes. The spearmint-smoke smell of Kools was like an old friend came back. Mama hadn't touched her cigs in two weeks, since that day she slapped me across the face. She threw away the rest of the pack she had been working on and the lighter too, like it was the cigarettes that made her lose her temper, the same as whiskey makes people mean.

She didn't turn when I opened the door. She kept smoking with her eyes closed like she was really concentrating.

"Mama," I said, "you put the tree up?"

She nodded. "It's December." Her eyes didn't look right. They were wet and swole like she was coming down with a sty, or maybe the pink eye.

"I woulda helped you with the tree," I mumbled. "Like always."

She carefully tapped her ashes into a bottle cap. "Sweet Pea, sit down and let me talk to you." Mama touched the chair next to her.

I sat on the one across the table, the one Uncle Kenny ripped open with a bottle opener that was in his back pocket. We fixed it with some magic tape Mama ordered off the Channel Seventeen. The seam was supposed to be invisible but I could always tell where it was at.

"Ray called." Mama looked hard at me, trying to see past my eyes into my brain.

"What he want?" I pushed up the edge of the tape with my fingernail. It was gooey like bubblegum.

"He wants you to come to South Carolina."

"For the summer?" The tape was between my fingers now. I could snatch it all the way off if I wanted to.

She shook her head and sucked on the cigarette. The bottle cap was full already so she let the ashy part build up on the end. If I breathed just a little hard it would fall into her glass of orange juice.

"What for, then?"

"He wants you to stay up there for a good little while. At least until this mess is over." Mama nodded over at a stack of newspapers. TERROR ON ATLANTA'S SOUTHSIDE. She said it like we know just when that would be. Like the child murderer called up Mayor Jackson and said, "Oh, I plan to stop snatching kids on the fourth of July," or something like that.

"But, Mama," I said. "They could be killing kids *forever!* Mayor Jackson's already offering a hundred-thousand-dollar reward. Even still, kids coming up missing almost every week."

Mama nodded her head like she was listening to me. "That's true."

I thought she was seeing my side. "And anyway, it's just boys getting killed mostly. So ain't really no reason for me to go away."

Her ashes fell off into her glass. She looked down at it sad, like she had really wanted to drink that juice. "What about those two girls? I heard one of their mothers speak at the tenant meeting."

"What she say?"

"She said maybe you should go on up to South Carolina with your daddy."

"No she didn't," I said, easing more tape up.

"No," Mama said. "I didn't speak to her directly. But when she got through talking, I called Ray back and told him alright." She put her glass up to her mouth before she remembered the ashes.

"But, Mama, I got things to do right here. I can't just move to North Carolina."

"South Carolina," she said, like that made a difference.

"But what about my friend?" I said soft. "What if something happened? How I'm going to know about it?"

She made a confused face. "Delvis'll be right here when you get back."

"Not Delvis," I raised my voice. "My friend what's missing."

Mama looked like she had forgot all about that. "I didn't know you were that tight," she said. She reached across the table like maybe she was going to touch me, but she didn't. Her hand just stayed in the middle of the table.

It was hard to explain how I felt so close with someone after just a week. That's how long me and Rodney actually talked to each other. So maybe we wasn't best friends. But if we had more time, we coulda got tight. I could tell it was coming like how you can smell sweet rain on its way on a hot afternoon.

And if me and Mama was tight, she would already know how I was feeling. It would be like when I was little, and she could look at me when I was tired and say, "You sleepy?" just from the sight of me. Now me and her just getting looser and looser. Like when the elastic give out on the waist of a pair of pants. They just keep sliding off until you end up naked.

"We was friends, Mama," I said. "I need to be nearby to find out what happened."

"I'll call you if there's news," she said.

But I needed to be there. Right there. Not just on the line. Ray lived on the other end of a phone and he wasn't

no daddy to me. How could I be a friend to Rodney from
through the telephone? If God worked a miracle and found
him safe, how could I be in South Carolina? And if he was
dead, I needed to be there to see him buried in the ground.
When Granddaddy passed away, they kept him in the funeral home for nine days while we waited for Uncle Edward to get train fare from Detroit. They said Uncle Ed
needed to be there so he could rest. I asked Mama if they
was talking about Uncle or Granddaddy and she said,
"Both."

"Maybe I could go and stay with Granny," I said. Macon
wasn't too far away. "They not killing kids in Macon."
Granny reminds us about this every time she call over here.
I yanked loose more tape.

Mama dropped the cigarette stump in the orange juice
with a sizzle. She pulled out another one. "No ma'am. You
not going to Macon. *Last* thing you need is to stay with
Mama. She'll have you sitting up in church all day, every
day. Can't nothing good happen in Macon, Georgia."

"But you from Macon." I had pulled the tape far
enough back that the stuffing jumped out.

"That's true."

"Ray from Macon."

"He not there now," she said. "Your daddy ain't crazy.
He was out of Macon on the first thing smoking when we
finished high school. He took his diploma like relay racers
take that baton." She turned her face to the ceiling and blew
white smoke straight up.

"Where did he go?"

"College," she said. "He used to write letters at first.

Then after a while he just wrapped the money orders in a clean sheet of paper. No note."

She smiled a little and shook her head, staring off at the Christmas tree. I was near enough to touch her. I smelled her soap and lotion. "Can't I just stay here? I'll be safe."

She put her hands on my shoulders, like she was going to pull me into a hug. But she just squeezed my shoulders and spoke slow and careful.

"It's more than just safety, Sweet Pea. Ray *got* things. He send money every month. That's more than a lot of them do and I respect that. But what he really got, he can't fit in a envelope."

I thought she was talking about hugs, kisses, and mushy stuff. "I don't need to go all the way to South Carolina for that," I said.

"How else you gonna get it?"

"From you?"

She was tugging on her blue robe and something ripped. "I don't have what Ray and them got. He teach at a college. If you staying with him, ain't no way you not going to get to go."

"Well, we live nearby to a college, right here." I passed the iron gates of Spelman College every time we walked to the store.

Mama touched her side through the hole in her robe. "Sweet Pea, look at me."

I turned my face in the right direction but locked my eyes at the Christmas tree behind her head.

"Octavia." She called my given name.

I looked at her face for real this time. The hot-comb scar

on her forehead was healing up bright pink. I watched her lips red with lipstick and brown from smoke.

"Ray wants to give you something real. It's a shame that fourteen kids had to die before he offered it. But now he got his hand out and you don't have no choice but to grab it."

But there was too a choice. All she had to do was call Ray and say *No way José. You not taking my baby.* And then Ray would be the one with no choice but to back up.

Mama didn't unplug the Christmas tree before she went to work. It flashed on and off like a silent alarm. I put my hand on the TV to cut it on, but then I changed my mind. I was tired of dead kids, search parties, and reward money. If I never saw Monica Kaufman again, it would be too quick.

And I was mad at everybody I ever met in my whole life. Mad at Jashante for bringing bad luck to our neighborhood. I was mad at Mama for putting up the stupid tree by herself, for handing me over to Ray like a two-dollar gift swap. And she the one who sent Kenny away. I kicked the Christmas tree and one blue glass ornament landed near my bare foot. The lights kept up the on and off. I wanted to pitch a real fit like white girls on TV, throwing dishes against the wall, hollering and cussing between each crash. If I was a white girl, I would chuck a cereal bowl across the kitchen, cussing at Kenny for getting himself kicked out, for putting his hands everywhere when he tickled me. I might break a whole shelf of glasses screaming at Rodney for sharing his candy with me and getting hisself snatched two days later. And last I would destroy Mama's green punch bowl, cussing at myself for being too stupid to see that nothing lasts. That people get away from you like a handful of sweet smoke.

I turned my eyes to the ornament on the floor. I put my foot on top of it. Lightly. The bottom part of my foot bent easy over the curve. I pressed down a little bit. The glitter scratched the soft space on my sole. Then I pushed with my whole weight. The glass broke with a solid crunch. It wasn't the same as destroying a whole cabinet full of china, but it was enough.

It hurt. I hopped on one leg to the couch and examined my foot. It was dark in the room except for the Christmas lights, but I could make out a piece of blue glass sticking out. I pinched it with two fingers and yanked. The blood came then.

Walking carefully with one hand on the wall, I limped to the bathroom to tend to the wound I could see.

———

Sometimes, I have too much on my mind and I need somebody to help me think about it. On the last day of school before Christmas, I went down to the second-grade class to look for Mrs. Grier.

The second-graders must have had some kind of party. There was wrapping paper everywhere and little bits of candy cane mashed into the floor. Mrs. Grier looked wore out like she had been working double shifts.

But still, when she saw me, she smiled. "Octavia! Merry Christmas!"

"Merry Christmas," I mumbled back.

She straightened her back after bending down to pick up some of the wrapping paper. "What's troubling you, Octavia?" Mrs. Grier always talks like a book.

I waited a second because I wanted to answer back with the same kind of words. But finally, I used my regular way of talking. "My mama say she sending me off to stay with my daddy."

She smiled. "For the holidays? That's lovely."

"No. For ever. Or at least till they catch the child killer or till I'm too old for a child killer to kill." I started moving the desks back into rows.

"Oh, I see." She took off her shoes and stood in a chair to pull down a red streamer. "Where does your father live?"

"Orangeburg, South Carolina."

"Oh? Is he affiliated with the university there?" She got down from the chair and sat in it.

"I don't know."

"Well, what does he do?" She looked kind of worried. "I don't know of much industry in Orangeburg."

"He teaches at a college."

She sat up in her seat a little bit and smiled. I knew right then that she was going to side with Mama.

"What a wonderful opportunity."

"Opportunity for what?" I crossed my arms over my chest. "I want to stay right here in Atlanta, Georgia."

"Don't stand so far away," Mrs. Grier said. "Sit here. I want to tell you about when I was coming up."

I sat down in the chair. She handed me a piece of foil-wrapped chocolate before she spoke.

"We were poor when I was a girl." She looked at me with her eyebrows up, nodding her head a little bit. She didn't expect me to believe her. And it was hard to picture. First off, it was weird to think that she had been a girl before. I tried to get it fixed in my imagination, but the best I could do was to get her real short. But even still her wavy hair was silver-white and cheeks hung low. The poor part was harder. Mrs. Grier don't seem like she know where the projects are at, let alone that she used to stay there.

"My hometown is Sugarloaf, Alabama," she said. "A town so small that there isn't even a caution light to tell people when to get off the highway. There were twelve of us children, but only nine survived."

"Kids was getting killed way back then?" I was shocked. The way people carried on here lately, I thought that child murdering was invented in 1979.

"No. Back then, many children didn't survive infancy. One of my brothers died in his crib from a spider bite. The twin girls had whooping cough. All of this happened before I was born. My brother, Everett T, was murdered, but that was much later."

"Twelve kids is too many," I said.

"That's the right attitude, Octavia." She smiled. "Two is plenty in this day. But back then, children worked the land. We were a sharecropping family and Father was a proud man. He was determined to pay off the debt."

"What about your mama?"

"Mother worked cotton too. She was strong, taller than father and nearly as broad. People never knew she was expecting until it was time for the babies to come. And they only knew then, because she took two days away from the field. One day for birthing and the other day to marvel at what she had done."

Mrs. Grier stared out the window behind me. The merry-go-round and swing set reflected in her glasses. She was quiet as a library.

"Do you want me to clean the blackboard?" I asked, just so somebody would be saying something.

"That would be nice."

I went down the hall to ask the custodian for warm water and rags. When I got back, Mrs. Grier picked the story back up.

"I was the youngest. My sister Livonia, who watched after those of us too small yet to pick cotton, made quite a pet of me.

"Every night Mother would tell us that she loved us. She might say, 'Livonia, I love you like a cup of cool water. Everett T, I love you like the morning. Edna Lee' (that's my given name) 'Edna Lee, I love you like a bunch of grapes.'

"I had never tasted grapes. But I knew they would taste like love. When I was in college, my roommate gave me some fat ones from the farmer's market. I expected them to be bright purple like the pictures in the primer, but they were dark as Mother's knuckles. When I tasted the sweet juice, I knew what Mother meant about love and then I bit into the bitter seed and I knew better. Do you understand, Octavia?"

I didn't have no idea what she was talking about. My mama always gets the light green grapes with the seeds taken out already. "Yes'm," I said.

"Mother and Father passed away on the same day. Father was a race man. He walked eight miles to Troy to get dry goods. There was a mercantile on our place, but the store in Troy was colored owned. Someone knocked him off the road as he walked back pulling the cart. He fell in a ditch and drowned in two feet of water.

"At the same instant, Mother put down her sack, complaining of a headache. She laid under a magnolia and died."

I had the whole board wiped down but soon as it dried, traces of the chalk letters started showing through again. I dunked my rag in the water and started over.

"We children were separated. The older boys, Everett T and Burnett W, stayed behind. All the rest of us were sent, one by one, to live with relatives. My aunt Lee asked for me since my mother gave me her name. She came with Uncle James in a blue Packard and took me to Atlanta.

"I was just six years old, and had never ridden in a car before."

"You was used to catching the bus?" I asked. Me and Mama always be on the MARTA.

"No, Octavia. We were sharecroppers. Everything we did, we did right on the farm. A plantation, really. Understand?"

I nodded and she went on with her story.

"So there I was in the backseat of the Packard. I didn't realize we were moving. I thought that the *trees* whipping by the windows were passing *us*. After we were on the road an hour or so, I needed to use the lavatory but I was afraid to ask my uncle and aunt to stop the world so I could get out." She laughed at this. Her mouth was the same pink as her fingernail polish.

I stopped rubbing the board and stared at her. Grown people love to tell the saddest stories and laugh about them.

"By the time we got to Atlanta, naturally, I'd had a little accident. Aunt Lee was angry. I burst into tears, not because I was about to be whipped but because Livonia had told me that Mother was always watching me from heaven.

"My aunt didn't live in a mansion. The home I have now is larger. But to my Alabama eyes, it was amazing. Running water was some kind of miracle. I was scared to flush the commode.

"I shared a room with my cousin, Twyla, who is a few years older than I am. I had seen Twyla only once before when she came to Sugarloaf to meet us—her country relatives. We had all gathered in the front room. Twyla, who had never seen such a big family, whispered to Aunt Lee, 'Mama, they have *company*.' All of the adults had laughed and we children were confused. When I got to Atlanta, she was like a stranger.

"When night fell, I tried to climb in the bed with Twyla. I couldn't imagine sleeping alone any more than you could imagine a single person eating an entire ham.

" 'Not in here with me,' Twyla said, as though bed sharing was disgusting. I tucked my little head and went to the other twin bed. The pretty spread was butter colored and I was afraid that I might spoil it. I was as lonely that night as I have ever been in my life. But I didn't cry because I didn't want to wet the eyelet pillow slip.

"Somehow, I managed to sleep well that night. Drowsiness relaxed me and I spread myself all over that bed. Every time I moved an arm or a leg, I felt cool cotton. In a year's time, I hardly thought about Sugarloaf at all.

"When my sister, Livonia, came to visit me four years later, I hardly knew her. By then, I was about your age. I saw Livonia like Twyla did, a country cousin that we both felt sorry for. I remember that she wore run-over brogans and a man's belt around her dress.

"Livonia stayed for dinner. She wrapped her roll up in a paper napkin with a chicken leg and stuffed it in her bag. Before she went outside to wait for her people to pick her up, we had a moment alone. Livonia hugged me to her chest. I smelled the cocoa butter she used on her face and hands mixed with the chicken in her bag.

" 'I love you, Sister,' she said to me. 'Like a bunch of grapes.'

"I held on to her neck and did all the crying that I didn't do that first night after I left Sugarloaf. Livonia gently pulled me free. 'I gotta be going now,' was all she said.

"I never saw her again."

"What happened to her?" I asked.

Mrs. Grier rubbed the back of her neck and shook her head. "She stepped on a rusty nail and died of lockjaw."

"For real?" At first I couldn't figure out why she was telling me this story. But then I thought that maybe she was taking *my* side. She was telling me this so I could get Mama not to send me to South Carolina. I almost smiled, but I thought of poor Livonia with her jaws locked up. I rubbed that chalkboard with a straight face.

Mrs. Grier took a deep breath. "But that's not the point," she said. "While I stayed with Aunt and Uncle, I had to make myself useful. I washed all the clothes every day when I got home from school and ironed them in the morning before I left. Everybody in school admired Twyla's clothes, but I was the one who had to iron in all those tiny pleats. I was the one with burned fingers from the curling irons I set her hair with twice a week.

"Oh, you should have seen me huffing and puffing under my breath about how things would be different if my parents were alive. I felt like a little colored Cinderella." Mrs. Grier smiled.

"But didn't you want them to still be living? Nobody wants for their mama and daddy to be dead." I didn't hardly know my daddy but I didn't want him to be *dead* in the ground. And if something happened to my mama I'd probably just hop in the casket right along with her.

"You're right, Octavia. I grieved for my mother and father. My brothers, sisters, and I have never again been under the same roof. I mourn that. But what I am trying to tell you is that I made myself *useful* in my aunt's house and good things happened as a result."

"What good things? They treated you like a maid. My mama said she ain't sending me to South Carolina to be nobody's maid. She said slavery times is over." I crossed my arms again.

"Hush, child," Mrs. Grier said. "I'm not finished. Your mother is right. Your father *should not* treat you like a servant. But I'm a little older than your mother, and I have had a few more experiences, so listen to me when I speak.

"Often people don't do what they should. And if your father and your stepmother make you earn your keep, earn it. They won't send you back if you make them need you. By the time you finish high school they will be obligated to sponsor your education.

"My aunt and uncle didn't send me to Spelman College with Twyla. I went to Fort Valley State. But I took advantage of opportunity. I didn't have money for movies and hamburgers like other girls, but I completed my teaching certificate just the same. I met my husband there too. He may not be a Morehouse man, but he works hard and we made a good life for ourselves. Understand?"

I still had my arms folded tight across me. "No."

She got up from her chair and pulled my arms apart. Tugging on my wrists, she said, "Octavia, when you're poor you don't always have a choice."

I wanted to snatch my arms away and tell her that me and my mama are not poor. We don't stay in the projects. We stay across the street from the projects. But she let me go all of a sudden and gathered up her things.

"I'll drive you home."

We didn't hardly say nothing while we were heading to the burgundy Cadillac. I was still mad about her calling me poor. But she didn't even look over at me to ask why I had my lip poked out. Mrs. Grier was so far into her own head that she messed up three times trying to get her keys in the car door.

The inside of the Cadillac smelled like Christmas because of the little cardboard tree hanging from the mirror. Mrs. Grier turned on the radio and played the kind of music that don't have words.

"Where do you live?" she asked.

"Down by Fair Street."

Through the shaded car windows, everything we passed from school to my house was dirty brown like an apple with a bite out of it. People had their decorations up, but the stockings wasn't red enough and the green of the wreaths was faded as old socks. A dog had knocked over a trash can, throwing empty egg cartons and tin cans every which-a-way. Running over it sounded like crunching a squirrel. I wanted to tell Mrs. Grier that a mutt was to blame. The people who live there put it in the can. They can't help what a dog do. But I kept quiet.

"Right here," I said, when we got to my building.

Mrs. Grier was looking out the wrong window to the project side of the street.

I tapped my window. "On this side."

She turned, but her mouth was still bent into a sad clown line. How come she didn't smile to see that I didn't live over where she first thought I did? Probably because of the rainy-day windows. I followed her eyes to the flowerpot Mama and me put marigolds in last spring. The blooms were long gone. Now, it looked like a bucket full of dry dirt.

"Mrs. Grier, we had flowers in that pot before." I had to tell her. "They not really dead. They'll be back come spring, Mama say."

She nodded like she understood, but the corners of her mouth bent down.

"Well, thank you for the ride." I put my hand on the door. I wanted to get from behind the smoky windows. From where I was I couldn't hardly tell my building from those across the street. Both were made of dirt-colored bricks with windows without cute shutters like in schoolbook pictures.

"Do you want me to go with you and tell your mother you were with me?"

"No ma'am," I told her. "It's not too late."

I opened the car door. I thought that light was going

to flood in from the other side of the glass, like when God speaks, but maybe everything had got dingy just that fast.

I turned around and waved at Mrs. Grier once I was on my sidewalk. Weeds grew bushy in the places where the concrete was broken up. In the spring there would be dandelion flowers there too. I thought maybe I should have hollered that to Mrs. Grier. But it's not ladylike to holler. And dandelions are not much to talk about.

"Think about what I said." Her voice was loud but not hollering.

"Yes ma'am. I will."

Mrs. Grier waved and rolled up the window and watched me through dark glass until I went in my door.

Mama was sleep when I got home. She was stretched across her bed diagonal. One arm hanging off the edge, her fingers barely touching the rug.

"I'm here, Mama."

"Okay," she said. "Put the teakettle on for me, okay?"

"Alright," I said, and went into the kitchen.

In the refrigerator was a plate of crackers and cheese but the cheese wasn't cut into little chunks the perfect size for a Ritz cracker. I broke the hunk of cheese into smaller bits and ate a little of it while I waited on Mama's water to heat up. Mama took some days off to spend time with me, but all she been doing is sleeping and sewing. She want me to carry all the Nikky dresses with me.

The teakettle started whistling.

"Mama, your water ready," I said.

She came in wearing her blue robe. She poured the hot water over brown coffee pebbles. She stirred in some sugar and took a deep sip. I don't know how she can drink that hot stuff without burning her mouth.

"Go and put on that pink dress. I want to make sure I got it pinned right before I sew it." Her eyes were crusty.

"Mama, you going to wash your face?"

She nodded as she sipped.

"Why do I need to take that pink dress with me? I'm just going to be up there for a little while, right?"

"Right," she said.

"So why I need all those clothes? And where I'm going to be going to need that many good dresses?"

"I just want you to have them. To let them know you used to nice things."

"Cause she quality?" I asked.

"Who?" Mama said.

"Granny say Gloria is quality," I explained.

"Mama just color struck," Mama said. "Now go get into that dress."

"When I get through trying on the dress, can I go outside?"

"For what?"

"Talk to Delvis."

"Alright," she said. "But you better be back in here before the streetlights come on."

It was just four days before Christmas and nine days before I was supposed to be leaving and I didn't even tell Delvis yet. I know I was supposed to tell him. Because when everything is counted up, he is my best friend. Almost my only friend. So I shoulda gone running over to tell him as soon as Mama told me. But something about it ain't quite fair. Your best friend is supposed to be like your best friend out of all the friends that you might ever meet in the world, not just the best one you got right now, where you at. But still, I needed to tell him. It seemed like a lie for me to run around with him and the twins talking about what all we going to do next year when I know good and well that I ain't going to be nowhere around here. Two times already, I meant to say something. Now I'm shamed of having waited so long.

I walked across the yard to his building. The wind was kicking and I didn't have on my hood. I remembered it when I was on my stairs, but I wasn't going to go back in my apartment until the streetlights came on.

Delvis snatched open the door before I even knocked on it.

"Come in and see," he said.

I paused a second. I wasn't supposed to be in people's houses if they mama wasn't home. But Delvis said, "Come on," again. So I followed him. What could Mama do to punish me now?

Delvis squatted down about six inches in front of the TV. He had the sound turned down extra low. He waved his hand for me to sit down.

"Turn up the volume," I said.

He shook his head. "I don't want the twins to see what's on."

I looked hard at the screen. There was a lot of static, but it looked like they were showing a forest. Like the kind on TV when families go to chop their Christmas tree by hand.

"What is it?" I said, knowing that the words SPECIAL REPORT didn't have nothing to do with the holiday season.

Delvis put his ear to the speaker. "It was out in De-
catur."

"Somebody else got snatched?" I pulled at the dry skin
hanging from my bottom lip.

"Naw," said Delvis. "It's a body."

"Who?"

Delvis said his name right when they showed his
photo.

You can't be surprised by something that you already
know.

"Aw, Sweet Pea," Delvis said. "Why you crying? You
didn't think they was gonna find him still living, did you?"
He put his hand on my shoulder, then took it back and put
it in his pocket.

"No," I said. "I'm not stupid. But—" The tears started
coming heavy. I wanted a Kleenex so I could blow my
nose and stop swallowing snot. "It's not fair," I said.

"What?" Delvis said.

"Just get me some tissue," I told him.

I was cleaning off my face when he said, "You think
you'll get to go to the funeral before you go to South Carolina?"

I stared at him with my teeth clamped tight together.
He knew this whole entire time that I was leaving and he
had been spending time with me every day like wasn't
nothing going on but the rent.

"You know that?" I said like a dummy.

"Yeah."

"Why you didn't say something?" My ears were heat-
ing up with anger.

"Don't be hollering at me," he said. "You the one perpetrating like you ain't going nowhere. I just didn't want to bust you out in your lie."

Sticks and stones are not the only things somebody can throw at you. Telling a lie is bad enough. It's embarrassing in a private way. Like if you wet the bed but can change the sheets before anyone gets home. But when someone takes your lie and throws it in your face, it's embarrassing like catching a whipping in front of your whole class.

Mama was going to go to the wake, but not me. That don't make no sense, since I'm the one that knew him.

"Wakes are not for children," she said, putting on her earrings.

"Tell that to Rodney," I said, going into the living room and flopping on the couch. The Christmas tree was gone already. She took it down right after dinner on Christmas Day. Most people leave theirs up until New Year's. But most people don't give their children away.

"Sweet Pea, how many times do I have tell you to put your things in your room? Come and get your shoes from in the bathroom."

I went where she was. I kept my eyes on the ground so she couldn't see how red they were. I picked the shoes up by tucking my fingers in the laces. I used to really like these shoes, canvas ones that everybody called "white girls." Mama washed them with bleach when they started getting dingy and now they look like moths got to them. They were cleaner, but how much longer would they last? If I wore colored socks, you could see them through the holes.

Mama was still walking around messing with stuff.

Now, she was in the kitchen peeking in the cupboards like she wasn't sure the glasses were still in there.

"You alright, Sweet Pea?" Mama said, without turning around.

"Yeah," I said.

But that was a lie. I just didn't want to talk about it. When somebody die, people like to sit around and say all the things the dead person used to do. Like with Grand-daddy. But I didn't really have that much to say about Rod-ney in that way. We only really talked three or four times, but I could tell that we were fixing to be friends. And not just because he didn't talk to nobody and I didn't really have no friends either. But because we liked each other. I don't mean like people that be going together. When a girl go with somebody she start acting like somebody else. Putting all this Vaseline on her mouth and stuff like that. But when you just friends with somebody you start really acting like yourself. You can be in public the way you can be at home. And that's how it was with me and Rodney. Well, that's how I think it was going to be, at least. And when somebody die, you not supposed to sit around talk-ing about shoulda, coulda, woulda. You got to say what ac-tually happened. And I didn't have nothing to say.

I took my sneakers to my room and shut the door.

Mama had just left when the phone rang again.

"Hello."

"Hello Miss Sweet Pea, let me talk to Yvonne." It was just Granny.

"She's not home," I told her.

"She working?"

"No ma'am. She at the wake."

"Wake?" Granny said. Mama told me not to tell Granny about Rodney or Jashante. She was still trying to act like nothing was going down where we live at.

"Yes ma'am. She gone to the wake for one of them children that got killed."

Granny caught her breath. Then she said, "Somebody y'all know?"

"Yes'm. One of my friends from school." Granny was breathing with little shocked breaths. Mama was going to be mad when she found out that I told, but I didn't care. She needed to learn something about the truth.

"Bless your heart," Granny said.

"And Jashante who stay next door to us, dead too. Snatched."

"Lord have mercy," Granny said. "Baby, you alright?"

"No'm," I said. I was meaning to say I was fine, but once the truth gets rolling it's hard to stop it. "I'm sad." Granny didn't say nothing right then and the truth kept coming. "I don't have that many friends at school. They pick on me. I got Delvis, but he not in my class. My library card got took back because I dropped a book in the bathtub. It was a accident. The librarian said it cost seventeen dollars to make it right and Mama can't pay. I'm too shamed to even go back in there." I was talking and crying at the same time. "And the one who died was getting to be my friend. He gave me candy and stuff."

Granny said, "Let it out, baby." But by then I didn't have no choice. It was like when you have the flu and start throwing up. Ain't no stopping it.

"I didn't mean to make Mama put Kenny out. I was

trying to do something nice. I liked having him here. It
was like having a daddy in a way. A fun daddy that like to
talk to me without having to say *so* all the time. He used
to kiss me too hard, though. But I was so little then."

"What?" Granny said. "Say that again."

"I gotta go, Granny," I said. I was glad to have the
words out of me. It was like drinking the last of the juice.
Selfish, but those last drops taste good in your mouth and
cool when it runs down your throat. But the empty bottle makes you shamed of yourself. "I'll tell Mama you
called, alright?"

"You alright, child?"

"Yes'm."

"Alright. Tell Yvonne I'll call her later."

Mama got back from the wake at nine o'clock. I was already in the bed when I heard her turn the lock, but I
wasn't sleep. I closed my eyes and tried to look peaceful
when she came in my room. She took off her shoes to be
quiet but I could hear the rub of her stockings on the floor
and I could smell her perfume. When she got closer I
could smell cigarettes too. It was like roses were on fire.
The floor creaked as she got down on her knees beside my
bed and started kissing me. She kissed both my cheeks,
touched her lips to my eyelids. There wasn't no use in pre-
tending to be sleep. She was *trying* to wake me up. I opened
my eyes.

"Mama," I said. The light coming in from the hall
made her face shine. I wanted to feel her cheeks to see if
what I saw was tears, but my arms were pinned under the
covers.

"Sweet Pea," she said, not like she was calling me but like she was talking about me to somebody.

"Ma'am?"

She sniffed. I knew for sure she was crying. I could just tell it from the way her shoulders hung low. "You scared, baby?"

I didn't answer because I didn't know how much truth I could tell without telling all of it.

"Don't worry," she whispered.

She stood up, slipped her dress over her head, and hung it on the back of my chair. I scooted over to make some room for her in my skinny bed.

"It was so sad," she said, laying down. "That little boy." She started crying hard now. "And that lady. How do you say good-bye to your child?" I didn't have to touch her face to know it was slick with makeup and saltwater. She cried loud, not all quiet like TV ladies who have to wipe their eyes to show that something was wrong. My mama laid on my bed and cried like kids with their head busted open. She cried like she was the one who knew Rodney Green and I laid stone still like I was the mama.

At ten o'clock, she got up and changed clothes to go to work. She kissed me again before she went. When the door closed, I put my hand on the wet place where her face had been. But I didn't sleep.

Once you seen your mama cry, everything is different. Kind of like when you see a picture and it looks like one thing. But then you find out there are twelve apples hidden in the drawing. Once you find the apples, all you can see when you look at the picture is apples. You forget the main picture you were looking at in the first place. That's how it was with Mama. When I look at her now, I can always see the tears.

———

The day I was leaving, my picture was in the paper. On page three. I couldn't hardly recognize myself. I knew it was me because I saw the white trim on my dress, my black shoes with the strap. The girl on the paper had her hair like mine, curled up tight with a headband holding it back. But it was like the pictures they draw at the Omni for three dollars. I looked like a joke on myself.

"Mama, that's me?" It was the first words I had said to her all morning.

We were in my room. I was wearing a new cotton slip that itched. Mama was looking through my new suitcase trying to figure out which one of the dresses in there I should put on. She had changed her mind twice already.

"That's you." She pulled out a blue wool one that looked like something a deaconess need to be wearing.

If she asked me what I wanted to put on, I would have told her to let me wear my soft blue jeans. I would have told her to wash my hair so I can get my naps back. But nobody asked me nothing so I just squinted at the gray picture of myself. I know my shoes were not as nice as they were last Easter, but in print they looked like they had been handed down a thousand times; but Mama had bought them new from Baker's downtown. And Nikky's dress didn't look like I just needed to grow into it. It hung off me like I was starving to death. "But I look funny."

"No you don't." Mama came to the side of the bed

where I was sitting and took the pink rollers out of my hair. "You look fine."

"Ouch!" I said, when she touched my ear. It didn't really hurt, but I wanted her to remember that she burned me there with the curling iron.

Didn't none of us look fine in the gray photos. We looked poor as a whole neighborhood of church mice. The only people who looked the same on paper as they did at Rodney's funeral were the people who be in the paper all the time. All the people who worked for the city looked like they worked for the city. But all the rest of us were all over page three looking crazy.

I turned over to page one. There was a picture of Rodney's mama with crying eyes.

"Mama, did you see Rodney mama crying?" Every time I looked over at her, she looked beautiful and calm as Coretta Scott King. She had the same long hair and the same black hat with a little net over her face. And even a little girl laying across her lap.

"No, she wasn't crying," Mama said. "She was too busy trying to be Jackie Kennedy." She turned the brush as she pulled it through my hair, making the curls smoother.

Why did she sound so irritated? Granny always said that Kennedy was the best president we ever had. He was even friends with Dr. Martin Luther King Jr. "I thought we liked the Kennedys."

"Jackie not crying is one thing. When your husband die, and you don't cry, that's good. That's strength. You see what I'm talking about?"

I nodded my head. "Like Coretta Scott King?"

"Hold your head still," Mama said. "But when you lose your *baby* and you don't cry? Then you got a problem."

"Why everybody always say you lost somebody? Rodney not lost. They make it sound like you mislaid your lunch box or something." Now I was the one irritated. People need to say the words they mean. Rodney not *lost*, he *dead*. And Mama need to stop tearing up because she not about to *lose* me, she throwing me away.

"Sweet Pea." She pressed her lips to the top of my head. "You lose your child not like you lose a watch. You lose your child like you lose your sight. Lose your mind."

"Like Miss Viola?" The sadness in her voice pressed against my chest, stealing my air.

Mama let me go and pulled a cigarette from the pack on my dresser. "Just like Viola." She turned her lips to the side so as not to blow the smoke right in my face.

———

From the church's balcony, Rodney's funeral was like a service for Jashante too. Everyone knew Jashante was dead, but since they didn't find him yet, Miss Viola couldn't have a funeral for him. Rodney's family and all the money people were down on the bottom floor where the casket and choir was. But everyone that stay where we live, took a place in the balcony. When we got there, Mama didn't even check to see if there was any seats down below; we just climbed the stairs. When we got up there, that's just where our people was. Nobody up there knew Rodney Green except for me. But all of them knew Jashante and Miss Viola, his mother.

When Cinque Freeman starting singing "Lord I'm Not Asking" in a voice so full of tears that the music sounded wet, the ushers downstairs stood four on each end of the family pew. And Miss Darlene and another neighbor moved in closer to Miss Viola. Cinque didn't get too far into the song before he started crying all the way. It spread like measles.

I had never heard a whole room full of people cry before. The sound is loud and rolling, like when I cross the street halfway and have to stand on the yellow line while cars whoosh by on either side. A dangerous sound. I wiped my face with my sleeve and looked down from the balcony. Almost everybody held a fan with Dr. Martin Luther King Jr. on the front and the funeral home on the back. As the fans flapped, the crying got louder like it was a train and the fans pushed it on.

Then Miss Viola said, "Jesus." The first time, she said it like He was standing at the front of the church and she was trying to get His attention before He went back up to heaven with Rodney. I looked at the black Jesus in the window glass. Then she hollered it out how like when you call after somebody and say *you know you hear me.* The window Jesus wasn't black like anybody I know. His skin was just a little browner than a regular Jesus and His black hair hung straight to His shoulders.

The casket that Rodney was in was silver-gray and closed. I knew he was the one in there because, after all, it was his funeral. And the program in my hand had that same photo of him on the cover. But if you don't think too hard about it, it could be anybody in that box. Anybody that you don't know where they at.

Miss Viola didn't wear a hat with net, but her sadness covered her face just as well. And her daughters looked like mourning women, not seven- and eight-year-old girls. Each one sat on one side of their mama, wrapping themselves around her like kudzu. Miss Viola held her hands up in the air. "My child." She heaved forward like she trying to get up to go downstairs. But the girls held her tight like they were trying to hug each other but their mama's body was in the way.

Miss Darlene and the other ladies from our neighborhood moved in around Miss Viola as she called Jesus out of His name, and the little girls reached for each other. Then my mama held me to her. She grabbed me fast and suddenly like she was sweeping me out of the way of a crazy driver. She squeezed the air out of my chest and I thought that maybe she was killing me. "Lord," she said into the top of my head. Then she sang one of the songs we sing at our church. Moaning songs that don't have words.

Mama sang her song until everyone around us joined in. Downstairs, the choir sang, "I'll Fly Away," but the people sitting around me paid it no mind. The music from the balcony was the kind of music that was meant for crying like some other kind of music was meant for dancing. I was crying too, now. I wanted to keep my mind on Rodney so my tears would fall for all the right reasons. But I cried because it seemed like everything good in the world was locked in a box, like a backward Pandora. "Mama, let me stay," I whispered.

"No," she said. "I can't." She pressed me closer to her,

hurting my neck. I felt tears dripping from her chin onto my freshly pressed hair.

———————————

Tears dripped from her chin right now too. But they weren't landing in my hair. Mama caught these tears in her own empty hand. I watched her like she was someone on TV. Not like she was my own mother sitting here on my own bed crying like somebody just died.

I got up from the bed and stepped into the heavy blue dress. I reached around my waist to scoot the zipper up. Then I stretched my arm over my shoulder to finish closing it but I couldn't reach.

"Come here," Mama said. "Let me help you."

She was still sitting on my white bedspread and I stood between her knees. She pulled the zipper and I felt the dress tighten around me. Mama hugged me hard at my middle, leaning her face against my shoulder blade. "It's gonna be okay," she whispered. "I'm not sending you up there to be nobody's maid. Nobody's baby-sitter. You his *daughter.* You *family.*"

I'm her daughter too. *We're* family. What about that?

"I love you," she said.

But she lies. Her words are like a chocolate mint, soft and delicious, melting on my tongue; but I can't swallow it.

I wiggled out of her grip. "Taxi be here in a minute."

———————————

The wind is mean as me and Mama stand on the corner waiting for the yellow cab.

"You look pretty," she says.

What she means is that I look like someone else. Nikky's dress, new Sears and Roebuck coat. Frilly panties that never touched my body before.

"One thing is missing." She digs in her purse and comes out with a little bottle of her perfume. Mama sprays my neck and wrists with her favorite scent like she's sending me to the kind of party I never get invited to.

The smell of my mother is all over me now. It rises from my skin and forces itself up my nose and down my throat. I try not to take in air, but I know that I have to breathe her in or die.

I take small sips of Mama and cry. The water in my eyes blurs her like a dream or a ghost.

She speaks and the lies curl from between her lips like smoke, getting into the fabric of my clothes and twining through my hair. "I love you," she says.

Today is an ugly day. The clouds, dark and cold, hang close to the ground, like they might start raining gray ice and broken glass.

I turn my face away from Mama and look toward Fair Street. I don't see the yellow taxi. For Mrs. Grier, all it took was a car trip and a eyelet pillowcase to make her forget home. But not me.

I'll be missing my mama for the rest of my life.

Author's Note

Though the events and characters in this novel are fictional, the serial murders described on these pages are based on a string of ghastly murders that began in the summer of 1979, when the bodies of fourteen-year-old Edward Smith and thirteen-year-old Alfred Adams were discovered in Atlanta, beginning the official investigation of what became known as "The Atlanta Child Murders." Over the course of the next two years, at least twenty more African American children were murdered. (There were several other child killings in Atlanta during this period, but they were deemed "unrelated" although many of the victims matched the demographic descriptions of the "official" victims.)

On June 1, 1981, Wayne Williams, a twenty-three-year-old African American, was charged with the murder of two adults, twenty-one-year-old Jimmy Ray Payne and twenty-seven-year-old Nathaniel Cater. Though he is officially accused only of these crimes, it was largely understood he was believed to be responsible for the two-year killing spree. On February 27, 1982, Williams was convicted of the murders and sentenced to a double term of life imprisonment. The next month, the "child murders" task force officially disbanded. The courts have rejected all appeals filed on behalf of Wayne Williams. Many Atlantans believe that the child murderer is still at large.

I have made slight alterations to the chronology as it suits the purposes of the novel.